RUN FOR YOUR LIFE!

Machiko dropped her gun and ran.

Her breath came in ragged gasps, echoing inside her helmet, her heart drumming a machine gun beat in her chest. Her feet pounded a counter rhythm on the steel floor of the nesting chamber.

She barely heard any of it.

All she was aware of was the sound of the alien Queen's pursuit.

She ran for her life.

She could feel the heat of the creature's breath on her neck. She certainly heard the clank and clack of its chitin, the stretch of its tendons.

Up ahead was the door . . . the passageway to safety.

Standing on the other side, hand at the controls, was one of the Predators. She could not see his expression because of his mask.

His arm twisted.

A "chak" of controls.

The door slammed down hard, cutting off her only exit. . . .

A L I E N S
vs.
PREDATOR
HUNTER'S PLANET

DAVID BISCHOFF

Based on the Twentieth Century Fox motion pictures,
the designs of H. R. Giger
and the Dark Horse graphic story by
Randy Stradley.

MILLENNIUM

First published in Great Britain in 1994
by Millennium
The Orion Publishing Group
5 Upper St Martin's Lane
London WC2H 9EA

Millennium Paperback
Number Twenty-nine

ISBN: 1 85798 228 2

Printed in England by Clays Ltd, St Ives plc

For Donald Maass

Special thanks for the able editorial input from Kij Johnson and Janna Silverstein

ALIENS vs. PREDATOR

HUNTER'S PLANET

PROLOGUE

*D*tai'k-dte sa-de nav'g-
kon dtain'aun bpide.

"The fight begun would not end until the end."

Tarei'hasan shit.

Nat'ka'pu illustrated how silly the old yautja saying
was by feinting to the left, then slipping around the
sparring spear thrust out by his opponent. With aston-
ishing speed the Leader followed through with a lightning lunge, grasping the edge of the student's mask
and ripping it off his face, shearing off a couple of
tightly bound ringlets of hair in the process. Yellow
eyes blazed with surprise. Mandibles clicked with
shame. The student yawked with displeasure, at-
tempting to slap Nat'ka'pu back with the blunt side of
the spear. But with a creaking heave of his armor the
Master took advantage of the cocky student's bad po-

1

sitioning, hacking down on the elbow with the blunt
edge of his leather gauntlet, forcing the weapon to
slap down onto the floor. Then, before the snot-nosed
fool could even begin another sorry howl, the expert
reached in and boxed the warrior's right tusk so hard
that it looked to the others as though the young one's
head would be ripped from his muscle-grieved neck.
The student could only give to the force so adroitly
positioned. With a gasp he toppled to his knees.

"Nain-desintje-da."

The pure win, of course. Nat'ka'pu expected nothing less of himself. However, he spat upon his victim
with open contempt. The fool should have lasted
longer in battle. For all his young pride and strength,
he was one of the more thoughtless sparring partners
that the Leader had ever faced.

"You have much work before you if you wish to
feel the sting of the Hard Meat's *thwei* upon your
brow—if you survive that long."

The student—a snarly, oily fellow named Ki'vik'-
non—just glared back silently and woodenly.

"Get away from my sight," snapped the Leader. "Go
and wash disgrace and defeat from your eyes. And
cleanse your ears as well. You smell of childbearer's
musk. Hurry, Ki'vik'non—or your betters will wish to
mate with you."

The cruel joke set the others on the deck of the
ship into a braying, clicking laughter—derision. With
as much dignity as he could muster under the circumstances, the fallen would-be warrior rose to his feet
with a clatter and creak of his *awu'asa*. Sunken deep
in their orbs, his yellow eyes shone hatred and disre-
spect before he clanked back into the ranks. Something was wrong with this one, Nat'ka'pu thought.
This Ki'vik'non lacked the sense of honor that drove
a good warrior. He bore watching. Nor would it be a
good idea to turn his back on Ki'vik'non when they
were alone.

Suddenly the enunciator in the wall of the *kehrite* blared.

"*Kainde amedha!*"

The Leader's mandibles rippled with satisfaction, even anticipation.

He turned to the younglings, his eyes blazing with challenge.

"Prepare your souls for some *true* action!"

The ship of the yautja descended from the clouds and skated across the tops of trees. This was a fertile planet, which suited yautja purposes just fine. Besides its variety of terrain, it had plenty of species of life, many quite vicious and dangerous, making it prime Hunting material.

The yautja were Hunters who traveled from world to world, proving themselves with the skill of their kills. Nor was Hunting just sport for them; it was a way of life. It was the Path. The philosophy that bound their bones more surely than did their sinews. They were Predators, and they often ate what they could, but more often they collected and preserved only trophies to testify to their prowess. They were Predators of meat physical, meat spiritual, and below their ship now was one of their favorite tastes in predatory effort.

Kainde amedha. Hard Meat.

And Hard in more ways than one.

Upon this Hard Meat, sown in chosen areas, the youth of this race cut their tusks. Upon this Hard Meat, the inexperienced learned the Truth of the Path, turned experience into value, came of age, became a true yautja and could father younglings with pride and pass on the courage and honor that separated Beings of Will from the dross of mere instinctual life.

The Hard Meat was valuable prey for the Hunter, because it could turn the tables with a flick of a claw.

There was no more valuable target for Predators than other predators, for in difficulty is there courage and honor. And honor and courage were of paramount value in these creatures' lives.

Their ship looked like a combination between a fish and a huge engine tube. With a strange flash of greenish hue, it landed in a clearing. A broad ramp extended from it, and down the ramp the Hunting party strutted. Seven of them there were: four students, the Leader, and two adjutants. The students and Nat'ka'pu carried only spears; the adjutants carried burners.

They were giants, these warriors. Their average height was two and a half meters, and even the shortest, at a mere two meters, had broad shoulders and biceps that strained against their leather jerkins. They wore armor and masks, and their tough, wirelike hair hung in dreadlocks from the back of their necks. The first step toward becoming a warrior was the agony of the pleating of these locks, a process that took months of ritual and scalp pain, performed in public sessions. If there was any sign of tears or even the tiniest voicing of pain, then the intricate weavings would be undone, and the candidate had to start from the beginning.

Nat'ka'pu was in the forefront of the party, as befitted his rank. The two adjutants held sight-amplification equipment. They quickly scanned the terrain. The short one grunted, then pointed.

The prey was spotted.

Nat'ka'pu called for the binoculars. He trained them on the bushes, saw the squatting, partly hidden form of the Hard Meat.

How odd. It was not a Queen, and yet it was discernibly larger than the average drone. The Leader tapped his mandibles thoughtfully against his mask, then turned to face his charges.

"Who demands the honor of facing this fresh Meat first, alone?"

They all brandished their weapons as one, fiercely and yet quietly. This was all part of the ceremony.

Nat'ka'pu laughed mockingly. "You are fools, all of you, and yet at the first part of the Path lies the door of the fool."

"Perhaps you should show us the door, Leader," suggested Ki'vik'non.

"Perhaps I should show your intestines the point of my spear!" barked the commander.

"It is true," said the short adjutant, whose name was Lar'nix'va. "These are rank beginners and have never sucked Hard Meat before. It is not fitting that a few feints be made by the Blooded—especially when the Blooded is said to have fought the Hard Meat bare-fisted."

"And torn off its head!" spat Nat'ka'pu proudly. "Very well. But mark my methods, for I will leave the final killing to you, my students."

That said, the Leader turned and walked jauntily. He'd weaken the thing so that his charges could dispatch it easily. It had been a long day, and he was looking forward to going back and selecting a bulb of *c'ntlip* to drink with his bloody meal, to the relaxation it would bring and the pleasant dreams of his wives, waiting for his valiant seed back home.

The yautja called this world Var. It was used only off and on for Hunting, despite its merits. The Brave People were vagabonds of a sort and had a wide field in which to range, touching on a variety of worlds. Too long in one place created stale *kv'var*—exercises. It blunted the warrior's soul, and made the Path rocky and illusory.

When a flotilla of ships had returned to Var, however, there was a distinct change. There were *oomans* here now, that new growth of intelligent Soft Meat who were colonizing worlds. Nat'ka'pu knew that yautja lore spoke of many expeditions to the homeworld of the *oomans* with delicious results. Ad-

ventures to make a warrior smack his lips. The notion
of performing *kv'var* on a world where humans had
settled—albeit only in one small area, and with odd
purposes and circumstances—stirred his blood. At the
very least, hiding their activities from the Soft Meat
would give him a sense of superiority. And if
Nat'ka'pu actually encountered them and was forced
to hunt *oomans*? Well, then, all the better. Nat'ka'pu
could use some *ooman* skulls to dangle from his trophy cages. Perhaps that would even gain him some
new conquest with females.

The thought stirred his seed within his loins and
churned up his blood. He could feel the aggression
knotting in his muscles, and his great heart beat a
song of battle.

He advanced, his spear held out in front of him,
part of the ritual of Readiness.

The Hard Meat did not stir behind the covering of
the bush, which was not unusual. It was daylight, and
though the Hard Meat was not nocturnal, it preferred
to slink through areas of darkness. That it was out in
the open at all was a wonder, but then, Nat'ka'pu had
seen them in such circumstances before. Nor did they
usually travel alone, though the detectors showed no
other Hard Meat in the area. Just as well, however.
The situation suited him perfectly. It was as though it
were tailor-made for such a training exercise, and
Nat'ka'pu was never one to push away a challenge of
fate, even when it was presented upon a tray of precious metal.

Had he merely wanted to kill the beast, he would
have approached it in his shiftsuit and turned a
burner on it. There was no valor in that, though, and
certainly no lesson for the snot-noses.

No, he had to face the thing full on.

However, for the beast to be fought properly, it had
to be aware of his presence. This one seemed to be in
an odd and awkward kind of repose. If it had been

dead, their sensors would not have picked up its signs.

So what was wrong with it?

Carefully, his warrior's instinctual antennae out and questing for information, Nat'ka'pu advanced, his spear firmly placed before him, ready for any sudden charges.

He came into full view of the creature.

The Hard Meat was indeed a large one.

It looked like the obscene skeleton of some larger monster, and Nat'ka'pu could feel the familiar worm of fear threatening to wriggle in his gut. His said his *kantra*, though, which kept the fear at bay, and used the spurt of adrenaline to sharpen his senses.

Yes, the monster was obscene in every sense.

Part reptilian, part insect, part arachnid, and all evil, with no glow of nobility or honor whatsoever. Just sheer vicious need to kill and procreate.

Its head was like a banana with teeth. No eyes. It had a reptilian tail, and long mantislike limbs. Pipes rose from its back like periscopes out of hell.

Something different about this one, thought Nat'ka'pu. Something odd, besides its large size.

His boot stepped on a dry twig.

Snap.

The response was immediate.

The Hard Meat rose up like a vehicle on hydraulic crane legs, and a soul-chilling hiss escaped from its mouth. Thick saliva dripped from its jaws, and it reared up for what looked like the beginning of a charge.

Nat'ka'pu went immediately into the Warrior's Stance, the position from which all martial-arts moves in such Hunt battles derived. His mind spun ahead, calculating the maneuvers that would be necessary when this creature attacked.

The Hard Meat always attacked. These were not shy creatures. They were vicious fighters, albeit with limited intelligence. They were tenacious and cunning, with a terrible focus, and deadly weapons at their disposal. Even in Death they could be deadly; their blood was acid that could eat through some yautja armor, all yautja flesh.

The review flashed in his mind.

When facing Hard Meat with only a spear, the best course of action was a penetration into the thing's inner defenses and then a quick upthrust through the bottom of the head, into a portion of the brain that would paralyze it. At that point, one could carve the thing up at leisure. The challenge in this situation was to duel with it only awhile, perhaps slightly incapacitating it, so that the students would have an easier road to the final victory. A wound to the thorax perhaps, or a lopped-off limb.

Hiss.

The thing rose up and down, almost challenging.

Nat'ka'pu's mandibles bristled. He could taste the blood of victory in his mouth, even against the harsh, fearful smell the thing was exuding.

He raised his spear and chanted that most Holy of Holies, the Warrior's Song, that blast of wind and rain that terrified greater prey than this.

Then, pride and joy brimming in his veins, he advanced upon the next leg of the Path.

The *kainde amedha* suddenly stooped.

When it came back up, it was holding something in its limbs.

That was one of the things that was different about the thing, Nat'ka'pu realized. The limbs were different. At their ends were structures very like hands.

And in those hands now was a weapon.

No! Was this a dream? Hard Meat couldn't hold weapons.

But before he could think anymore, the weapon gave off a blast of fire that cut through Nat'ka'pu like a giant saber, and the Great Path suddenly dropped away like a trapdoor into pitiless darkness.

Lar'nix'va watched as the explosive bullets rammed through his commander's armor, watched as they blew his head and chest apart like ripe *naxa* fruit.

He did not watch for long, however, for action in the life of the warrior was the stuff of survival. This was no longer an exercise, this was the real thing, and something incredibly unexpected had just happened.

Raising his burner, he ran forward, calling out a terse command for the other adjutant to do likewise. The moment he was within striking distance, he pressed the trigger. A stream of power and flame streaked out, attaching itself to the Hard Meat before the creature had the chance to swing its weapon around.

The thing screamed and fought against the power, but it was blown back, blazing, pieces of its chitinous body tearing off.

The blast of his fellow adjutant pushed it over, finishing the destruction. The Hard Meat was soon a pyre of death.

When the flames died down, the group walked through the gory ground, littered with the blood of their commander.

"I am Leader now," stated Lar'nix'va matter-of-factly. "Is there any challenge?"

There was none. Astonishment hung heavy amid the stink of Death.

When the dead creature had cooled, one of the students stirred the remains with the end of his spear.

Lar'nix'va looked down, deeper astonishment filling him at the remains of the creature.

A guttural snarl tore from his lips.

"What is happening upon this planet?" he said.

None of the others had an answer.

Lar'nix'va swung back and walked to his ship through the splattered body of Nat'ka'pu.

The flotilla would need to be contacted.

This business bore evil portent, and from his life experience, the short yautja suspected who lay at the root of it all.

For whenever there were *oomans* on a planet, there was always trouble.

1

eace can kill."

Machiko stared at the blocky letters she'd just written on her blotter for a moment, then with a red pen commenced to illuminate the *P*, like a dusty old monk at work on some Gothic Bible.

The cursor of her desk-bulb computer blinked blindly at her. A stack of input crystals lay inert atop her IN compartment. A mug of coffee with a dead multilegged, multieyed insect afloat on its turgid surface sat to one side, beside a half-finished piece of dunktoast. The gray, flat plains of Alistair Three stretched out from her window like nothing, squared.

The warrior was bored.

The memories of battle lived inside her like bloody monuments to a time when she'd been truly alive.

A time of danger, nobility—

And yes, honor.

She'd been a different person then.

Buddha, how she'd changed.

Ryushi had changed her. Her time with the yautja pack had changed her. Both to the better, she thought. At the core of her soul, before, there had been shame. Her father had brought shame upon her Japanese family in Kyoto, embezzling from his company and then taking a coward's way out by killing himself before he could be jailed. "You are my flesh, Machiko," he had said. "You must restore the family's honor."

And then his blood had spilled.

Machiko Noguchi had tasted honor when the bugs had been loosed upon her town of Prosperity Wells, fighting alongside Dachande and his warriors. When she had joined the Hunter Pack, she had literally *become* honor. But then, later, her humanity had called to her upon that miner's world, and although honor demanded that she fight against the pack to save her *ooman* genetic kin, it had meant betraying her place in the pack. And now, stuck back in the muddle of humanity again, she had lost that sense of honor, become merely quotidian.

And oh, yes—a little snarly, a little bitter.

She stared morosely at her vague reflection in the computer screen. A few lines had formed beneath her dark Japanese eyes, and her short black hair was a little gray, but otherwise she was an attractive woman. Small-breasted, muscular, a compact beauty. It was lost on her, though. She longed for more.

She sighed.

You'd think the Company would at least let her bring Attila on shift. At least then she'd have someone to talk to. She wouldn't have to resort to doodling. However, the last thing the Company was interested in was her mental health. As far as they were concerned, she could *drool* and doodle here, just as long as she got her job done. Just as long as she stayed out of trouble.

If only they didn't have that contract hanging over her like the sword of Damocles. If only she had money, a ftl-ship—a business plan . . . !

If only . . .

A high-pitched voice from a grille molded into the framework of the desk beside the computer facet interrupted her reverie.

"Ms. Noguchi!"

She started, then immediately realized who it was. How many times had she wished that she could yank this infernal radio-comm from its mooring and toss it into the garbage blaster? Freedom would break out. Peace from the incessant whine of the planet's Company president . . . a man who made certified anal retentives seem relaxed and carefree.

"Yes, Mr. Darkins."

"How's that oversheet coming?"

"It's going well."

"Good. Glad to hear it. I need not remind you that it's due in my office at the end of the week. Company heads are expecting a subspace transmission then, and a comprehensive one. I trust that it will be a better job than last time."

"I think it will satisfy them."

"Good. Glad to hear it. You've got an important job, Ms. Noguchi. An important job, on an important planet."

The transmission ended, with a faint buzzing sound like the annoying song of a rat-fly.

Sure.

Important, her *butt*.

Alistair Three—also known as Doc's World—was a planet with a perfect rotation, a perfect distance from the sun, a perfect atmosphere . . . perfect, that was, for a blandly uniform surface, with bland cattlelike grazers on its vast plains, few mountain ranges. Its

weather was boring, its oceans were dull and luster-
less; all its specifics were the epitome of monotony.
One of these days humans from other planets would
get around to fully populating this planet, but for right
now there were far more appealing planets to go to,
with much less distance between them and the rest of
the human part of the galaxy.

What interested the corporation enough to dip its
tentacles down into Doc's World (named after one of
the men who'd discovered it, Doc Warden, an alcoholic ne'er-do-well whose ship had gotten lost, and
whose comment on Alistair Three was "Makes me
want another drink") was simple.

The mining.

Not that Doc's World had anything like rubies or di-
amonds or unusual precious gems.

No, what it had was *narkon* ore, a curious grade of
ore created by Alistair Three's unique mineral vulcan-
ization process, which the corporation liked to use in
its starship engines. Thus it had set up this Blakean
"dark satanic mill" to mine and process said ore, then
to transport it to satellites and moons where the ship-
building was accomplished. Almost ten thousand people lived here in Solitaire City. Many were miners who
took a daily troop train twenty miles south to a mountain range where they worked. Many were the miners'
companions who often as not went with them. A few
were supervisors and managers. A few more were bu-
reaucrats. Machiko was one of those few—albeit on a
top echelon—and she loathed it.

And to think of what her past had been.

To think that she had once run with a Predator
pack.

Oh, how the Mighty had fallen.

She sighed and tapped up the spreadsheet. She began to examine the data that had been entered by others, and to send the computer through its analytic
paces so that the corporation would have the pre-

cious vital statistics it needed. She stared awhile at the screen, and then she put in another crystal, adding a new matrix of information.

Juggle, juggle.

Toil, trouble.

After a while, she saved her work. She sipped her coffee. And then she stared off into the plain plains of this nothing world, remembering what it had been like to fly with lightning in her wings.

2

achiko, warrior, looked around and found herself surrounded by Death.

The bugs.

For a brief moment fear exploded inside her. Then she realized that fear was her friend. It helped limn the borders between life and death, light and dark. It plumbed the depths of her soul and biochemistry, bringing up the thunder of valor and the controlled explosion of adrenaline.

Up ahead Top Knot, running point, aimed a strafe of plasma. The fiery stuff raked across a line of the aliens, cracking their chitin into cinders. Lethal acid splashed back, boiling into acrid steam.

Others of the pack added to the fire, tearing a wide hole in the jumble of the bugs, the swelling ranks pouring forth through tunnels to protect their hive.

The pack had just landed on this planet in the majestic and silvery craft that was their starship. Their
mission was simple: secure this hive's Queen for their
own purposes. Simple though their goal might be, the
road there was not.

She was working with a pack of yautja on perhaps
one of their most dangerous objectives—indeed, so
dangerous that the Predator Hunter's normal codes of
conduct in the pursuit went right out the window.

For this expedition, anyway, the ritual laws of
matching the quarry weapon for weapon were sus-
pended.

The naginatas and scatterguns prescribed for hunting the *kainde amedha*, the Hard Meat, were replaced
by plasma-casters and lasers.

This was no Hunting trip.

This was war.

Just as it had generally been in the history of her
own *ooman* peoples, there are no rules in war.

Only objectives.

Machiko, warrior, was no longer Machiko Noguchi.
No longer a streamlined ramrod for the corporation
on a planet of alien cattle. She was Dahdtoudi, proud
and brave warrior, who had proved herself on the
planet called Ryushi and was Blooded by no less than
the great Dachande, a great Predator Leader.
Dahdtoudi. "Little Knife." The lightning scar that he
had etched on her forehead just before his death with
the acid of a broken bug finger, partly neutralized by
his bloody spittle, marked her glory for life. When the
pack searching for Dachande and his ill-fated mission,
headed by the valiant Vk'leita, had discovered
Machiko, she was Dahdtoudi, and she bore Dachande's mark and had a Queen's skull hanging above the
door of her home. She'd been one of the surviving
oomans—humans—on Ryushi. She had no particular
reason to stay, seeing as she no longer felt committed
to the Company, and every reason to go with the

yautja. With the alien Hunters she found the core of honor, a state that eradicated the shame that had descended upon her family when her father, having been caught embezzling funds from his family, had committed a bloody seppuku. But a suicide without honor. Though she had excelled scholastically and then corporately, this was a pain and shame that had always hung over her, crippling her relations with other people. She had found it difficult to get close to people, but there was always the desire. Now there was no reason to get close to the yautja. Here, thus released, she could test herself, test her courage and skills, test all the things that would lead her into the state of grace shown her by Dachande.

As a Blooded One, she'd been entitled to come for Hunts.

She felt a real and profound need for that now, a vital desire to pursue honor and valor and the ways of the yautja.

A desire she needed to explore.

And so now, here she was—

They moved through the birthing chambers. Remains of ill-fated denizens of this foggy world— apelike creatures with four arms, big jaws, and elephantine ears—hung from the walls, their chests burst, their innards in various states of decomposition. The smell was beyond description, beyond bad— cloying and gagging. If not for the filters in the mask they'd given her, Machiko would not have been able to make it through that funk. Well, perhaps ... After all, she was no longer Machiko, she was Dahdtoudi, and she had not yet fully tested what Dahdtoudi could take.

Whatever it was, she knew it was going to have to be a lot. She'd braced herself for this raid. She'd braced herself when she'd gone off with the pack. Her whole life now was one big Brace—

Payoff time now.

The big guns having paused momentarily for their metaphorical breaths, the Leaders stepped aside, staggered English-line style, for their backers to let loose their volleys.

Machiko and the youngers to the rear discharged their weapons, cutting into the throng of aliens, slicing, dicing, and generally churning up the Hard Meat into chunky-style puree, acid flavor.

Machiko wore the yautja armor, sleek and economical and oddly comfortable. The material worked well in the movements of her lithe muscles, and the air circulation was superb. The armor was blessed, and it felt almost like augmenting prosthetics, as though the lines converged into power that boosted her own. Her hair was worn now in the ceremonial ringlets, rather like neat dreadlocks bouncing energetically at the back of her head as she moved forward, her discharges blasting through the dying, spindly creatures.

They broke through.

As though this knowledge was as instinctual as it was empirical, the pack moved as one through the opening presented to it. The wedge of the older, valorhogging frontmost went first, and the others, including Machiko, allowed this. All were equal in honor, all were esteemed. However, Machiko had quickly glommed on to the fact that these Predators were pretty much like an Earthly predator pack. The members jostled for dominance, and the older, smarter, and more experienced members were generally either given deference or simply plowed past the more awkward younger members.

"Ha ha ha!" whooped one of the younger warriors, a snot-nosed kid about a head shorter than the others; a difference in height was almost made up for by the chip on his shoulder. This dude had bridled at Machiko's presence in the pack from the word go and had been on her back ever since. He took guff from

the others for his lack of stature, then handed it to
her coated with a little shit for good measure.

"Ha ha ha!"

It was garbled laughter. He'd heard Machiko laugh
once, and he would imitate her from time to time, out
of spite. She jostled right back generally; jostled just
short of a set-to: no reason to make unnecessary
waves, when all she wanted was to sing in the band.

No, especially right now, smack in the middle of a
den of the most vicious killers in the galaxy.

"Ha ha ha!"

The tide had let up under the slash and burn of
their weapons. The elders were hurrying along, intent
on their goal, the other youngers tagged along, just
behind them.

She called her tormentor Shorty, though before
she'd assumed he didn't know English.

Now, though, she wondered.

He turned around and shoved her.

"Ha ha ha!"

She went back a few feet, surprised at the push.
She'd already figured out that the very last man had
the least honorable position in battle, albeit a necessary one. That must have been what Shorty intended:
to make sure that she came up in the rear.

"All right," she said, "let's just go," hoping her tone
was understandable, if not her words.

"Ha ha ha!"

Shorty fairly skipped ahead, waggling his locks at
her in a defiant, teasing manner.

Oops.

She saw the thing way before he did. It was coming
out of a tubing in the ceiling: a mean-looking bastard,
its diseased banana head already dripping saliva, its
claws outstretched and ready to jump.

"Watch out!" she cried, pulling up her plasma gun.

Shorty may have been young and stupid, but he

was quick. He spun around, looking up immediately at the trouble.

She waited.

Not because she wanted to see Shorty killed.

Worse. She wanted to let him sweat a moment, until she did something much, much worse. . . .

Fast as he was, the bug was faster.

It jumped down, leaping for the certain kill.

Machiko fired.

The blast caught the bug in midsection exactly at the point she had calculated, not only smashing the thing to fiery bits but blowing back those pieces and their acid blood against the wall, preventing them from falling on Shorty.

Shorty stepped back away from the devastation. He had stopped laughing. Through his mask Machiko could see the ice of his glare.

"Ha ha ha!"

One of the other youngers, up ahead, had stopped. A brawny arm pointing an accusing finger.

"Ha ha ha!"

They'd learned the laugh, all right, and now the derision was being heaped on Shorty.

A bark of communication. Shorty turned and stormed off. Machiko followed into the harsh acridity of the smoking advance.

Time to get back to work.

Sometimes, at lulls like these, when Machiko felt a little sick to her stomach, more than ill at ease with her companions, she wondered about how the bugs had spread across the galaxy. Simultaneous evolution? From what she could gather, Hunter folklore seemed to indicate that. But could that folklore have been created to mask a troublesome possibility? Could the bugs have spread because of the Predators' blooding rites? Could "accidents" have occurred on many others worlds—"accidents" of containment, like that which had occurred on Ryushi?

Of course, the cultural pride of these Predators could never stomach that notion, and so the possibility was washed over with insistent folklore. Besides, who could really say? The bugs had a way of spreading, like disease. And interstellar-vector theory really had no bearing on what they were doing now, on this planet.

The bugs had this planet. That was all that mattered. The Hunter mission now was not to dispute the bug domain, but to appropriate their Queen, for their own purposes.

And their destination was not far away. Machiko could sense that much.

Breakthrough was imminent.

The elders, honor and glory and ego etched in flesh and bone and armor, blasted their way through one last tissue of defense. By the blaze of their weapons, Machiko could see a much larger chamber, lit in a feral spectral glow.

Closer, she could see that it was like a chamber of the devil's heart.

And squatting inside that chamber was its own particular demon.

The Queen was about normal size. Which was to say, *big*. It hunkered in its hold like a cornered jabberwocky, its fingernails-on-blackboard hiss already aroused by the surrounding Hunters.

As rear guard, it was the youngers' duty now to keep the Queen's drones away while the more experienced Hunters did their jobs.

Machiko performed that duty, but made sure she didn't turn her back on Shorty. These creatures were supposedly made of honor, but she'd never really trusted young males of any race, and now was *not* the time to begin.

The Predators knew their prey well.

One of the bugs' collective strengths lay in their complete subjection to their Queen. Another was their total dedication to the proliferation of their species.

But within these strengths was the key to their one major weakness: the warrior-drones would do nothing to endanger the life of their Queen.

In turn she would do nothing to endanger the lives of her unborn brood.

Armed with that knowledge, the success of the Hunters was assured.

Still, it wouldn't be easy. Trouble along the way was virtually guaranteed, despite the strutting self-confidence this pack had displayed toward the effort from the very beginning.

As the youngers picked off any of the drones who dared to poke their misshapen, horrific heads into the chamber, the elders expertly shot off their grappling devices around the numerous limbs of the Queen, around her neck, effectively hog-tying her.

The mighty weave of the cords pulled tight. The Queen raged and heaved, but her powerful huge body was held in vague check. Even though she wobbled and surged from time to time, it would have to do.

The Queen thus reasonably subdued, the drones seemed to check themselves, keyed intuitively to her vulnerability.

Now came the most dangerous part. . . .

The capture team had to maintain control of the Queen as Top Knot, their brawny leader, prepared her for travel.

This was a ticklish business, as it consisted of separating her from her egg sack.

Top Knot advanced, his long, sharp blade held high and glistening in the halogen portable lamps carried by the others. He raised it high, tensed himself, aimed—

And brought it down like a surgically trained executioner upon the fleshy interstitial connective tissue.

The blade cut down and through the stuff hard. There was a shriek from the Queen.

Unfortunately, the Hunter whom Machiko called Three-Spot was caught napping. His stance had been improper, and so when the Queen unexpectedly threw all her ample strength into that limb and pulled it away, he was lifted bodily into the air by the rope curled around his arm.

The Queen hurled him around like a yo-yo and dashed him down onto the hard ground.

Stunned, the Hunter could not move.

But the Queen could.

With a vicious vengeance she brought down her own scythelike claws directly onto Three Spot's chest. So sharp were the claws, so much momentum did the Queen have in her blow, that they drove down directly through that armor, burying deep into the warrior's chest with a sickening splash and thunk of released blood.

Three-Spot wriggled and spasmed for a moment. Then he was dead.

That's what tended to happen in these situations.

On their way out of the unfortunate Hunter's body, the razor claws slashed through the rope.

Part of the Queen was free.

This wasn't good.

The situation was pretty obvious to Machiko. The capture party's continued safety rested on their ability to control the Queen. Her freedom would be the signal for her brood to attack.

Back when she was corporate ramrod on the planet Ryushi, Machiko would have examined the situation ... weighed her options.

People would have died.

Now, instead, she simply acted.

Dropping her gun, she leapt for the loose rein. She had a split-second grab for it before the thing whipped back out of reach. Her leap was automatic, but there seemed to be magic in it, talent in it, a skill and precision that she hadn't owned before her experience on Ryushi.

She'd leaped out of her position, darted past the others, still seemingly frozen in the confusion of the moment—

Her fingers folded around the rope, grabbed it, held it just long enough for the other mesh-glove to grab it, wind it around her hand. When the thing went tight, it felt almost as though her arms were being pulled out of their sockets. . . .

Fortunately, she'd dug in and was pushing down with all her power.

Just hold it, Dahdtoudi, she told herself. "Little Knife," the name that Dachande had given her. Her handle on strength and pride and honor.

Just keep that thing in control. The others will do the rest.

Mere moments seemed to stretch as long as her arms wanted to. Sinews creaked and her bones felt close to cracking. The feral alien smell of the place threatened to overwhelm her. However, she concentrated on stillness. She would not be moved. She pretended she was sitting *zazen,* totally centered, totally within herself, and lashed her mind to this planet's gravity.

She sensed more than felt the others gaining control. And then two Hunters took her place.

She stepped back, breathing hard.

The Queen was still straining at the ropes, but she was in control again.

By stepping in like that she'd prevented a possible disaster.

Top Knot approached her.

She expected . . . what? A pat on the back? A bend of the mandibles by way of smile? Some kind of medal of honor?

No. She didn't expect that at all, not from this race of beings, and she braced herself.

Top Knot slammed his arm against her chest with such power that she was knocked down. Despite her preparation her breath was knocked from her lungs. She did not offer resistance, she did not take offense, she did not complain.

What she'd done, besides saving these Hunters, was to go against her station in stepping out to grab that rope.

By abandoning her post she had disobeyed Top Knot's orders. Though she helped avert disaster, she had revealed herself as untrustworthy.

Her insubordination might be forgiven, but it would never be forgotten. These crab-faces might not have been around to forget without that insubordination, but she'd still flown in the face of tradition, honor, and authority.

Oh, well.

They started to haul the Queen back to the ship.

She picked herself off the ground and simply stood for a moment, waiting for the chamber to stop spinning around her. Eventually, on their way out, Top Knot turned his attention to her.

He gestured forward, and she understood.

She was to take position at the advance guard.

She picked up her gun and hobbled ahead.

It was a token position at best. The Queen's pheromones would do the work of scattering her brood before her. It was rather like pulling out a hostage with a great, big, sharp machete held to her throat.

The older, more experienced members of the troop—the ones with the necessary muscle and alien-wrangling experience—hauled the reluctant Queen forward toward the ship.

As much as Broken Tusk/Dachande's mark allowed

her entrance to this society, her behavior that day had branded her as an Outsider.

She still had much to learn about the ways of the Hunters, but nonetheless, she knew that had she had choice over again, she would have done the same thing.

The haul back seemed to take forever, what with the bitch digging in from time to time and needing a quick stun to take some of the fight out of her.

And what a job they had ahead of them, to boot:

According to Top Knot's briefing, bringing a captive alien Queen onto a ship was the most dangerous part of any capture mission.

When they got to their destination, Machiko soon found out why.

The ramp was lowered by remote control. It was narrow and posed quite a problem. She could see that the tight confines of the ship would allow no margin for error, no room for slack.

According to Top Knot, many times the captive Queen made a suicidal last-ditch attempt at the door of the nesting chamber.

With great effort the Hunters hauled the Queen up the corrugated ramp. They pulled her through into the area that would be her prison—a chamber separated from the rest of the ship.

Machiko took up her position by the end of the ramp. She could not help but cast concerned glances back at the progress the others were making, getting that monster into her own private suite.

She expected it to make a last break for freedom at any moment.

What she did not expect, what came as a surprise, was that the bid for that freedom came not from her, but from her children. Somehow she got off an unseen signal or a silent call that spurred her offspring into action. They came roaring out of the cavern, more fiendish than ever. Their cries spurred Machiko into action.

She swiveled around, took stock, reacted instantly, swinging her weapon around and spraying streams of bright death into the burgeoning hordes. In conjunction with her fellow youngers, they must have killed thirty of the bugs in the next fifteen seconds.

The aliens just kept on coming.

Top Knot bawled out a retreat order. . . .

A bawl that turned into a howl of consternation.

Machiko had already started up the corrugated ramp. The bugs seemed to pay no attention to the fact they were being slain by the score. A few broke through the fiery onslaught and started up the ramp as well.

Machiko turned around to see what the commotion was and was horrified to see that the ranks of the brave, valiant senior Hunters were splintering. The Queen had turned into a raving fury, trailing lines. She leaped to one side.

Another cry.

In the confusion Machiko realized that Top Knot had called out for the ramp to be lifted, and not a second too soon. Even as the lip of the thing yanked from the ground, two bugs clambered onboard.

Fire from the retreating Hunters tore them off, but two more took their place.

Meanwhile the ranks of the Hunters frantically fought for control.

Machiko stood aside to allow the last of the youngers to climb onboard. She fired one last salvo, tearing the final bug off the edge and hurling it back into the frenzied roil of its companions.

And then with a chuffing sound, and the shriek of hydraulics, the ramp/door shut.

The bastards were outside.

The bitch was inside, though, and free.

Machiko turned. The Hunters were scuttling about

to the exits and their posts while the Queen howled out her frustration and anguish.

The Queen had only one path open to her—directly into the waiting nesting chamber. Behind her was a grillwork-covered vent from which a cable dangled, but it was too small for her to fit through.

The others knew this ship much better than Machiko, and they had hurried off to be out of danger. In her confusion and consternation, Machiko had simply stood her ground watching the Queen rampage.

The Queen turned and headed straight for Machiko.

Automatic response drew her gun up as the Queen approached at full bore. In fact the gun seemed to move of its own accord, expertly swinging into place, aiming directly at the Queen's head. At this close range one blast would tear even that huge head off.

Just a pull of the trigger would do it.

Her finger tightened.

But then she stopped herself.

No.

Too many of her companions had paid with their lives that day trying to reach the Queen. To kill it now would negate their sacrifices.

In this situation even honor offered only one course of action.

Retreat.

She dropped the gun and ran.

Her breath came in ragged gasps, echoing inside her helmet, her heart drumming a machine-gun beat in her chest. Her feet pounded a counterrhythm on the steel floor of the nesting chamber.

She barely heard any of it.

All she was aware of was the sound of the Queen's pursuit. . . .

And the implicit sound of her own mortality.

Leaving Ryushi and joining the Hunters had seemed like the logical thing to do at the time, the *right* thing to do. The yautja code, as she perceived it, seemed enviable, clean. As she had waited alone on Ryushi, she had waited for just such an opportunity, feeling herself changed in the crucible of her experiences at Prosperity Wells.

Now the decision just seemed stupid and vain. A romantic fantasy. Hard to think of anything but fear and survival when there were tons of drooling Death bearing down upon her. Whatever had made her think that she could match the ways of these half savages? What had she hoped to prove to herself?

She ran for her life.

It seemed as though she could feel the heat of the creature's breath on her neck. She certainly heard the clank and clack of its chitin, the stretch of its tendons.

Up ahead was the door ... the passageway to safety. It was round and small and could close quickly.

Standing on the other side, hand up and off to the side, was an unexpected figure at the controls.

Shorty.

She could not see his expression because of his mask.

Hell, she didn't know if these things had expressions—she just couldn't read mandible positioning.

Shorty's arm twisted.

A *chak* of controls.

The door slammed down hard, cutting off her exit.

In its very middle was a triangular window. Two of the Hunters—neither of them Shorty—moved up to that window and gazed into the chamber.

Neither of them moved a muscle to get the door up. Neither of them made an effort to save her.

They just stared at her, spectators of some deadly morality play.

Whatever had made her think that she could live by these creatures' bizarre laws?

Much less gain their respect?

She spun around.

The monster Queen was not as close as she feared, but neither was she far.

And she was gaining all the time.

Well, she'd worry about saving face after she saved her own skin.

She feinted in one direction, and the Queen quickly responded, shifting its weight in a twinkling and investing its momentum in its bid to make quick work of this available tormentor.

Then Machiko shifted, dodged, and sprinted for her true objective.

There was more than one way out of any trap.

She headed for the vent and the restraining cable she had noted before.

Machiko leaped with all her strength and began to scramble up this rough ladder.

She made the climb in record time, but even as she made the grill, she heard the beast below her. It apparently wasn't going to just sit around and watch her get out.

She didn't waste a moment.

Perched upon her shoulder was a laser.

She fired it, and its brilliant beam cut through the wires speedily. She turned it off and pried off the grill-work, making a hole wide enough for her slender body to slip through.

Just about it. A moment or two and she'd be out of—

Even as she was tasting her safety, she felt an awful tug on her hair.

The Queen had reached up and grabbed her dreadlocks.

Fortunately, the Queen wasn't the only one with sharp and nasty claws.

Machiko let go of one of her grips and twisted her wrist forward in a manner that triggered her retractable blades. With almost the same movement she slashed backward.

She cut off her dreadlocks.

She also severed most of the Queen's hand.

It shrieked.

She could feel it thump back onto the floor noisily and messily, the wound spilling acid, none of it, fortunately, over Machiko.

Machiko pulled herself up through the hole she'd made in the grating, her muscles performing the function smoothly and efficiently. She once more was grateful for her training, her workouts, her endurance . . .

. . . and her luck.

She wiggled through quickly, not giving that bitch down there any time to renew her attack. It was wailing pretty fiercely, and she could smell the acridity of its pumping blood wafting up through the opening.

She did not pause to make sure it was okay but scuttled through the pipes as quickly as she could. There was still the possibility, after all, that it would thrust its good claw through the opening and grab her foot.

Her dreadlocks were expendable. She wasn't exactly trying to attract male action among the Hunters. Hell, maybe they even had some glue-ons she could use.

Her foot, though . . . her foot was a different matter.

She needed her foot.

Too bad about the Queen's fingers. But the Hunters would be able to get control of the thing, and it would certainly still be quite able to do what they needed it to do: namely, lay the eggs they needed for their blooding exercises.

Negotiating her way through the air venting was a matter of relying on her intuition and sense of direction.

Over. Up. Down.

Eventually, she came to another grate.

She put her back against the wall, brought her legs up. Kicked. Kicked again.

The grate banged out of its fixture, fell back onto the floor.

She slipped out lithely and fell the few feet onto the metal deck, landing on the floor on all fours, sleek and ready as a cat.

The Hunters were standing there, watching her.

Just standing there in expectant repose.

She tore off her helmet and took in a deep breath.

She gave the ritual greeting of a warrior's victory.

She wasn't sure what she expected. A thank-you? As far as she knew, there was no such phrase in the Hunter vocabulary.

She'd saved their bacon, and they had nothing to say.

They just looked at her, as though trying to perceive what this strange Outsider that Dachande had Blooded was composed of. This honored companion they could never understand . . .

Then they did something remarkable.

They bowed.

She'd bowed for them before . . . something from her Japanese ancestry she'd shown them. They'd just stared at that, seemingly uncomprehending. . . .

And now they were bowing.

All but one.

The others turned and left to be about the business of taking off from this planet. Of dealing with this captive Queen . . .

All but one.

The one lingered. He took his helmet off and his eyes were like lit coals in the darkness.

Shorty.

His mandibles danced menacingly.

He took a step forward, quick and menacing.

Machiko stood her ground.

Just inches short of her, the young Hunter stopped.

Machiko did not move. She did not blink. She just stared directly back at her challenger.

The mandibles bristled.

But then the Hunter spun, stalked away.

His steps echoed in the hallway.

She'd stared him down. Shorty dared not challenge her now, dared not hurt her after her incredible display of valor, after she'd risked her life to ensure the success of this operation.

No. She wasn't one of them.

But they owed her more than ever now.

She felt the bliss of an endorphin rush. . . .

. . . *wings of lightning* . . .

3

. . . heart of thunder . . .

Machiko crouched, holding her blade steady, waiting for the first move of her opponent.

For a moment the samurai warrior, in full medieval regalia, was just as motionless. His own long blade gleamed in the late-afternoon sun like a slender medallion of death, pendant from an azure sky.

The samurai warrior stepped forward, pleated armor ajangle off an obviously immaculate build. She fancied she smelled the musky competence wafting off him.

She tasted a backbeat of fear.

He moved again, and he stepped forward with a familiar and startling arrogance.

He seemed in a hurry, as though he wanted to finish up this particular butcher's order of slice 'n' dice and move on to the next bit of delicatessen fun.

"Hey," she called in Japanese. "Are you hiding a salami in that codpiece, you miserable, impotent coward!"

The eyes shot open with fury.

The samurai raised his sword and, screaming, ran forward.

Machiko Noguchi feinted to meet him headlong, then at the last possible moment stepped aside. She flicked her sword down, then up and under the skillful but infuriated blow, and its blade slammed up the vulnerable break in the armor, cutting into the man's body.

The man's face grimaced a suitable expression of pain and surprise, and his mouth opened to let out a howl of extreme anguish.

Machiko's sword whipped through shimmering light, coming out on the other side at full speed.

The man disappeared in a snap.

Machiko had to control the sword. She deflected its passage so that it whacked down into the sod.

She took a breath and steadied her nerves.

"Excellent," piped a voice beside her. "Absolutely excellent, Machiko."

She turned and looked at the speaker. There he was, beside that rock, crouching down so as to be out of the scenario that he had so ably created.

The holo-tube was already retracting into its compartment in his forehead.

"Thanks," she said.

She suppressed a smile. It would not be advisable to give old A the H *too* much encouragement.

He stood up, dusting off his khaki knees, straightening his immaculate bush jacket just so.

"You've utilized the Sun Tzu's principles very well," pronounced the android in a clipped, punctilious tone that had an old-time mid-Atlantic quality to it.

"Pardon me?"

"Sun Tzu. The *Art of War*, of course."

"Oh, yes. I thought you were talking about some kind of disease-carrying fly."

"That, I believe, is the tsetse."

"Yes, yes, along with many other fine principles, Attila. You reiterate them to me constantly. I don't necessarily have to be able to cough up whole sentences at the drop of a nunchuck! At some point, however, it all gets assimilated into my subconscious. It looked like a pretty obvious opening, though. You made the samurai display the flaw of pride and anger. I'm well acquainted with those flaws, and I know how to use that weakness in others. It's a common trait, I believe, in men—and I traveled awhile with super— well, if not supermen, then at least *exaggerated* men."

Attila looked a little troubled. "I wouldn't know. I don't have a subconscious. Perhaps I should save my money and buy one some day."

They were about three kilometers out in the plains of Machiko Noguchi's workworld. It was the corporation's bureaucratic equivalent of Saturday, and Machiko used the day in her usual fashion.

Exercises.

Fighting exercises with Attila the Hun, her robot, to be precise.

Keep the body trim. Keep the soul sleek. Keep the old noodle *alive*. That was the ticket. Even when she'd been assigned out here in Zerosville, she'd realized that she was going to have to have some kind of trainer, some kind of companion, and since she wasn't quite certain of the human availability in these departments out here in the hinterworlds, she'd bought herself a robot.

Well, "android" was the proper term, really, but as far as she was concerned, Attila was a robot. He'd been a number when she'd bought him, and she'd renamed him. It wasn't often that a private citizen was

able to afford the expense, and she'd had to get the
Company's approval. However, she'd explained in no
uncertain terms what she'd needed the thing for, and
since the Company was quite aware of her past and
wanted to placate her as much as to get this loose
cannon off their main deck, they'd complied. She had
the money, and if she wanted to use it on a fabricated
companion, well, what difference did it make if she
used it to fight with or to fornicate with?

Attila the Hun was not the normal android used by
the corporation. He was not an Artificial Person in the
usual semiorganic sense, but rather a more mechanical sort. His strata of models was created to be af-
fordable to the average populace, and used for
commercial or private reasons rather than military or
space exploration.

She programmed Attila to her specifications.

Unfortunately, she didn't know quite what to do
with the personality that came along with the whole
package.

"A beautiful day, Miss Noguchi, is it not?" said
Attila, casting a smile across the plains.

Machiko grunted.

"Not feeling particularly articulate today?"

"I just get really annoyed when you call me 'Miss,'
dammit."

"You're not married."

"Look, we've gone over this a hundred times before. I wasn't aware that I hadn't had your previous
programs erased, okay? I didn't realize that you had
such a complex background. I realize that I can't
erase them now without erasing you in toto. Can't you
try to selectively erase habits—like calling me 'Miss'?"

"Certainly."

"Well, *do* it."

"You're not in a very good mood today, are you, Ms.
Noguchi?"

"Machiko. Please, just call me Machiko."

"Oh, excellent. I enjoy our informal exchanges. It's nice to relate to you when you unleash me from the closet to do your will with me."

"Right. Like you haven't got a life."

"My life is to serve."

"And to watch your tapes and catalog your music."

"One has to fill the spare moments."

"I should have had you programmed to clean and cook. That's what I should have done."

"I do my share."

"You can boil water and that's about it."

"You forget that although I have senses, they have to be calibrated to the proper specifications to cook to your taste. Also, I would clean more, if your odd meditation exercises did not call for such Spartan quarters and your regimen did not call for your cleaning it yourself, as part of your *kata*."

"Okay, okay. I'm sorry. I guess I'm just in a bitchy mood. Maybe defeating holographic opponents isn't quite as satisfying as the thunk of real flesh, the splash of real blood."

"I'm sorry. I'm not equipped with those sorts of simulations. Again, you attempt to make me feel inferior."

"Nothing of the sort."

Attila suddenly smiled, and it was a revelation. Usually when in repose that face was dark and dour. With a dark complexion, dark eyes, a natural frown, and a sharp, perfect nose set in a thin face topped with a perfect short gentleman's haircut, Attila looked more like a mopey Neapolitan young man than a Germanic Hun. However, when he smiled, showing perfectly shaped white teeth, the entire face seemed to light up into a different dimension. Moments like this made Machiko forget entirely that he wasn't a human being.

Moments like this also made her remember that *she* was a human being.

She'd always prided herself on her cool, her control. Her glacial characteristics had caused associates to dub her "Ice Princess" or "Snow Queen." She had had very few friends. Her pride in life was remaining tough, cool, and efficient.

She had changed somewhat after her experience with the yautja. True, she had been more comfortable in some ways with creatures who had rules of behavior among them and who generally obeyed those rules. However, they were alien, and she was human. Her experience on Gordian made her realize that she had a deep instinctual love for, and loyalty to, humanity. She respected the yautja. In many ways she had become one of them. But she had discovered that she would have to do so in *human* terms and so was now trying to explore different dimensions of her humanity. This did not mean that she could deal with other people that well. However, she was trying. One of the best parts of being with Attila was that she felt comfortable with him and could be playful or bitchy, cold or charming, and experiment with emerging aspects of her personality.

"Oh, good," said Attila. "Then you'll snap out of your funk and agree with me that it's a beautiful day. I mean, all the evidence is here before you."

Machiko looked around.

The scent of her own exercise had dissipated somewhat, so she was able to notice the smells around her. Prominent, of course, was the grass. Not Earth-type grass, but on the same principle, short and green and cast over everything like a luxuriant rug. It was this area's version of summer here, pleasantly warm, just as the area's version of winter was pleasantly cold. In between were the long, long autumn and spring, king and queen of this world of the bland and the mild.

Flowers.

That was what Attila was talking about, of course.

The floral addition was truly pleasant and combined with the odd shadings of color combed into the
surroundings, poking out of unexpected spots in
ochers and magentas and bright slashes of camellia.
That, along with the uncommon blue-green of the sky,
the way the cumulus clouds navigated the vasty, silent
reaches of it, and out beyond the reaches and humps
of hills and flats, the faint suggestion of mountain
peaks.

A slight, fragrant breeze ruffled Machiko's still-
short black hair, cooled the still-hot blooding mark on
her forehead, that afterimage of lightning. . . .

"Nice."

"Nice?" The robot's eyebrows rose with surprise.
"Merely 'nice'? Where are your aesthetics?"

She shrugged. "It has a kind of unruly, boring at-
tractiveness, I suppose. You forget my background,
though."

A curious cock of the head. A finger lifted in understanding. "Ah, yes. As Japanese, you must prefer the
more regulated and disciplined beauty of a garden."

"I'm not saying I don't enjoy wild beauty. I learned
to thrill at the wastes of Ryushi, the violent dawns,
the harsh sunsets. . . ."

"Perhaps your opinion is presently reflected by
your state of mind."

"Oh?"

"You are not a content individual?"

"Oh, right . . . and you *are*?"

The robot shrugged. "As an android, I am merely
content to be an individual."

"Freedom in bondage, eh?"

"I do not consider my service with you as bondage,
though I suppose legally and technically it might be
considered so."

"Oh, for emancipation! Let my people go."

Attila's face assumed a rather hurt expression.

"Perhaps we should continue our exercises."

Machiko took out a scarf and wiped away a residue of sweat from her exertions. "I think I want to break for lunch. Maybe we can do some war maneuvers later this afternoon."

Attila shot an arm forward and made a show of scrutinizing his wristwatch. "I believe I can fit you into my schedule."

"Well, how thoughtful of you. There's a nice little bistro in town I thought we could go to."

"Well, since there's only one bistro in town, I believe I know the one of which you speak. It's a shame you didn't bring a picnic lunch. We could have lingered and enjoyed the day. . . ." He slapped his chin with exaggerated revelation. "But oh, my. How could I have forgotten?"

Attila fairly skipped over to the omniterrain vehicle, opened the trunk, and pulled out a basket covered with a red-and-white-checked towel. He whipped this off to reveal sandwiches, apples, and a bottle of red wine.

Machiko gave a grudging smile. "I didn't realize that you were programmed to be thoughtful."

"All androids have areas of latitude within which to move."

"It's the areas of longitude that trouble me."

Attila sniffed with fake huffiness. "Perhaps you should just partake, enjoy, and then criticize if the fare does not meet your high standards."

She laughed. "Come on, Attila. You're just trying to cheer me up." She followed him over to the boulder, where he motioned to a place where they could sit.

"Yes. I confess. And with good reason. Life is so much more pleasant when you're in a reasonable mood." He began to unpack the basket and place the meal on the tablelike rock. He lifted a small vase, complete with diamond-petaled flower, and made it the centerpiece for this sumptuous display. "There. To your liking?"

She nodded. "A pleasant surprise."

"There is more to existence than the *Art of War*."

"That's nice to know. What kind of sandwich is this?" She began to unwrap the cellophane.

"Taste it. Guess."

"I hope this isn't some kind of new martial-arts exercise."

"What? Sandwich karate?"

"Complete with the Movement of the Lettuce and Mustard?"

"And the Pickle on the Side Kick? Hardly. May I suggest that you taste it?"

She did. From one look at the contents between the rye slices she was able to guess that it was some kind of meat pâté, and the color was liverish—but surely not . . .

She bit into it, and her eyes lit up.

"Foie gras!"

"The genuine article."

"But where—"

"Oh, a little barter with the gentlepeople in Shipping and Handling. I thought it would go well with a picnic, and you seemed so down in the dumps lately."

She took a bite of the delicious fatty pâté and just let it linger meltingly in her mouth. She closed her eyes and savored it.

"Can you blame me?" she said finally.

"I had thought that you were happy when you were dating that mining foreman."

"Who? Edward? That was a laugh. Just a diversion. It's all pretty bland now, Til. It's all anticlimax."

"Hardly a very positive attitude. Surely those Predator sorts didn't have foie gras sandwiches?"

"No. They ate their liver raw."

"Surely they didn't have clever and valuable android assistants?"

"No, and they didn't have robot slaves, either. They were quite resourceful, those fellows."

"Hmm. Sounds like they ate honor and valor for breakfast, lunch, and dinner."

"Oh, no. There's a biological reason for their interest in Hunting. They're quite carnivorous. You can pretty much tell by their breath."

"What a lovely bunch. And you say you actually miss them?"

"Miss them? I wouldn't go so far as that, Til. They're not exactly the lovable sort. No, they hardly inspire much sentiment." She sighed and thought of a different way of putting her feelings. It pretty much came out exactly the way it came out before. "I felt *alive* then."

"You're alive now. You want me to engage my diagnostic functions?" He grabbed her wrist. "Ah, a pulse. A very good sign."

"Sorry. I felt fully alive. Fully in the *now* of existence."

Attila shrugged. "Dangerous sportsters report the same kind of rush. It's all the human body's internal drug system. I'm told that they have some nice rushes on the black market as well."

"No, no, you just don't understand."

He nodded. "No. Perhaps I do. Perhaps, with all this proving of your mettle, your own honor and valor in this society of hypermacho creatures, you were able to somehow momentarily blot out the shame and guilt that rest so heavily upon your family's name because of what your father did, and what that means in the culture that you cling so stubbornly to."

"I hate it when you get like this."

"Get like what?"

"What—did I buy a psych-bot for God's sake? What kind of bullshit are you handing me?"

She got up, red-faced, and threw the half-eaten sandwich at him.

Attila flinched.

"Simply pointing out things we've already discussed."

She was immediately sorry.

She realized the reason why they didn't call these things robots anymore. Robots didn't have feelings. Androids did. And though perhaps those feelings weren't as screwy and cantankerous as human feelings tended to be, they deserved respect and consideration.

"I apologize, Attila." She went over and picked up the sandwich, biting into it as though she were eating the words she'd previously spoken. "A delicate area." She brushed some dirt and grass from the sandwich and took a large bite, masticating with emphasis. "Hmmmm. Lovely."

Attila the Hun folded his arms. "Perhaps I refuse to be tricked in such an obvious way."

"Oh. You won't forgive me?"

"I was never upset. What's to forgive?"

"Oh, *now* who's dissembling?"

"I find our course of conversation extremely unproductive and will now resume my role as your trustworthy, faithful, and *silent* robot servant."

"In other words, you're going to sulk."

"Precisely."

"Well, before you do that, maybe I can have your input on what I'm presently looking at over there."

She directed her finger skyward.

Attila swiveled his head, responding immediately to the seriousness of her tone.

The spaceport lay to the west of the makeshift town. They had driven immediately south. Coming down on incandescent impellers was a starship, flashing in its own exhaust and in the exultant sun at its zenith.

"A moment."

There was a click and hum as Attila's oculars focused on the object and made the appropriate telescopic adjustment. Attila had shown her some of the mechanical aspects of his composition. All truly impressive. Hidden compartments. Perhaps even hidden weapons? He even claimed that portions of his body could operate independently of one another—by remote control. At his more exasperating moments, Machiko sometimes felt like testing this out with her sword.

"Well?"

"Impatience is not a virtue of a warrior."

"My humanity is leaking. So . . . spill."

"Your metaphors are mixed."

"Come *on*."

"It's a most curious spaceship, Machiko Noguchi. Some kind of KX model."

"KX models . . ." She whistled. "Those are exclusive *yachts*."

"Indeed."

"Why would anyone who owns a KX want to come to this godforsaken planet?" wondered Machiko Noguchi.

4

It didn't take long for her to find out.

"Well," said Livermore Evanston, hoisting his own glass of fine wine to his guest, "here's to health, happiness, and a mutually beneficial business arrangement."

Machiko looked at him suspiciously. She sniffed the brimming crystal glass of startling red he'd just poured. Superb. This, coupled with the foie gras, would just about make her gourmet quotient for the year. Nonetheless, she managed a noncommittal expression.

"I only know your name and that you zoom around in a big private starship. As for business arrangements, that remains to be seen."

He smiled, his red cheeks glowing like cheery

Christmas bulbs. His merry eyes were wide and open and seemingly wanted to hide absolutely no secrets.

"Oh, I think what I've got for you, my dear, will be of emphatic interest."

She sipped the wine. Truth in advertising on this. It was the best burgundy that had ever crossed her lips, a glow of grapey warmth with a dry yet clever finish.

She took another sip, though, just for the alcoholic content.

"May I sit?"

"Certainly."

He gestured to the streamlined though well-appointed seat before her. Everything on this ship was sleek and streamlined, but with touches of quality and class that could come only from wealth.

She sat, and the cushioned chair was very comfortable indeed, ergonomically accommodating her body.

"More wine?"

"Why not?"

She put her glass out and had it topped off.

"Excellent stuff, no?"

"I see nothing on this ship that's not excellent."

"I'm so happy you could take the time to come here and visit me."

She shrugged. "I miss out on a frozen dinner, my vid, and my robot. You owe me a lot."

"An attractive woman like you, not being wined and dined on the evening of a weekend. Somehow the very notion appalls me. I am happy that coincidence brought me here today."

She took another sip and leaned over, all politeness wiped from her face now, replaced by a pure business expression.

"So. Let's cut to the chase."

"Gladly." He sipped at his glass. "I have an offer for you, a business proposition, that I think you will find most interesting."

She leaned back to listen.

When she and Attila had returned to her apartment, there was a message waiting on her communications module. It was a man's voice, requesting her to return the call to a certain number.

She did not return the call.

She had a bath. Time was a luxury, and always after a strenuous workout she took the chance to have a languid bath, filled with scented oils and topped with delicious bubbles. She'd never taken time for them as a corporate ramrod in those frenetic pre-Ryushi days. Just quick showers. Her baths on Ryushi had been generally cold water. And with the Hunters ... well, they seldom took baths, and so she'd just learned to live with her own true grit.

Now, though, her baths were opportunities to shut out the universe. Machiko-time she called it. She had all kinds of interesting gadgets in her bath.

Dried off and in her synthsilk robe, she'd been in a reverie that she liked to think of as meditation but was actually a regretful daydreaming that she'd started at this dead-end job here, when the phone had rung.

She ignored it.

Attila, however, had not. Attila had answered and then had insisted she take it. This made her think seriously about selling Attila. However, she did take the portable phone and placed it to her half-listening ear.

That was the first time she had heard the name Livermore Evanston.

It was only after she'd rung off and discussed the phone call with Attila that she realized, with the android's help, that the address she'd been invited to that evening was a docking bay at the spaceport. In all likelihood she would be heading that evening to the spaceyacht she and Attila had witnessed landing. Attila had been all atwitter about the possibilities, but Machiko remained stoic and suspicious.

There was too much to lose if any kind of hope crept into the mix.

"Let me put my cards on the table from the beginning," said Livermore Evanston. "I know quite a bit about what happened on Ryushi than most people. And I know more about *you* than the corporation does."

She raised an eyebrow. "Oh? You want to spell out exactly what you mean by that?"

He knew about the Hunters? That seemed unlikely. They kept a low profile, and their maneuvers through human as well as universal history had been veiled with secrecy. That, after all, had been part of their Game.

Her time with the yautja was officially "unaccounted for" in Company records; the Company didn't know what had happened in the time she was missing, but they knew enough to bury her someplace safe. They'd thought they had done that when they left her on Ryushi after the colony was moved.

"I know about your experience with the alien *arichnida.*"

"The bugs, you mean."

"Yes. They are, frankly, the reason I'm here."

Something sparked in Machiko. She could not help but move forward. Doubtless, interest flamed in her eyes. It wasn't a good poker face anymore. Fuck it. Bugs were Bad. Anything that had to do with squishing them was worth paying attention to, and every little bit of help she could extend to eradicating them from the galaxy she did not begrudge.

"I'm listening."

"You seem to have a reaction to the creatures."

"I do. They need to be destroyed."

"So your dossier would indicate. And if your survival on Ryushi proves anything, you're quite talented in that area. Although your settlement was all but wiped out, your experience, your skill, and your valor

were noted—however, you disappeared for years . . ."
He let the sentence hang, waiting for her to fill in the
blanks.

She sipped her wine and left them empty.

". . . and then suddenly you reemerged on that mining planet, in better shape than ever."

"Yes. Gordian."

"A planet with a bug problem."

"Yes."

"Along with some sort of other mysterious problem. . . ."

Again she sipped wine. He did not probe.

She remembered how it had been on Gordian—
another human colony world seeded with bugs by the
Predators she hunted with. She had to make a decision there. She had to choose between the yautja she
Hunted with for two years and tried so desperately to
win honor from, or the colonists, creatures of the
painful race that was her own, that had caused her
and her family so much shame. Her sense of humanity
had won out. She had thrown in her lot with the colonists and beside them had fought off the Hunters.
The margin of victory had been slim.

Evanston had assumed a serious, closed aspect,
sealed with a frown during these last sentences. Now,
though, he smiled and assumed a jolly openness once
more.

Livermore Evanston was a round and pudgy man,
but there was no sign of a lack of strength, either
physical or mental, in his face or body. He exuded a
vitality of power and enthusiasm beneath his mask of
indolence. He wore beautifully tailored and color-
coordinated clothing in a business-suit ensemble that
looked as comfortable as it was neat. Expensive, like
everything else around here, no doubt. His hair was a
lovely mass of artfully coiffed curls—dappled brown
and gray—and he wore a tastefully cut goatee. He
smelled of lemony sandalwood cologne and pipe to-

bacco. He was the epitome of the excesses and might of civilization, and Machiko Noguchi had to admit to herself that she was very, very intrigued.

"Ah. I'm getting ahead of myself. I am a creature of curiosity. I forgot my promise to you. I have the advantage here. I know far more about you than you know about me."

He paused then and slipped his hand into his pocket as though he were digging around for a pipe. Then, as though deciding against it, he pulled his hand out again and reached for his glass of wine.

He did not drink it, just stared into its clear, deep red as he spoke.

"A little rectification, then, is called for."

A scratch of the nose, as though an aid to considering the best phrasing.

"I have this planet, you see . . ."

That was a little too much for Machiko to take, right from the start. "Wait a minute. You're clearly a wealthy man—but you're telling me you own a *world*."

"Hmm. Yes. A bit off the beaten track, but then so is this wonderful little place."

"Never has sarcasm been so truly used. You mentioned before you're not a member of the corporation."

"No. I *trade* with the corporation. I got my start in the Rigel system, you see. A huge inheritance and I've been nothing but a pure entrepreneur since I can remember. All sorts of businesses and technologies and conglomerates. Much of what constitutes the modern starship engine was designed in *my* engineering think tanks." He shook his hand expressively and dismissively. "Enough of that. I'm loaded, okay? So loaded that I personally sent out an expedition in an unsettled and unexplored region of the galaxy, personally colonized it, and set up an enterprise unlike anything in human history." He took a deep breath and exhaled through a tentative, chagrined smile. "However, we've got a problem."

"I suspected as much."

"Yes. There's been a sudden and unexpected bug infestation . . . and the hell of it is that we don't know where they came from or how they got there." He looked at her with an arched, bushy eyebrow. "A situation very similar to that on Gordian, right down to the mysterious and unexplained deaths. Also similar to Ryushi. It's been said, you know, that planet is haunted."

"Yes, I've heard that theory too."

He tapped his fingers on the table, looking at her expectantly, as though she were going to solve his problem with a pronouncement of some sort.

She, however, said nothing, even though the interest still burned in her eyes, undisguised.

"I suppose you'd like to know what sort of planet it is I own."

"Something that would make money, I presume."

"Oh, yes. But it's something that's important to me as well." Tap tap tap. "I have your dossier. I'm aware of your abilities with weapons, and your excellence in martial arts. However, your write-up is not complete. Have you ever *hunted*, Machiko Noguchi?"

She smiled. "Yes."

"What?"

"Bugs."

"That wasn't sport, that was necessity."

She let that go. He said it, she didn't. The further away the subject stayed from the Predators, the better. She smelled possibilities here, and there was no reason to louse them up with a little jaunt into Alienland. Let that business be her little secret. It was bad enough, betraying her pack to save her humanity. She didn't want to broadcast that little personal bit of mixed courage and shame.

She shrugged. "I went duck hunting once."

"Then you know something of the thrill of the sport."

She nodded.

That was the understatement of the year.

Hunting with her pack had come to make multiple orgasms feel mild and mundane.

"Good. I had that feeling about you."

"Is this suspense thing to keep me interested? I mean, I came to your ship, didn't I?"

"I'm sorry. A bit of sales technique. I've never quite gotten out of the habit." He leaned back and rubbed his pudgy hands together gleefully. "You see, it's a hunter's planet, Machiko."

"I kind of guessed."

"Good. I suppose you're aware of the restrictions that have been placed on blood sports on many worlds."

"You have governments and they tend to make laws. You have corporations and they make laws too."

Evanston nodded soberly. "Yes. And as civilization proceeds its dizzy climb up the ladder of Progress, the elevated few who think that they can legislate morality have lost track of some of the needs of humankind."

"Like hunting."

"Precisely. It's in the fiber, the very marrow, of humanity. The *hunt* . . . Instincts die hard." He winked at her and patted his chest. "I know. They're right in here."

"Hmm. I'm catching the drift. You find and colonize your own world. You go and shoot its creatures without any threat of reprisal."

"That's not the whole story. I import creatures as well . . . fine, ferocious creatures. Worthy of glory. I then sell tickets to people who can afford them."

"Ship them out, let them chase beasties about."

"Yes."

"Sounds ideal."

"That's what I thought, Machiko. I didn't bargain, though, on the arrival of the bugs."

"A bit more than your hunters can deal with."

A grave nod. "At the moment I'm pretending it was all planned. There have been deaths, but that just adds spice to the sporting. However, deaths are one thing . . . catastrophe's another. I'd like to hire you to avert catastrophe."

"One little problem, Mr. Evanston. As the song says, I owe my soul to the Company store."

"Ah, yes, the beloved corporation. They didn't know quite what to make of you when you came back, did they? They considered you a loose cannon, and so they put you out to Pasture World. Yes, yes, I'm well aware of the confines of your life, Machiko. However, I'm a man of means—and a man of contacts. If you'll sign on to help deal with this alien manifestation on my planet—with the understanding, of course, that you'll be well remunerated for your effort—I will not merely get you leave from this backwater nothing of a planet"—he smiled—"I'll get your contract torn up."

She blinked. "You can do that?"

Evanston nodded.

"Hmmm." She stood up and paced.

It was too good to be true. There had to be a catch. She looked the gift horse in the mouth.

"How do I know that I won't be stepping from the frying pan into the fire?"

"Oh, it's a fire, all right. But you hate the frying pan, I know, and it's my take on you, Machiko, that you *love* fires. Your element, so to speak."

"I don't know. You're telling me the whole story here, right?"

"No. Of course there are details . . ."

"Details that would make me regret my decision to jump on your horse?"

Again the shrug. "You'll have to wait and see. Look, I'll tell you what. Come with me, and I'll make you an

advance. Work for a week or two. If things aren't to
your liking, the advance will be enough to start a new
life somewhere."

"You'd pay that much up front?"

"Indeed. And you won't even have to spend any of
it for ship fare. I'll put you on one of my ships."

"I can get this in writing."

"Yes, and I'll be legally bound to let you free."

"You must know I hate it here. How do you know
I wouldn't just use the opportunity to get out of this
bureaucratic hell and then skip?"

"Like I said, I have a dossier full of information on
you. Including your family history. That would be a
shameful thing to do, Machiko, and you know how
shamed your family's name is already."

Machiko nodded. "Yes."

"And may I also suggest that a successful comple-
tion of this task will not merely make you an independently wealthy individual . . . it will add just about all
the honor and self-esteem to your individuality you
crave so much."

She sat back down. "I wonder if there's enough in
the entire universe." She looked up at her prospective
employer. "You've certainly done your homework."

"Money buys a great deal."

"You certainly want it to buy me."

"As I said, I think I understand something of your
psyche. I'm not buying you. Money isn't your thing,
Machiko Noguchi. I'm offering you freedom . . . and
self-respect within human society. You'd be able to go
home again, Machiko. Go home, with your head high."

She thought about the offer for a moment more.

And then she gave him her answer.

5

The yautja danced.

Lar'nix'va danced the dance of Death. Not just a Path dance, but The Path dance.

His opponent hissed and clacked before his spear, seeming aware of the importance of this battle. Beyond life, above Death. It smelled of its acid, though it had not bled yet. It had just been detected with a sensor and then beaten from the bush where it had been hiding.

The pack had challenged Lar'nix'va's assumption of the role of Leader. The *kainde amedha chiva*, the Hard Meat Trial, would prove his worthiness.

To Lar'nix'va, though, it was just one more step on his personal path, a path that had engraved itself upon his soul at a very early age.

The Hard Meat lunged.

Lar'nix'va dodged backward and performed a graceful flip. A showy maneuver, certainly, but then this kill wasn't just for sport or for blooding—it was to illustrate for certain that he was worthy of not just a questionable Leadership, but a brilliant and honorable Leadership with more than a touch of pride and swagger. Thus would he take the next step up the ladder, for the other packs that Hunted on this planet would surely have to take note. The situation merited extreme scrutiny, and by his careful and panache-filled Leadership, Lar'nix'va knew that he would attract the attention of the elders. Thus he hoped to command many yautja, not just a pack. Thus he hoped to attract many females, breed many children, and make such a name in the genetic pool as had not been heard in many Passings. To think that the elders had once considered him unsuitable for breeding, had even considered severing his gonads. It was not just ambition that drove this warrior, but outrage. Soon there would be many yautja a few *noks* shorter than the norm. But they would be superior warriors and good solid breeders, without question. His name would not just be in history books, but written in the annals of the genome.

With this fire of intention that burned in him, he took a couple of fancy steps, confusing the Hard Meat and impressing his fellows with his nimbleness. Then, before the *kainde amedha* had the opportunity even to consider the possibility of fleeing, he raced forward and with stunning speed lopped off one of its forward limbs. Even as the sword-sharp length of special steel sliced through the last bit of chitin, Lar'nix'va yanked it back and stepped away from the spray of acid blood, not merely in the prescribed training fashion, but with a glorious flourish and a deep bellow of victory.

The Hard Meat shrieked, but it bore forward, its long head darting out, drooling and snapping.

The good thing about the *kainde amedha* was that, while they could be wily and hard to deal with in the closed space of tunnels and darkness, out in the open they were highly predictable. They sought to attack and kill, and that was it. A warrior merely had to time his attack and defense in cadence to the instinctual performance of his prey.

Now Lar'nix'va played with that. This was his Dance.

The Hard Meat struck, its limb dangling horribly. Fortunately, the limb had ceased spurting acid, merely dribbling now, so that Lar'nix'va dared to dart in and attack once more. He saw a perfect opportunity to slash open the creature's thorax. However, the fight would have been over too soon then, cheapening his glory. He signaled with a whistle his decision to attenuate the battle, and then instead of making it a quick kill, he whacked down with the blade upon the thing's leg.

The limb was tough. The blade bit into it but did not sever it. The spear was stuck. Acid streamed out. Rather than pull on the spear and risk a slash from the jaws or remaining limbs, Lar'nix'va abandoned it, leaping back with fancy footwork.

Then, rather than receive another spear from his fellows, he did the glorious thing.

Lar'nix'va pulled out his short blade.

He heard the mandibles of the pack behind him chatter with disbelieving approval. This was an insane thing to do, but a little insanity in the Leader was always respected.

Lar'nix'va capered around the Hard Meat speedily, and then, before it could do anything in defense, he jumped. His leg muscles drove him up onto its back, and with a powerful blow the new Leader brought the blade down upon the back of the cranium. The sharp steel pierced the armor, driving perfectly into a node that controlled the creature's reflexes. Before he could be grabbed, Lar'nix'va bounded away.

The Hard Meat screamed.

It rolled and convulsed.

Maddened and in terrible pain, it tried to leap toward the warrior responsible, but its limbs would not respond. With a clatter and clunking it fell into a hellish heap.

Lar'nix'va darted in, grabbed his spear, which had fallen away, and with a fluid motion rammed the weapon down and through the thorax with such force that the Hard Meat was pinned to the ground.

Then Lar'nix'va leaped away.

With the life of the thing leaking into the dirt, he turned to his fellows.

"Can you doubt now that I am a Leader?" he said.

"No," said a tall warrior named Bakuub, sullenly. "We cannot. However, there is more to a Leader than an individual feat. You well deserve your skull here, and the honor that this kill heaps upon you, a milestone on your Path. However, we must see how the pack works under you. Times are serious, and we cannot hazard a bad choice."

Lar'nix'va could feel the blood rush to his head. However, he controlled his temper. By rights all he had to do was call this a challenge from the troublesome fool and defeat him in a duel. However, Bakuub was correct. They were in a troublesome position. Most likely Bakuub would be killed in such a duel, and the pack—Lar'nix'va's pack—would thus lose efficacy.

This, after all, was the pack that would lead Lar'nix'va to greatness. It was a good pack, and the yautja knew it well. No reason to dismantle it when such was not necessary. What was the saying? *Thin-de le'hasuan 'aloun'myin-del bpi-de gka-de hasou-de paya.* "Learn the gifts of all sights, or finish in the dance of the fallen gods."

Lar'nix'va had no intention of moving his feet and shaking his spear in that particular festivity.

"Very well. We should have an exercise. A portrayal of teamwork."

"Yes," said Bakuub.

"A Hunt!" said another.

"A challenging *Hunt*," chimed in a third bellow.

"But what is worthy of such a Hunt? What will truly test our merits as a working unit?"

Lar'nix'va's mandibles clattered together in a sly yautja smile. "The most truly worthy prey. The other creatures who hunt on this planet, who have no doubt caused the death of our Leader. A prefatory foray into their realm."

"Yes."

"Pyode amedha," cried another.

"Wait," said Bakuub. "Is it wise to do this before we know what truly transpires upon this planet?"

"You are not revealing cowardice, are you, Bakuub?" said Lar'nix'va.

"Soft Meat!" cried a warrior.

"Yes. A true challenge," echoed another.

Lar'nix'va nodded. "The others agree. We must hunt the *oomans*. We must hunt the clever hunters. And we shall hunt our loosed Hard Meat at the same time." He grabbed a spare spear and waved it in the air. "Hunt and thus our glory as a pack will be restored!"

The cheers of his companions buoyed his spirits, and his soul began to yearn for killing.

6

 don't know about this," said Attila the Hun. "I don't know about this at *all*."

"Don't know about what, Til?"

"This entire enterprise. It smacks of duplicity. It smells of trouble. It reeks of—"

"I think the phrase you're groping for so literarily is 'It's very suspicious.'"

The android looked taken aback. "Well, don't you agree? I mean, from out of the blue comes a Greek bearing a gift. I believe the dictum states clearly that one should be chary of such."

"I don't think 'Livermore Evanston' sounds very Greek, do you?"

"The fact that he didn't come with a bloody Trojan horse doesn't change the fact that ... that ... well, that this whole thing sounds not only *fishy* but *dangerous!*"

The look on Attila's face was so sincerely chagrined that Machiko Noguchi slowed down to a walk. She halted her assistant and trainer, who was of course not at all winded. She herself spoke breathily, and a light patina of sweat covered her forehead.

"Aren't we wading a little deep into the ancient kingdom of mixed metaphors?"

Evanston had agreed that Machiko should keep in shape, and as there were no exercise machines or rooms devoted to same, she was allowed to avail herself of the circular corridor on the second deck, which was pleasantly similar to a short track.

Round and round and round . . .

Puff and puff and puff . . .

The thing was, if Machiko didn't do some strenuous exercise as well as her *kata* and her little soft-shoes with holographs thrown up by good ol' AH, she'd be so antsy she'd be in a thoroughly nasty mood and probably insult or hit someone. And if not him, then one of his several toadies who ran this boat.

What had happened was this:

She'd signed on.

That simple. She'd accepted Livermore Evanston's offer, laid down her Joanna Hancock right by his own squirrelly scrawl.

As promised, it took only the weekend for all the red tape to get bleached and snipped. Evanston had advised her to take the day afforded her to pack and make arrangements for what she wished to bring with her.

All she'd wanted to take with her were a few paintings she'd grown fond of, some phones and some music cubes, a painting set she found helped her meditate . . .

And, of course, Attila.

Attila was a little trickier, since her license for him

extended only to Company territory; and Evanston seemed a little nonplussed about taking a training android to Hunter's Planet (that simple term seemed to be the favored appellation, spoken with a wide range of irony and emphases and melodrama by both the impresario himself and the crew). However, once assured that Attila would not only help keep her in tip-top fighting and physical trim, but, with his multi-faceted abilities, actually be of help in the effort, the Boss agreed.

Besides, he *adored* the name.

People at the office were appropriately stunned and impressed by her company and her swift departure. She gave them a quick toodle-loo and showed them her backside, though not quite in the way that perhaps she would have preferred.

She and Attila were ensconced in luxurious quarters aboard the spaceyacht. Evanston asked if perhaps "the Hun" wanted his own room, or perhaps just a broom closet somewhere, and when Machiko had answered that Attila always slept in the same room, like a "big teddy bear," the fat man had just leered.

All to the good, if it kept the guy's mind away from the possibility of any midnight peregrinations. Machiko honestly doubted that Evanston had any designs in that direction. Doubtless, money, power, and sheer personality kept him deep in whatever sexual activities he pleased to partake of. No, he surely hadn't taken ages to trip out to Buttlick, Milky Way, to try to jump a scarred, overmuscled, stringy-haired gal's bones, no matter how sexy she might be. He had come because she was, in his words, "unique."

That didn't mean, though, that he wouldn't try, the lech.

Actually, Evanston was fortunate.

Starships could go lots faster now than in days of yore. And though Blior, in the Norn system, was a far way out of the normal sphere of interstellar activity, it happened to be in the same Einsteinian neighborhood as Dullworld, relatively speaking.

"I'm as much a warrior in the land of mixed metaphors as I am in any other land," said Attila. "But truth to tell, I rather liked it back where I was."

"Even though I was miserable?"

"Ah, but you would have been so much more miserable without me. I had a purpose, a positive value reinforced every single day. What being, biological or manufactured, can truly look for comfort in his duties?" Attila sighed. "For a while I could." He looked off sadly at a stolid bulkhead, as though staring through some imaginary porthole into the depths of space. "Now I'm just a bag carrier."

"Come on. You're my trainer, my associate, my secretary, my alter ego, my—"

"Your robot slave."

"No . . . that's absurd. Again . . . you're my . . . my . . ."

She wanted to say "friend and boon companion" or something sweet and supportive, but somehow the words stuck in her throat, like peanut butter.

Maybe that was why she'd run off with the yautja. They had hard and steely emotions, just like her. Honor and valor were all, and emotions soft and tender or simply good-natured were nonexistent.

A reality where shame and weakness could be fought with and defeated, and a noble Death was as much a victory as a noble conquest.

"My better half."

"Oh, dear. Don't strain yourself." But Attila the Hun was smiling, happy with whatever crumbs of genuine approval she threw his way. "Still and all, I *am* on record: This is a bad idea. You will regret it, and I already regret it. But, then, I have very little choice in the matter."

"That's right, guy. And don't you forget it." She smiled. "Would you rather have assumed my lovely job back there? How well would you have done on a mining world without me?"

Attila was silent for a moment. "Very well. Point taken."

"We do this job, make some money . . . and we can start up something on our own . . . our dream, Til. . . ."

"*Your* dream, you mean." Truculently.

"Hey. You came up with it, not me."

Still walking, round and round and round.

"A suggestion, merely." The accompanying sniff was affected, Machiko knew. Attila didn't have sinuses.

"Our own school of martial arts and 'Spiritual Training through the Physical.' That's the exact phrasing you used. I liked it then and I like it now."

"What, back on Earth?"

"Still a world of opportunity. . . . That, or some other older civilization. With culture. Plays, musical events . . . *art*, Til. Real art, not just books in some dank library. Panoramas, cities, things to do . . ."

Although he was fighting it, the android clearly was brightening. "Yes . . . yes, I do admit . . . it all sounds very tasty indeed." Darkness again, lowering of the prominent brow ridge. "But we've got to survive this next leg first. And we don't know exactly how long it will be."

Machiko shrugged. "I told you about my experiences with the Predators, Til. I told you about what I had to do to reconnect with human beings again. I told you about the hell on Ryushi. My anguish on Gordian. I survived. I'll survive again."

A look of profound thoughtfulness had taken hold of the android's face. "Yes, but it all proves that you're a magnet for trouble."

"C'mon, Til. If that's true, you'll actually be able to prove out all these great fighting theories of yours . . . and actually see me in action."

A sheepish look appeared on Attila's face. He said nothing, and Machiko did not needle him.

It had always been one of Attila's private embarrassments that he'd never actually had a fistfight or a street scuffle, let alone been involved in anything like a battle or a fight for his semilife. That was, as far as he knew. All the war stuff, after all, had been fed into the neural complex center of a practically tabula rasa android. His body had been around for a while, and his personality and odd subaware stuff were still clinging to his artificial neurodes and dendrites and synaptic colloids, but he had no substantial memory of his past. Machiko used this fact to reassure him. Perhaps, she claimed, he'd in fact been a valiant warrior in some antilitter campaign and had been taken captive by the slobbish enemy, his brain hastily and poorly scrubbed of memory. Identity he'd never felt in short supply of; memory was an entirely different affair.

Not that Attila was ever in short supply of things to do. While Machiko was doing her forty-hours-plus of bureaucratic nonsense per week for the corp, he would read, paint, master musical instruments, and compose music, becoming a well-rounded—indeed, a renaissance—robot. However, when Machiko was around, his focus of attention was entirely upon her, as if he were some sort of faithful Labrador retriever. At first ever-single and self-sufficient Machiko found this annoying. However, she rapidly got used to it and now actually enjoyed it.

Attila was along on this trip as much for company as anything else. She enjoyed the surprising aspects of her personality that she displayed around him. It was like discovering a new Machiko inside her, a funny and clever Machiko, though more vulnerable, more hurt than she'd ever admit to anyone else.

"Maybe that's what I'm afraid of," said Attila.

"Okay, okay. This kind of mopey attitude is not the

sort of thing I'm in the mood for. Maybe I should just take the dry sleep that Evanston offered."

Attila shook his head adamantly. "Not and stay in any kind of trim or tone."

"Ha *ha*! There's the drill instructor I know—*that*'s why I need you. Had I gone alone, chum, you can bet I'd be snoozing in one of those chambers right now, with a nice little sleep aid for company."

Attila seemed to take that well.

They continued walking along the hallway, chatting lightly as was their wont. The corridors of the ship had nothing of the metal-and-glass sterility usually associated with Long Drag boats. In fact, they were more like an odd penthouse, what with the colorful and tasteful wall patterns and artwork, along with the occasional piece of antique furniture. Livermore Evanston tended to prefer rococo, baroque, and Victorian decorations, and the principal rooms had a strangely cluttered look for a starship. But, then, it was all very homey, especially the fireplace in the dining hall, and it *was* the private spaceyacht of a rich man. Machiko thought it fascinating.

Attila's mouth made a slight tic, a sure sign he was consulting his internal chronometer. "All right, that's fine for the exercise."

"Anything special you'd like next?" said Machiko.

"Yes, as a matter of fact . . ."

"Be my guest. Your choice."

"Actually, if you don't care to accompany me, you need not," said Attila.

"You're too kind. No, actually, I'm enjoying seeing what you get up to when I'm not around. Go ahead—shoot. What did you have in mind?" said Machiko.

"Hmm. Well, maybe we *should* go over some exercises . . . can't be too careful about preparation."

"Nonsense. I'm up to here with exercises, anyway. Let's have fun. *Your* kind of fun."

Attila brightened considerably. "Yesterday I did

have a peek into the library and thought it most interesting."

"Oh."

Attila nodded his head emphatically. "Not boring old microfiche or computer screens. Real volumes. Some with leather binding and marvelous illustrations. Exquisite."

"So you'd like to pore over some antiquities."

"I'm sure you'd be bored."

"Not at all. Let's go."

Attila looked positively ecstatic. "I'm sure there are rewards. I thought I saw a volume of haiku that would interest you. You are aware of the poetry of your ancestors."

"Oh, yes. I think I wrote one or two in my romantic youth. Certainly, Til. That all sounds quite grand."

The library was on the second level. They took the antigrav pneumatic tube box to get there, one of the few items on board the craft with streamlined modern design. The first thing that Evanston had done was to give them a tour of the boat, including a brief glance at the library and art room. He'd given them access to these throughout the trip; at their destination Machiko placed her palm on a light strip. It read her DNA pattern. A door whisked open, revealing a room full of shelved books. The place had a wonderful, comfortable old booky smell.

Attila immediately gravitated to the poetry section, poring over a vellum volume with great awe and reverence.

Machiko discovered a whole section devoted to classic comic books. Now, that interested her. She was looking over a collection of ancient Superman stories when Attila looked up suddenly from his reading and said, "Machiko." Softly.

"Yes."

"Shhhh. We're alone, right?"

"I didn't see anyone in the corridor, and unless

they've got visibility dampers on, there's no one in here."

"Good. I believe that this library has an annex."

"No, it doesn't. Evanston showed us just one room."

"I'll bet he has more books. I bet the truly interesting ones are in the annex."

Machiko got a little annoyed. "*What* anex?"

"Shhh. I detect no observation equipment in this room, but I've noticed that voices do tend to carry through the corridors in this environment." He got up and walked over to a shelf of books. "My sensors picked up a control box here, behind these books." He carefully took the books down and placed them on a table. Sure enough, there was some kind of electronic switch on the wall—nothing like on the outside, either.

"Hmm. Curious. Purely mechanical. No identification required."

"I really don't think you should fool with that." Normally, Machiko would be just as curious as Attila. However, she didn't want to go ruining a good thing by getting caught snooping around where she didn't belong.

"Come on. If it was all that important, it would have an identity access seal. My spatial and analytical sensors detect a room next door, along with more paper and leather." His eyes seemed to glow with enthusiasm. "That must have some true antiquarian prizes."

He began to touch the controls.

Machiko got up. She could order him to stop, she supposed, but somehow it didn't seem worth it. Attila seemed interested and intent, and it was good to see him so fascinated with something.

Besides, she was getting a little curious herself.

Suddenly a complete panel of the library shelving opened, revealing a door.

Attila looked totally delighted. "Just like in the movies. A secret room."

He turned another switch, and a soft yellow lambency spread through the new room.

Machiko stepped forward to have a look.

Sure enough, there were books lined on more shelves.

Attila stepped forward, examining spines.

Machiko had noticed something else besides books.

"Fascinating," said Attila. "How very curious ... our benefactor seems to be a war buff. He's got extensive biographies of generals from Julius Caesar through Napoleon, Rommel, and even Lickenshaun from just a few decades ago. He's got all the books of John Keegan from *Face of Battle* to *A History of Warfare*. He's got all of von Clausewitz's writings. Of course, the *Art of War*. Many first editions. My goodness, he's even got things by Maenchen-Helfen, the most meticulous collator of Hunnish data concerning my namesake. Perhaps he's some sort of war-gamer. He's got that sedentary look about him."

Machiko walked to the other end of the small room. There was a glass case there, like those used in museums. Set inside the case were several items.

A glove.

A broken javelin.

Half a bloody mask.

And a knife.

"An interesting collection," said Attila. "And extensive. If he just wanted the data, it would all be stored in—"

"Til," said Machiko in a sharp, hushed tone.

"My goodness. A first edition of—"

"Til!"

"Coming, coming."

The android moved to her side. She pointed down at the display. He blinked at her.

"So?"

"Til. The pack I was telling you about?"

"Yes. The yautja. The Predators."

"This glove . . . these weapons . . . theirs."

"What. The pack's?"

"Not necessarily. I mean, these are part of their general war culture."

"I thought their whole culture was war."

"War. Hunting—all to gain honor, prove themselves."

"Yes. I've heard all your stories." He looked down through the glass case again, clearly mulling over this new turn of events.

"You know what this means, don't you?"

"There are a number of possibilities. The one *I* favor is that you're being taken for a ride. I knew that Livermore Evanston was no good the moment I met him."

"These only mean that Evanston's got some relics of the yautja. Nothing more. Although it *could* mean that he knows *something* about them. . . ."

"Care to list the possible speculations?"

"One step at a time . . . right now . . ."

There was a sound of voices. Distant voices, fortunately.

Machiko and Attila looked at one another for a split second and then immediately hopped back out of the room. With remarkable speed and agility Attila punched the necessary buttons and closed the door behind them.

They reassumed their places in their chairs, perusing books. A crew member walked past, gazed in for a moment, nodded good day, and then left.

"Shall we go back in and take another look?" Attila asked after the footsteps had echoed away.

"Maybe later. We've got a few more days' passage." Machiko nodded thoughtfully. "I need to think about this."

They went back to their respective reading.

7

he hunt was on!

Abner Brookings, Esquire, lawyer to the bright and the powerful, and gun-fancier extraordinaire, strode through the *yanga* trees, a beautiful antique rifle cradled in his arms like a well-oiled baby. The sun of this world, a purplish, splotchy affair, was just topping a magnificent frieze of mountains in the distance, and the colors the rays made through the swirling mists against the leaves and vines and flowers and trees were spectacular. Brookings took a deep breath, tasting the sweet and sour life of this world, and again he felt the charge that the hunt always brought:

Total Hereness.

How often, in the docket of some musty judge's quarters, or even in rich corporate boardrooms, did his mind wander. *Thereness*, he called the state, and he decided that human beings lived most of their lives in that quarter-conscious state.

Some people woke themselves up through Zen meditation. For some, music rang their chimes. Others—well, the list was endless, from grav-skiing to poga-licking.

For Abner Brookings, though, it was the hunt.

For him it was the Prospect as well as the Act of killing something.

Today, though, the sensation was particularly acute, for the something was the sort of beastie who could just as likely turn around and kill him.

"Watcha think, Ab?" said the woman walking abreast of him. "Pretty good day. Think we're going to bag that *zangoid*?" Petra Piezki grinned and shifted her hold on her large and heavy twelve-gauge shotgun. She was short and stocky with big shoulders, and she liked heavy artillery. Piezki was a lawyer in the same firm as Brookings, a little younger, and not quite the snappy dresser that the dapper A.B. was. In fact, she looked a little like Jungle Jill in her silly khakis. She was dark and gruffly friendly in her Russki sort of way, and a good gal to have a vodka martini with after nailing poor suckers in legal coffins. They'd gone hunting before, but never on this kind of extravagant planet, never for this kind of big game. Brookings could see his own excitement mirrored in the flushed cheeks and the stance of his partner.

"I think we'd *better* bag that *zangoid*, or we're going to have to buy drinks for the whole bar tonight."

Petra grinned. "We did boast last night, didn't we?"

"Like the drunk legal eagles we are."

"Well, it's not as though we haven't had any experience in this kind of sport."

"Ducks and squirrels, some deer, one mountain lion."

Petra looked taken aback. "Not! They were alien, fearsome creatures!"

"The equivalent of the above."

"Come on, Ab. Give us some credit."

"What we've actually killed, Piezki, isn't much."

"The sims, though. The sims!"

"True—but 'virtual reality' in my humble opinion is a term that should be changed to 'verisimilitude reality.' I assure you it's just not the same thing."

"We'll see."

"Right. After pointing that gun down the jaws of a charging *zangoid*, I'm pretty sure that we'll both have different views of this entire business. And goodness knows, on the plus side, it will be a bigger rush."

There was a long pause, and Abner Brookings took the opportunity to gaze over the party, taking comfort in the numbers and the fact they had a couple of guides, looking competent and hearty as they surveyed with keen eyes the murmuring alien savanna.

"You know," said Petra Piezki, "maybe we should have taken along heavier armament." She looked down at her beautiful shotgun with its elaborately carved handle and its beautiful metalwork. "Like a many-millimeter blaster or something."

"Ah," said Brookings. "Getting a slight bit of jitters, are we?"

"Of course not. It's just that—well, from what those guys were saying about the particular *zangoid* that was being let loose this morning—I don't know. Maybe the first time out here on Blior we should have been a little more cautious, a little less sporting, huh?"

Brookings hefted his own rifle. "Look, these guns are part of our collections, right?"

Petra nodded, looking a little pale.

"We paid plenty of money for them, right?"

"Oh, yes."

"So let's use them!"

Petra thought about that for a moment as the sun burned through the mist and an exotic bird with rainbow plumage thrashed up out of the foliage.

"That's the sort of game these things are suited for." He shook his head. "Man killers ... I dunno."

Brookings grinned, showing his perfect teeth. Some of them were implants, and they were all personally attended to by an expert dentist at extraordinary price. However, Abner Brookings had learned that nothing befitted a good sharky lawyer like a flashy set of choppers. "Petra, Petra! This isn't paddle tennis. This isn't null-grav ball! We're here for the challenge. We're both gun collectors, right?"

"Absolutely."

"And a sport gun isn't truly a sport gun until it's been christened by the blood of a challenging kill."

Petra cocked a civilized eyebrow. "So you say."

"I speak from a long tradition of gentlemen hunters. Believe me, there will be absolutely nothing like the feeling of composure, contentment, and satisfaction you'll feel in your old age when you sit down in your study with your snifter of cognac and view the trophies on your wall, right beside your tasteful gun collection." He coughed and shivered exquisitely at the very notion. He pointed over to the guides, two brawny extrafabs slightly bent under weaponry and powerpacks. "Besides, should we run into trouble, we've got friends here with blasters." He pulled out a bit of Tartonian snuff and snorted it up his nostrils. "People don't pay the money they do for this expedition to get *killed*. They pay for the illusion of danger."

Petra shook her head. "I don't know. I'm feeling somebody squatting on my grave, doing something obscene."

"How amusing. It's called *fear*, my good friend. It's fresh and original and primal, and when you're through it, you'll go back to your normal humdrum— and then, before you know it, be back for more."

"I just want to get through this now, and maybe later I can buy you a drink, pat you on your back, and tell you how right you were."

They were an odd couple, Abner and Petra. When they did criminal law work for the corporation, their nicknames were Bad Cop, Bad Cop. When they did any other kind of work, they were called Shark and Sharkette. There were a whole raft of names they were called behind their backs, but in Brookings's opinion when you were called nasty names as a lawyer, that just meant you were doing your job well.

Abner Brookings was a full head taller than his compatriot in torts, and blond to boot, a handsome devil. He was forty-five years old, although with his rejuv treatments and his regular exercise and vitamin injections, he still looked a rigorous though experienced twenty-seven. There were those who whispered that Brookings sucked blood to stay young, and he would always air these statements to his office and colleagues with the addendum that if he indeed sucked blood, it was only metaphorical—and could you undo that collar a bit . . . I can't quite get at your jugular.

He had a straight nose and a square chin; he almost looked prefab. Money had bought him his good looks, and he made little secret of that either—although he added that this way he didn't have to buy women. This was the one area of modesty in a generally arrogant and immodest individual, and he cherished it. He'd had a few wives here and there through his life, and a few children, whom he saw irregularly. Mostly now what he had was an exciting and fulfilling life and lots of money, beautiful women, adventure: a life, in his opinion, far beyond the dreams of lesser human beings.

In truth, his allusion to "paying" for this expedition had been mere rhetoric, since there were actually professional matters to which the corporation had sent him here to attend.

Business mixed with pleasure, so to speak.

However, as true as that may have been, he was

quite impressed with what had been done with this
planet. As a hunter himself, when he'd heard about it,
he'd been intrigued, but he'd had no idea of the true
wonderland old man Evanston had concocted on this
world so far from the system that laws didn't matter.
This made the lawyer in Brookings nervous; but the
man, the hunter, it excited.

Anything was possible.

They walked through the warming day a little farther in silence. The other hunters in the party chat-
tered; Brookings could smell their jitters. And no
wonder. These weren't true hunters; not even true amateurs. They were just rich wanna-bes who thought by
plunking down cool credits they could put on some
macho, some stink of *cajones*.

Ha!

There were ten of them, ranging from scrawny to
obese. Some Company people; mostly remoras, entre-
preneurial hangers-on to corporations or to the Independent Man himself, Livermore Evanston. The Man's
dream, of course, was to make this world a business-
man's rite of passage—all corporation flunkies, all
"free market" sorts; anyone with a couple million to
rub together and make some money to burn, money
to spare should they want to get away and blow apart
some unlikely game.

Chances were, when those Disneyland days came,
it would be a cream-puff planet, with no edge. Brookings would have to look for his thrills elsewhere.
However, right now he'd get his kicks while he could.

"So, Nickelson," he finally said, calling out to one
of the prefabs. "Any sign of our guest of honor?"

Hank Nickelson turned and looked through heavy
lids at the lawyer. "Yo, Mr. Brookings." He lifted one
of his brawny arms and indicated. "I got a reading
from about five hundred kays ahead." The man's accent was gilded in Bronx. Brookings wasn't sure it
was real. It was a pure tough-guy accent, and maybe

The Man had trained his guide especially to talk in Tough Guy.

Take the other hunt leader, Hans Beinz.

"*Ja.* Ve haf der pheromone tracker on high. She is in our sights." Big teeth shone through a scowl on the Wiener-schnitzel face.

A fake German accent, no doubt learned from old World War II films.

Give me a break, thought Brookings.

Then again, maybe it made the excitement and uncertainty more entertaining for the others. For Brookings, though, it was like being in a bad VirtReal Adventure.

Oh, well, when the actual shooting started, *real* reality would take over.

"Good," asserted one of the newbies, a twitchy little geek in glitter-blue sunglasses and mousy mustache. Name of Sherman something, and he'd drunk milk the night before at dinner. "I ... I can't wait for the action to start."

"You sound as though you're trying to convince yourself, friend," said Brookings, unable to resist the opening.

"Going to be nasty, I can just feel it," said Petra. "I just hope we all coughed up the insurance premiums that were strongly suggested. Particularly the mauling-and-lost-limbs charge."

That got some eyes bugging.

"Hey, goofball," said Hank. "We don't need none of that, now. Everybody's gonna be safe, long as they follow the rules. And rule number nine is, Keep your big mouths shut if your group head tells you to." Glare. "And I'm tellin' you."

Petra shook her head and laughed. She looked over to Brookings for backup, but the lawyer just gave her a "This is *your* shit you just stepped in, colleague" look that he'd perfected with partners in court.

Petra shut her mouth.

After a while Hans looked up from his machine-encumbered arm, a puzzled expression knit over his meaty face. "Funny. I'm not getting anything on the motion sensors."

"Maybe the *zangoid* is asleep."

"What? With the sun up? The thing had a good rest last night. Morning is its most active period."

"Maybe it's caught something, and it's chowin' down."

Hans tongue-probed his cheek thoughtfully. "*Ja. Ja.* Must be!" His eyes, though, did not look sanguine.

"What you think, Petra?" said Brookings, drolly. "Perhaps the fearsome critter has found a perch on a tree somewhere and is presently patiently waiting to feast on your liver."

Petra smiled. "No, on your brain, good buddy. It likes soft food."

Brookings let off a hearty chuckle and slapped his colleague on the back. "That's the spirit. Stupid jokes. Bonhomie. Bonding. That's what makes this a hunting safari of some quality and note."

With renewed vigor they advanced to the forefront of the party, following immediately behind the two leaders. The others in the group, though, did not look so reassured. In fact, the general consensus, if expressions were to be read, was that perhaps they should all just go back and play something lighter and less troublesome, like a few holes of golf.

The *zangoid* had been beacon marked. Hans and Hank followed their sensors and tracers into a large copse of tall trees, a denser part of junglelike terrain. The smells were more pungent here, the rising damp steam more oppressive.

They filled out into a small clearing.

There was something in the middle of a clearing, and Brookings could see the digitals and dials grow excited.

Hans pointed. "*Ja.* There."

"What's it doing?"

"Just lying there," said Hans.

"Odd," said the other leader. "*Zangoids* prefer to remain in the brush. You generally have to flush them out. What's it doing in the open?"

"Maybe it's a retarded specimen," said Brookings.

Both leaders flashed dirty looks at the lawyer. They were big and dominating enough that Brookings cringed a bit at their obvious displeasure. He'd have to be a little more discreet with his quips out here. He couldn't hide behind the robes of a judge, and these boys could kick his tail, easy.

Still, it gave him a little thrill to be so saucy with them; a part of the dare of this whole expedition.

They approached the *zangoid*.

The beast was lying prone on the ground, on its back, quivering.

Zangoids are generally feline in principle, with a lizardy head and hide and six limbs—four legs and two arms. Some called them "snake centaurs" because of their resemblance to creatures of Greek mythology. They were fearsome beasts with talons on mobile limbs, claws on their "hands," and sharp teeth in their head. They were most definitely carnivores, preferring their meat from the fresh, quivering, and bloody counter. Although they hunted in packs, a *zangoid* on its own was a far more fearsome and dangerous beastie, which made it an ideal hunting animal. Thus it had been imported to Blior, and thus it was being used for preliminary safaris. The leaders had hunted lots of *zangoids* before and knew their habits, making this a reasonably safe expedition, despite the obvious snarling viciousness of the things.

However, Abner Brookings could tell from the expressions on Hank's and Hans's faces that lying down on its back in the middle of a clearing was not generally one of the *zangoid*'s known habits.

"What's it doing?" piped one of the subamateurs.

"Is it having some kind of attack?" asked another.
"Maybe it's sick."

There were other suggestions, including calling it a day and going home. However, Hank put up his hand for silence.

With his gun poked forward, he took a few steps closer to the creature.

Brookings watched, his own safety off, as the *zangoid* went through what appeared to be a series of seizures. Its wide eyes were rolled back in its head, and its splayed legs trembled spastically.

"Look. There's something growing in its chest," whispered Petra.

"Looks likes a pulsing growth or something," added another hunter.

"Shhhh!" said Hans with full Germanic sibilance.

Brookings watched with interest and disappointment. There was plainly something wrong with the *zangoid*, which, while interesting enough, meant that in all likelihood they weren't going to be able to hunt the thing.

A bulge had indeed formed in the creature's lower chest, and it seemed to pulse, as though the *zangoid*'s heart was beating far too hard. The animal's mouth had opened and snapped closed, and it had bit off part of its tongue. Rich red blood streamed down its side.

Every movement of the beast screamed its clear state of delirious agony. Its lizard eyes seemed expanded to the point of popping out of their sockets. It stank of blood and urine and feral fear.

The whole atmosphere around it was charged with an electric precognition of terror and violence; Brookings could feel it thrumming through the very ground. It raised his hackles.

He thrilled.

He could tell that Petra felt it as well. The young, stocky woman looked on the verge of bolting and running. Brookings placed a comforting grip on her arm, staying her. Then he turned his attention back to the event at hand.

"Stay back," cautioned Hans. "We don't haf any idea what's happened."

"Shit, man. The Boss pays a lot of money for dese things," said Hank. "He's gonna wanna know just what went wrong with dis one and—"

"Jesus Christ!" cried one of the new women.

With good reason.

The chest was expanding again, this time not retracting, just growing like some fleshy, bony balloon. A bulbous, puslike, veiny head formed at its peak, as though it were some kind of gigantic carbuncle in bad need of lancing.

It burst.

Blood spattered in all directions, a particularly large splatter falling and drenching Hank. But this was all peripheral to the main show, which Brookings watched with horrified fascination, rifle down and ready.

Emerging from the hole came a crimson-drenched wormlike creature the size of a heftily muscled arm.

"What the hell is that?" cried Petra.

"Some kind of parasite, it would seem," said Brookings. "Some kind of creature on this world they don't know about? If so, it has an amazing gestation period if the beast was just let loose this morning."

"*Nein,*" said Hans. "This *zangoid* was let loose several days ago to adjust to the environment. Experiment."

Both the hunter-guides looked as though they were undecided about whether to try to capture the creature or just blast it.

The creature didn't wait for their decision. It squiggled out of its host—clearly dead now, damaged tongue lolling, ribs spoked up like tombstones—and scurried for cover.

"Quick," cried Hans. "Hank—shoot it!" He raised his own blaster.

Hank wiped off a layer of blood and raised his own weapon.

Before either could twitch a trigger, however, something tore through the shrubbery. It was going almost too fast to see, but Brookings, who had excellent eyesight, made out the dim outline of some kind of boomeranglike device.

It whooshed through the air.

It sliced into the thick worm creature, cleanly lopping off its head.

The wormthing writhed in death throes.

The device that had killed it whisked back into the bushes, disappearing from sight.

"What the hell—" said Hans.

Brookings crouched, looking around. "It looks as though we're not the only ones hunting today."

"What do we do?"

"For right now, we just stay put and see what happens."

The others, however, paid no heed to this advice.

Two men broke and ran back in the direction in which they'd come.

"No, you idiots. Wait!" cried Hans. "There could be danger! Stay *together*!"

Neither listened. They cut through the quickest way back to the savanna, to civilization.

"Let 'em go, man," said Hank. "We've got our own problems."

"What's happening—"

"I dunno. Those weird signals we been getting. The tech boys have been saying that something weird's been going on for a while now, but the head honchos have been just forging on, you know. Turn on the cameras. We better get this down for posterity."

"And posterior holes, from the sounds of it," said Brookings.

"Camera's been on ever since I saw that thing," said Hans, backing away slightly, as though just in case something else was going to blow out of that chest cavity, or even the head maybe. "Bad stuff." His blaster was up, and his eyes were easing back and forth, catching a wide arc of vision. Feet apart, ready. A professional's stance.

"What do we do?" asked Petra.

"I suggest we see how our guinea pigs do in their path, eh?" said Brookings.

"Stalking horses of their own making?"

"Precisely."

The stalking horses were galloping along, indeed, at a rapid clip.

However, they did not make it.

Before they were halfway through the glade, immediately under a large palmlike tree, something shuddered in the foliage, and something black, something netlike folded around them from beneath, hoisting them into an elastic-gripped ride. They bounced in their tree-prison only once, before other things rippled through the foliage.

Spears.

Simultaneously these javelins transfixed the attempted escapees. One through the head. The other from shoulder through groin.

Both men had just enough time to let off a yelping screech and wiggle a little bit before the streams of blood started streaming out like beet juice through a colander.

"Oh God, oh God, oh God," cried one of the newbies.

"Shit and damnation. That fuckin' tears it!" said Hank. "This ain't supposed to be happenin'."

"Hank! Stay in formation!"

Ignoring his fellow hunter, the well-muscled man ran forward, spraying a huge plume of energy up into the treetops from where the javelins had emerged.

Defoliation on a massive scale. The leaves did not even have time to burst into flame. They were simply blown into carbon along with many of the surrounding trees, leaving only blackened skeletons behind.

Hank turned around, a satisfied smile broadening his lug's mug. "There. That should hold the bastards down awhile, so we can see what the hell's going on. Hans, what are you showing on your sensors?"

"Nothing."

"Can't see anything up in the trees, either," added Petra.

"Maybe we got whoever it was," said Hank.

"I thought I saw something hopping from tree to tree up there," said a slender, bespectacled woman, who in Brookings's estimation wasn't quite as geeky as the others.

"What—now?"

"No, before."

Hank shrugged. "I guess we're just going to have to sift through the ashes. What do you think, Hans? Some kind of assassination attempt on one of dese worthies here with us?"

"I don't know. Any of you have reason to think somebody's after you?"

"Maybe they were after Blake and Alvarez," suggested Petra.

"Those guys. Unlikely," added a jowly man named Gustavson, profusely sweating.

"May I, as a lawyer, remind you gentlemen that we are presently all on audio and video, and doubtless this may be used in some sort of hearing," said Brookings.

"You can turn *that* off, buddy," said Hank. "There's no law out here but The Man's."

Brookings shrugged. "Sorry. Guess I'm just on automatic."

"What are we going to do? Take the bodies back with us?" said Hans.

"I'm afraid that I kind of blew them apart as well."

"Pick up the pieces, then."

"May I suggest that we pick up our own pieces and get out while the getting's good?" said Gustavson.

"We could send back an armored vehicle to paw through the wreckage," said Hans.

"I think that would be wise."

"I just can't figure out what went on there," said Hans.

"I really think we should leave that to the experts," said Hank. "We'll just get the data on this situation now, then get the hell *out* of here."

"*Ja.* I'm working on it, I'm working on it."

"Christ, you rube. You're going to have to get a little closer than that to get anything."

All this time Abner Brookings had been growing increasingly nervous. Before, the prey had certainly been capable of turning back and biting, but that was all part of the fun. Before, this place had been alien and strange, but that had been the frosting on the cake, fun stuff as well.

Now, though . . .

Now, with an armed and *civilized* menace mysteriously skulking about among the trees, things were profoundly altered into the truly unknown. Abner Brookings generally faced intelligent opponents in court, and those were not armed. Now he was in quite uncomfortable territory, and the threat to his mortality was not thrilling; it was unsettling on a deeper level than he knew he had.

"Perhaps you should be thinking about a higher calling, gentlemen," said Brookings.

"Yeah?" said Hank absently and brusquely as he made his way closer to the unharmed trees, holding out his sensors to get the best possible reading. "Like what?"

"I'm talking about your charges. You're responsible

for twelve lives here, two of which have been extin-
guished."

Hank shrugged. "Look, buster—you signed the
agreement. Did you read the thing?"

Brookings was a lawyer. Brookings read everything
he signed. Only as a consultant of the corporation, he
hadn't signed anything—this trip was free for him and
was all included under his umbrella agreement with
the corporation.

"Well—er . . ."

"What it says, Shylock, is you fucking pay your
money, you fucking take your chances."

Voices raised among the group. Voices that seemed
to be in general disagreement with that sentiment.

"Shit. Fuckin' Sunday hunters."

Hank shook his head sorrowfully and waded out
into the unknown. He directed the sensors in a wide
arc.

He stopped in his tracks.

"Shit, Hans."

"Vat?"

"There ain't just something out there . . . there's
several somethings out there, *moving,* and I can't see
a goddamned one of them."

"Look—over there . . . ," cried one of the Sunday
hunters.

Brookings followed the pointed finger.

Yes. There looked like something fuzzy and dis-
placed among the trees. Leaves shook and a branch
visibly bowed.

"Get your asses down here," shouted Hank. He
pointed his blaster up at the trees. "Or I'm going to
mow those trees down, just like I did—"

There was only a brief flicker.

A thunk, and a tearing.

A sharp intake of breath.

The next thing Brookings knew, Hank staggered,
equipped with a new appendage.

A javelin just like the one that had killed the others had almost magically appeared, transfixed in his chest, bloody barb sticking out of his side.

Hank looked down at the spear.

For a moment he tried to pull it out of his body, and then he keeled over dead.

"Damn!" Hans said no other words of benediction for poor Hank's departing soul. He just ran forward, screaming, pouring out a blast of energy from his gun.

For his trouble he was rewarded with one of the boomerang devices. It sailed through the air, again seemingly out of nowhere, and cleanly sliced through most of his neck.

The head whipped back on the remaining strands of skin and muscle. A fountain of blood whooshed up into the air. The blaster scorched the earth harmlessly under Hans's clenched fingers. Upside down, horrified and stunned eyes stared at the party for a moment, aware . . .

And then the light died in them.

The body toppled over, still twitching. A gout of fire churned up some more dirt.

And then it was over.

For Hans . . .

A rush of adrenaline and panic suffused every cubic centimeter of Brookings's body. He looked down at his antique, expert rifle—and it seemed as useless as some stick.

The stink of death was in the air, and Abner Brookings had no desire to add his own to the mix.

He reached over with his rifle and tapped Petra on the shoulder.

"I don't like the turn of events. Let's go."

"Maybe we should grab the blaster."

"Uh-uh. That's going to invite another attack. Let's see how fast you can run. Follow."

So saying, he turned and started running back the way they'd come.

The remaining hunters were mostly frozen, transfixed with terror. Their protectors, after all, had been
killed, and now they were effectively alone in the wild
in a confrontation with an unknown enemy.

Two of them began firing randomly into the brush.
Mistake.

Deep in the pit of his instinct for survival, Brookings knew this was a mistake. Exactly *how*, he had no
idea ... but there was *something* ...

He didn't dwell on the subject. He just ran on it, offering absolutely no resistance.

Petra's footsteps and huffing sounded behind him.
The woman was smart. Follow the lead of your betters ... a practice that Brookings had always used
personally.

He was in good shape, a good runner, and he felt
the chemicals of his fear charging through his muscles like well-oiled, high-octaned pistons.

The path back was beaten, and the other 'end was
clear and free. If he could make it back there, Brookings had the feeling that he could make it.

Behind him he heard the shrill sounds of shots and
screams.

The massacre he'd foreseen was in the offing.

He put on a burst of speed.

Behind him he heard the sound of a trip, the stutter
of attempted renewal of balance, and the *chuff* of
bushes swept aside by a fall.

"Brookings. Give me a—"

A muffled yell.

Brookings's natural inclination was just to keep on
running. However, he sensed he was in an area of
safety, for now. He could spare a few seconds....

And boy, would Petra *owe* him.

It was better than money. It was a power that
Brookings actively cultivated. He stopped, went back
to where his fallen colleague was lying on her stomach, struggling to get up.

"Come on, chum." Brookings reached down and pulled Petra up by her arm. "No time for lying about. We've got to save our—"

He realized that the squelched screaming wasn't coming from the distance.

It was coming from Petra.

Affixed to her face was some sort of crablike creature. Brookings could see the ridges of blood where it clung, like some hellish mask.

Brookings let go and backed away.

There was nothing he could do. *Nothing.*

Abner Brookings was a man of quick, decisive powers, and he made a fast decision now. He was going to have to leave Petra to fend for herself.

The sound of the dying filling his ears, he turned and ran for all he was worth.

8

The planet Blior was an Earth-type world, fourth of seven planets around a GO sun. It had five moons, none of which were large.

When Machiko had read the specs on the computer in her prepping work, she had understood why Livermore Evanston had taken the time, the trouble, and the huge expense to settle and colonize this world for his own business purposes. It was an ideal world, with a nice atmosphere, a perfect axial spin, which gave it mild seasons, and a terrific balance between sea and land. There were twenty-nine Australia-sized continents distributed around the planet. Evanston had actually started his colony on only one, leaving lots of room for growth.

This island continent was called, arrogantly enough, Livermoreland, with its capital city dubbed

Evanstonville. When the rich man's yacht landed at the compound's spaceport, and Machiko stepped out onto the fresh tarmac and got a lungful of the air, any doubt of the planet's beauty and worth was immediately erased.

However, she was distracted by what was waiting for them: a group of twenty-one people, dressed in exaggerated military garb, reminiscent of the plumage sported by officers in the Napoleonic wars. They raised rifles and fired into the air in salute to the return of their obvious leader.

Evanston saluted them, smiling broadly.

"A little flourish of mine I enjoy. I employ a great many people, and we often have old-fashioned reenactments of famous battles from various parts of history. Gives my security forces a chance to exercise. We have an adequately trained force of two hundred people, with a hundred reserve. Of course, they also have other jobs and functions."

"Security force? You're in the middle of nowhere. What do you need a security force for?"

The smile became a frown. "You never know. The unprepared planet is the doomed planet." He brightened. "Besides, it amuses me. Warfare, after all, is a form of hunting. And re-creation of battles is a valid sport. No one is hurt—much less dangerous than what people pay me for. I'm hoping to make these kinds of re-creations a larger part of the entertainment here one day."

"Have you had any run-ins with belligerent intelligent life?"

"No, but that doesn't mean that I won't," he said sharply, momentarily showing a harsh side. He softened, allowing the charm to flow back in. "Please. Allow a rich man his paranoia. After all, I allow you a sidearm." He nodded down to the holster, which held an old-fashioned .38 revolver, a weapon that Machiko felt comfortable with and had requested permission to use.

"True. It seems to be a scary, unexpected universe." She nodded at the uniformed people. "If you've got all these guns and warriors here, what do you need me for?"

"You and the others I've employed recently are specialists, Machiko. My security forces are merely people with guns and a lot of time on their hands. You are a past master—an artist, if you will."

She let it drop and watched for a moment as the military sorts marched off to canned martial music. She was amused by this display, but mostly she was impressed by the scenery around her.

This was an *incredible* world.

She'd seen that on the way down, through the viewers. Evanston had shown them a special travelogue detailing some of the features. The usual panoply of waterfalls, crashing surf, sunsets, throbbing music, majestic mountains, jewellike jungles, purple waves of grain, et cetera. Machiko always just sort of tuned these kinds of things right out. You could doctor the hell out of images, and even though you could get some wonderful 3-D in-your-face special effects out of the medium, there was absolutely nothing like *being* there.

Blior had that pristine, rapturous glow of nature and creation and life and rock and water and pure air that the homeworld of Earth must have owned at one time, before Man and the alien infestation sullied it with agriculture, industry, and his own fungoidlike growth.

Even when she had been in a spaceship, she could almost smell it. Blior had that quality. It was a lifeworld, and to Machiko, despite her own difficulties with that particular state of being, these were the kind of planets to her taste.

"Very habitable," she said coolly, her reserve checking her enthusiasm.

"Rather nice piquant touch to the air, don't you think?" said Evanston, who had accompanied them down the ramp. Just on the edge of the launchpad, a large limousinoid carrier was pulling up. He gestured for them to move toward it. "Like an excellent year of Beaujolais, just decanted."

Attila sniffed tentatively. "Smells of exhaust to me."

"My goodness, Machiko. Your crony has an extraordinarily sour frame of mind for one embarking on such an exciting adventure." Although Evanston clearly didn't like Attila, he bore the android's presence with a bluff kind of humor that Machiko appreciated. Odd rich duck that he was, he was the kind of impresario whose language, carriage, and demeanor were at least always entertaining.

"You have to excuse Attila. He resents anyone who enjoys life."

"To the contrary. I applaud. I'd enjoy life a great deal myself—if I had one."

"Please, just ignore him. He really does have a heart of gold."

"Is *that* how they make androids these days? Well, I suppose gold *is* a good deal cheaper now."

"Sticks and stones, Mr. Evanston." The mouthy android shrugged. "Okay, okay. Actually, I say this begrudgingly, but it *is* quite a world, and from my stay on your ship—which I enjoyed immensely, particularly your library—I'd venture to say that the eponymous city we are about to behold will be quite something as well."

"Absolutely, absolutely. But I warn you both—don't compare the ship to the world. The city is most explicitly not constructed along classic masculine lines. You will see Victoriana or whatnot here and there, where appropriate—however, for philosophic purposes I've instructed the designers to dispense with most of the curlicues."

Attila shrugged. "Perhaps you'll allow me to have access to your yacht occasionally?"

Evanston beamed. "Certainly. Glad to keep you interested. Considering your disapproving intellect, I seem to have captured some of your imagination."

"Any warlike nature is just a program I employ when necessary. The purpose of war is to bring peace."

"Ah yes. That Chinese war philosopher said that, didn't he?"

Attila seemed impressed. "Yes, as a matter of fact. Lao Tzu?"

"Precisely. But didn't he also say, 'The purpose of peace is to prepare for war'?"

"Only in terms of balance."

"Your interpretation. Allow me mine." Evanston gestured. "Besides, this is not about *war*. . . . Hunting is far more primal, elemental."

"And these days, exclusive . . . ," said Machiko. She gave Attila a "Would you please shut up" kind of look, and the android nodded grudgingly.

"Also, this world is about far more than hunting. I'm not, after all, totally bloodthirsty." The irony was rich in his voice, and Machiko's chuckle was honest. "This world is about—enterprise."

"Free enterprise?" said Attila, taking on an interested tone.

"Well, it's certainly not *free*," replied Evanston. "You've got to be *extremely* well-heeled to come here. I suppose I'll eventually make a profit. You'll have to ask my business people about that. . . . On second thought, don't. They advised against it." He shook his head. "People with no vision. Still, business, hobby, whatever—it's a *magnificent* place, and I'm sure you'll be quite impressed with it. In fact, I'll give you the Cook's Tour, forthwith."

As soon as they arrived at the limousinoid, a man hopped out of the backseat.

"Good day, Mr. Evanston," the man piped. "Welcome back. And good day, Machiko Noguchi and Attila the Hun. Welcome to our magnificent planet."

"How does he know our names?" asked Machiko.

"I took the liberty of subspacing the results of my quest back to my highest officers. This, my new friends, is my personal secretary and entertainment director, Willem Cordial."

The man gave a brisk, self-mocking bow. "At your service. I'll be in charge of your personal needs during your stay here," said the man. "Anything you want, I'll get it. If this were a giant luxury hotel, I, Willem Cordial, would be your personal concierge!"

Willem Cordial was a short, slender man with blond hair, a perfect tan, and sunglasses. He wore khaki shorts and loafers shined to a glossy finish, a short-sleeved safari jacket, and a large rimmed safari hat. He had a clean-scrubbed, young look about him, and a squeaky, obsequious voice. There was a gap between his front teeth, and a feathery caterpillar of a mustache perched precariously below his nose.

"I sincerely hope that on your agenda for this stay will be the bagging of some big game!" said the man.

Machiko could only goggle. The guy seemed more like a comic parody of a hunter than anything approaching manliness and competence. She looked over to Evanston to see if this was some kind of joke, but for all intents and purposes Evanston was very matter-of-fact with the man.

No jester here, just another unusual facet of an unusual operation.

"I'm sure we'll take time for that, if time is indeed provided, Mr. Cordial," said Machiko. "However, we are here primarily to do a job, not partake of the obvious—ah—benefits of this world."

"Nonsense," said Evanston. "You're entitled to have a good time on your leisure hours and days, and Willem here will make sure you do. Isn't that right, Willem?"

"Entertainment is indeed my job."

"Excellent," pronounced Evanston. "Now, your bags will be along presently. In the meantime we'll show you Evanstonville and then take you to your quarters."

Willem Cordial gestured to the open car door and the luxurious leather seats beyond. "Please, just slide on into this climate-controlled vehicle, and we will endeavor to be of whatever service we—"

A sudden screeching of wheels got their attention.

A small sporty car was approaching them at high speed. The low car squealed to a stop just short of the limo, its bubble top popped, and a man jumped out of the car. He wore an expensive suit and tie, but looked disheveled and out of sorts. As he approached, Machiko could see that he had flesh-colored bandages on his face. "My God, Brookings. What happened to you? Abner Brookings, this is Machiko Noguchi. I have indeed retrieved her and she's in our service."

"Great. Nice to meet you. Sorry to disturb you, Mr. Evanston. I heard you were landing. I must speak to you personally."

"Well, of course. I should be in my office later on in the day."

"I'm sorry, sir. This is a vital issue and I must talk with you immediately. Important business . . ."

There was a wild and frightened look in his eye, and Machiko could sense that this man was not used to being frightened.

"Surely—"

"If I could just have your ear for a moment."

"Excuse me."

The two men walked back toward the car, out of earshot. The well-dressed man made a few heated gestures as he spoke in a whisper.

"*Some*thing's going on," said Machiko.

"Who *is* that guy?"

"He's a prominent lawyer, working on some high-level business here," said Mr. Cordial. "Now, then, if you'll hop into the car, we'll be all ready—"

"Has it got anything to do with my assignment here?" said Machiko.

"I haven't the foggiest, really," said their host. "Now, if you will get into the car—"

"I agree totally. Machiko should know," said Attila, turning as though to walk toward the talking men.

Cordial became noticeably flustered. "Please, no ... please cooperate."

"No need to rock the boat, Til," said Machiko, placing a calming hand on her android's arm. "After all, we're just hired hands."

The little man noticeably relaxed. "I think you'll find this vehicle very comfortable. We have a variety of music, snacks, and a full beverage bar for your needs."

Attila got in first. Machiko was about to follow when she realized that Livermore Evanston was clomping back to join them.

"No, no," said the big man. "Continue. I'm afraid I have to attend to something immediately, and so I'll be riding back with Mr. Brookings. Mr. Cordial, would you be so kind as to take my place in showing these folks around?"

Cordial positively beamed. "Why, yes, sir. And I think we'll actually be able to hunt up a splendid time."

"Good. Good. I will speak to you later, Noguchi, when you are comfortably situated in your quarters."

The usually affable, in-control Evanston looked quite preoccupied, thought Machiko.

She slid in beside Attila while Cordial spoke to the driver a minute.

"Wonder what's going on," said Machiko.

Attila wore a puzzled, worried expression. "I heard a few of the words."

"Well?"

But then Cordial was back, all smiles and goofy good cheer, and they were off on their tour, their guide yak-yak-yaking away.

9

Evanstonville was clearly more a settlement than a real city; however, it was spread out over a wide area, and there were many large and architecturally interesting buildings. It was set in a beautiful valley beside a meeting of two rivers. Trees and grass and plains surrounded it, green and vibrant.

As they drove along a road that crossed one of the rivers via a lovely old-fashioned bridge, Cordial explained that rather than allow his own city to grow in a haphazard fashion, Livermore had, with the help of experts, planned the whole thing out beforehand. Vital pieces—spaceport, essential roads, bridges, quarters and residences, storage places and parks—had been set in first, and as time and tide allowed, and actual colonists came to live and work on the world, the place would grow in a preordained and contained fashion. In this way there would be an aesthetic to every part of the city when in the fullness of time it was completed.

They drove past fountains and gardens and spectacularly designed buildings, many of which were just under construction. After viewing the city hall and main hotel, Machiko had to allow that she was impressed. There wasn't just money going on here, there was taste.

Then they stopped at a duck pond in the central park, and she had to reconsider.

Not that the park wasn't beautiful. It was. As centerpiece to the entire settlement, and to the future masterpiece city, it was already galaxy class. All manner of trees and grass and flowers and other blended botanical wonders were sculpted into a paradisal vision of nature, complete with rolling fields and swooping copses, glimmering streams and waterfalls, pretty ponds, and in the very middle, a splendid lake stocked with fish and graced with a collection of the greatest variety of Earth ducks and swans and other waterfowl that Machiko had ever seen.

"*Very* nice," she said.

"Rather like an interesting Western version of a Japanese garden, don't you think?" said Attila.

Mr. Cordial beamed with the compliments. "I think that all sorts of influences can be seen in this park."

"Well, I wouldn't go that far, Til," said Machiko. "I mean, where's the Zen garden, for instance?"

"Pardon?" said Cordial, brow furrowed.

"Zen garden. You know, sand, rocks, contemplation. Meditation!"

Cordial whipped out an electronic notebook, made a quick gathering of jottings. "An excellent notion. I'll make the suggestion. And please, any other thoughts . . . we'd appreciate them."

"Can we get out of the car and enjoy the fresh air by the lake?" said Machiko.

A frown from Cordial. "Well . . . actually, there are other things you should see, and we should be getting on."

"Nonsense. We need to stretch our legs, don't we?"

"Yes. After all, doesn't this vehicle make these stops? I mean, it *is* a stretch limo, isn't it?"

Cordial laughed. "Well, don't we have a sense of humor? Very well, but only for a few minutes."

"I'd like to take a look at some of these species of waterfowl," said Machiko as she got out. "You must have some sort of genetic and cloning biofactory here as well."

"Indeed, indeed. One of the features I was going to point out."

Amid the fresh floral and water smells, the sweet of grass and the sour of turned soil, they strolled down to the edge of the lake. Machiko produced a handful of crackers that she'd taken from the snack bin, gave some to Til, and together they soon had a flock of the things feeding and fluttering before them.

"Idyllic," pronounced Attila.

"Most disciplined," said Machiko. "And very interesting. I think I've already got a few questions I'd like to ask Mr. Evanston."

"Oh, I'm quite equipped with answers."

"No, I think I'll just use them for conversational fodder with our employer, if you don't mind."

"Of course not. Now perhaps we should be—"

"Say, look," said Attila, pointing to a rise just beyond the lake. "Another touring party?"

Machiko looked. She wasn't equipped with Attila's telescopic vision, but Cordial had supplied her with a pair of opera glasses to enjoy some of the scenery. She picked these up and examined the new arrivals.

They were a group of six men, all wearing stylized camouflage coveralls. Big hats and enormous goggles covered their eyes, and shoulder pads made them all look uniformly masculine and powerful.

"How peculiar. Who are these men, Cordial?" asked Machiko.

"Guests."

"Ah! So these are some of the rich men who've come to hunt."

Cordial nodded. "That is correct. Now, the limo is waiting, and there's so much more I want to show you."

Machiko put her glasses to her eyes.

"Wait a minute," she said. "These guys have guns."

"Shotguns, from the looks of them," added Attila. "How curious. Some sort of display of macho power. I also see holsters and bandoliers of ammunition."

"Yes," said Cordial with a forced cheeriness. "We of Hunter's World work to create an ambience of imagination and virility. Longtime symbols of power are utilized to create a sense of security and self-confidence in our guests. We also create exercises to prepare our guests for larger, more dangerous hunts and—"

"They're throwing bread to the ducks and swans," reported Attila. "They seem to be gathering in great numbers."

"What—feeding the birds is some sort of good-luck ritual before safari? I've never heard of that," said Machiko.

"Not exactly. This park, uhm, serves many purposes, all calculated to bring on various moods and satisfactions. In fact, if you'll just accompany me around to the other end, I'll show you something very interesting, something that—"

A gigantic, echoing blast interrupted his words.

Other blasts followed.

Machiko swiveled to see what was going on.

"Goodness," said Attila.

"Ha ha," tittered Cordial nervously. "Just a display of high spirits among our guests."

Ka-blam, ka-blam, ka-blam.

The men had lifted their guns and aimed them point-blank at the large gathering of birds trustingly partaking of the bready offerings. Now many of these ducks and such were just clouds of broken feathers and down, interspersed with a fine mist of blood and bone. Ruined duck bodies lay sprawled in the gory water. A flutter of wings took to the sky.

Whoops of joy.

Bloodthirsty success.

Ka-blam, ka-blam, ka-blam.

Flame and smoke poured from shotguns, and hard metal pellets shattered through a dozen more bodies.

The massacre was truly something to see, a Fourth of July of excess. As the shots ended and the ducks that had escaped flew away pell-mell, Machiko found herself gaping. The manly men were stomping around the flesh-and-feather detritus, laughing and clapping each other on the back.

The yautja had never done anything like this. Their prey were always hunters themselves. For food they would take down prey, yes—but never in such a dis- gusting display.

Machiko found herself sick to her stomach.

"My goodness," said Attila. "It seems a little exces- sive, doesn't it? And the waste!"

"Oh, the lab-and-factory folks can whip up more, I quite assure you."

"But the mess . . . hardly idyllic."

"A momentary thing, I assure you," said Cordial. "Look—the service robots are already coming."

A number of robots—true robots, of the servo-sort, of plastic and glass, waldo arms, and visible gears and equipment—appeared as though magically, hustling down on this barbaric scene. Quickly, the brave hunt- ers picked up a few of the less-damaged birds for sou- venirs and then let the robots deal with the rest. They set off for further park adventures, bloody and happy, tilting flasks and singing songs.

"Truly, where *else* in the galaxy can such exercises be discovered?" said Cordial. "Now perhaps another side of the park, and then on for the rest of the tour."

"Mind if my android and I take a little walk alone around the lake?" said Machiko.

Believe it or not, she thought to herself, *the brave huntress is feeling a little queasy.*

Cordial eyed his wristwatch. "I really do have to stick to my schedule . . . and we do have excellent drugs in the car that will doubtless eradicate any stomach or intestinal distress."

Machiko nodded. She'd be able to get Attila alone eventually and hear those words that he'd heard pass between Livermore Evanston and the lawyer. . . .

But apparently not now.

"That genetic factory you mentioned?"

"Yes?"

"The one that seems to be able to spew forth so many ducks and swans and all that expendable plasm and life things into this world?"

"I did mention such an establishment, didn't I?" He sounded a little uncomfortable, as though he hadn't realized the creature that had exited the bag had been a cat.

"If it's not too much trouble—could we have a look at that during our tour?"

Cordial, though obviously a bit discomforted by the request, said, "Certainly," with some of the verve and brightness returning to his speech.

Machiko followed Attila back into the car.

She wished she could talk this over with him now, without the ear of this flunky canting toward them.

She didn't feel real good about this "factory" thing.

Not good at all.

10

They drove past more houses, some built, some under construction, all dynamically engineered and brilliantly architecturally designed.

They drove past other parks, this time noticing roving packs of guests with guns, some bloody, some not.

They drove past a magnificent skeletal stadium, its promise explicit in the scaffolding that enclosed the growing shell.

All to the accompanying glowing descriptions of their guide, Mr. Cordial.

Finally, at the very end of the settlement, across a long field, crisscrossed by numerous fences, force fields, and other barriers and sentry posts, there loomed the most impressive building yet.

"Quite a building," said Machiko.

"More a compound, don't you think?" suggested Attila when Machiko made this statement.

"True, quite true."

In truth, there were more buildings than one, all of different shapes and sizes, but all were connected numerously by catwalks and gondolas and tubings and what have you, making it look like some gigantic monadic hamster colony. Machiko could see people walking back and forth, and a great deal of vehicular activity as well. It looked like a lively and productive industry, peculiarly stuck into a series of interconnected contemporary cathedrals. Glass and prismatic light; the occasional wisp of smoke stringing into the blue background of sky.

"Yes, there it is," said Mr. Cordial, gesturing absently. "Naturally we can't import the creatures we need for hunting purposes, so we grow and breed them there ourselves. A unique and still very experimental process, I might add, one that Mr. Evanston is watching over very carefully." He coughed. "Now, I'm sure that you're both tired and would like to make yourselves comfortable in your quarters before the other welcoming festivities our employer is preparing for you." He tapped on the partition between them and the driver, signaling him to drive past the intersection where a turn swung into the service road of the genetic-factory compound.

"We're here," said Machiko, "but we're not going to get to look inside?"

"I'm sure you must understand," said Cordial. "The activities inside those buildings are of a very sensitive and secret nature. Now, I'm certain that Mr. Evanston will allow you a tour. In fact, he probably wants to take you himself. However, we can't just barge in without warning. I sincerely hope you understand."

Attila said nothing.

Machiko nodded her head. "All right," she said. But

inside she still felt bothered. "Take us to our quarters, then."

Cordial relaxed. His entire attitude toward his guests seemed to change. Machiko sensed danger signals being dulled. Good. That was what she was hoping for.

"Thank you. I understand your curiosity, but I have my duties."

"Yes," said Machiko Noguchi, unmollified.

Their bags and clothes and other belongings were waiting for them at their room.

After all the luxury they'd experienced, the room itself was rather plain, one of ten lining a nondescript corridor in a brown-wrapper two-level building.

It was more like a barracks than a hotel, and while Attila seemed disappointed, Machiko was most emphatically not.

"We're hired soldiers here, in a way. I think that's what Livermore Evanston wants to remind us of." She sipped some tea Cordial had provided, looked out the window, and watched the limousinoid float away into the distance. The tea was iced, and it was exotic, rich, and cold; it sluiced away some of the stardust that had lined her throat.

"Okay, Til. Spill."

The android was sitting in a chair, looking thoughtful.

"I heard only a few words, but they were significant. I caught . . . 'hunting trip' 'all dead but me' 'bugs' "—he cocked his head—"and 'other hunters.' "

"That's all?"

"Yes."

"Well, that's what we're here for, right . . . the bugs."

"But who brought the bugs?"

"I believe you know what I'm thinking. . . ."

"I've heard your stories about Ryushi, but surely . . ."

"What do you think about that factory, Til?"

Attila shrugged. "Makes sense to me. Manufacture your own lions and tigers and bears."

"You think maybe Evanston was manufacturing bugs for hunting as well?"

"Why would he bring you to get rid of them?"

"Hell! They're bugs! Something always goes wrong with bugs!"

"I don't know. Why would he want to play with those things when he really hasn't even gotten Hunter's World off the ground?"

"Mysteries. Secrets." Machiko took a swallow of the slightly bitter tea, winked at her associate. "I like it. Puts some spin on the game, eh?"

"Makes *me* nervous!"

"Yes, well—it's a hell of a lot better than sitting behind some desk, monitoring mining operations."

"No comment here."

Machiko was about to ask him his opinion about the duck hunters in the park when there was a loud knocking on the door.

Attila got up and opened it.

Standing in the hallway were two tall, broad-shouldered men. Each gripped in his big hands a keg studded with microrefrigeration nodes.

"Hey, now!" bellowed one. "Welcome to Project Bug Spray. I'm ex-Captain Dick Daniels, late of the Colonial Marines, and this here's Ned Sanchez. Ned used to work for a security firm on Earth that dealt with the things." His eyes tracked from Attila to Machiko. "And you must be Machiko Noguchi." His eyes traveled over her firm, slim body in a taunting, hungry manner that she abhorred. She felt herself tensing: not another one of these jerks.

"Yes."

"Nice to meet you. We hear you're going to be

heading up this operation, so we thought we'd come over and introduce ourselves. Kinda been sitting around on our thumbs since we got here, and it's nice to know there's some action on the way, now that you're here." All said through an overfamiliar leer. He had a musky, hair-out-the-undershirt presence, and an overbearing, muscular aura that seemed to say, Let's get these formalities over with quick and then slip between the sheets, babe.

"Well, aren't you going to invite us in?" he boomed. He held up his keg. "We brought our own."

"I'm tired," said Machiko. "I only have a minute."

"That'll do!" A big grin split the man's swarthy, Roman-nosed face, and he lumbered in, handing the keg to Attila and offering Machiko a large, firm handshake. He smelled of hair and beery lunch, but he had a natural power to him, reflected in the firm muscles and the self-confident gait. His blond hair was tousled, but he was no spring chicken. It looked as though this guy had been in some heavy-duty scrapes and, from the scars on him, hadn't come out unbloodied. But unbowed? That was another story.

"Got some mugs or something?" he asked. Attila went to find something.

"Say, you're one solid woman. You'll have some beer with us, won't you?"

"I'm drinking tea."

"Oh, c'mon." He turned to Attila. "Get a brew for my new sweetheart, will you, guy?" he roared off at Attila. "We don't know what we're getting into here. Might as well party while we can, right, angel-eyes?"

With no warning Daniels stepped over and put his big arm around Machiko's back. She could immediately smell that he'd been drinking beer before he'd arrived. Somehow his big hand wriggled down to her backside and squeezed her right buttock as though testing the ripeness of a melon. The buffoon was large, probably weighing over twice as much as

Machiko, and probably figured he could get away with this kind of behavior by sheer intimidation.

Machiko barely thought about what she was doing; her reaction was automatic. She pulled the hand away, grabbed his arm by the wrist, stepped away, and with practiced ease flipped Daniels over. He landed heavily on the floor. Machiko stepped on his face as she twisted his arm at a startling angle, just short of damage.

"Next time I break it, chum. Understand?"

"Jeez. I was just joking!" objected Daniels.

"You didn't answer my question."

"I understand, I understand!"

She let him go, and he got up.

Sanchez's eyes twinkled, and there was a slight smile on his face.

"I told you to cut that kind of stuff out, Daniels."

"Yeah, yeah, yeah," said Daniels, getting up and dusting himself off. "Guess there's a reason you're going to be in charge." He grinned uneasily. "Can't really even say you're my type, but I'd park my butt behind your command any day. Nobody's gotten the better of Dick Daniels in a *long* time."

A rollicking partyer from the feel of him.

"I'm not here for anyone's amusement, Daniels."

"Cripes. Give me that beer. I sure need it now." He took the proffered glass and downed a large gulp. Attila handed one to Sanchez as well.

Keeping himself well away from Machiko, Daniels eyed Attila. "What—we got ourselves *another* teetotaler here?"

"Not really," said Attila. Rather than getting into android territory, potentially volatile if you weren't sure of your company, Attila took a beer. "I generally prefer to wait until dark."

"Good move," said Dick. "A smarter asshole than yours truly. Here you go, Sanchez—to the pretty powerful personality we've hitched up with. I feel sorry for the bugs."

"If Ms. Noguchi doesn't mind, I'd like to try some of the beer I noticed in the refrigerator. That's a local brew of some potency, I believe. And if I'm not entirely wrong, it's a nut-brown ale."

Machiko raised an eyebrow. "Good call, Mr. Sanchez. You know your beers, then."

"From porter to lager," said the man easily. "My favorite is bitter. At room temperature."

"An Anglophile?"

"Nope. Limey bastards are just as rotten as anybody. I just like their beer, that's all."

Ned Sanchez was slender, younger than his companion, and certainly darker, though there were suggestions of gray threading through his long black hair, tied in a ponytail at the back of his head. He was friendly and relaxed, but there was a hard and remote core of reserve to this man, and an unreadable nature to his fierce, empty black eyes. Otherwise, he had a face like a Greek demigod, and his beauty was not lost upon even so jaded a soul as Machiko's.

"Sure. I don't know about room temperature. The tea is cold. I don't generally drink beer, but once in a while I enjoy something of quality."

Sanchez shrugged. "I'll live through the experience of a cold ale. Little hot outside, anyway."

Dick slammed his big hand against his buddy's back. "Shit. Neddy and me, we done some heavy maneuvers today with the guys, just funnin', you know, but keeping in shape—and he barely pops a sweat. Quick shower, and he's ready for another evening of brews and babes." He straightened himself with feigned pain and examined a fancied bruise. "I don't know, though. Maybe just an evening of brews might be safe."

"I didn't realize this was Sodom and Gomorrah," said Attila dryly.

Machiko watched as the android sipped at his beer, amused. Attila could drink as much as he wanted without effect. He almost literally had a "hollow leg." And these guys hadn't seemed to realize yet he was an android. Of course, it was rare one could, unless the law was to have androids marked . . . and there was no such law here.

"What? You gotta be kiddin' me. You get in a bunch of rowdy and rich men to shoot it up during the day, and you're going to have to keep them entertained at night. Pretty easy, that. Some gambling, some girls—and lots of drink!"

"I can spare a little time," said Machiko. She felt herself relax slightly. Daniels's good-natured response to getting tossed on his face amused her. A yautja would have demanded immediate satisfaction of honor in a tooth-and-nail battle to the Death. *Calm down kid,* she told herself. *You've changed, remember?* She invited her guests to sit down. Sanchez sat quietly and compactly, but Daniels sprawled out over the couch, feet up on the coffee table, completely at home. "How long have you been in town?" Machiko asked.

"A whole three days," said Daniels. "We've got ourselves a company of about fifteen total now, including you." He belted a laugh, then a long swig of beer. "And let me tell you, I never did see such a mangy collection of misfits in my life."

"Oh? I'm pretty impressed so far by you two."

"Us? Oh, yeah. Mind you, we've all got the experience and pedigree and what have you, and I guess we've all seen our share of action. I'm just generally talking about the social level of the *other* guys. Mercenaries. Real pigs." He opened his mouth and let loose a long and satisfying belch without excusing himself. Then he took another drink.

"Did we come for a tiddledywinks tournament?" Machiko asked.

"Well," said Attila, "perhaps tiddledywinks and tea."

Dick Daniels looked at Attila for a moment, mouth open. Then he started laughing, and slapping his knee. "Good. Damned good. Tea! Hey, Ned, you think that Evanston can rustle up some tea for—what did you say your name was, guy?"

"I didn't."

"I'm sorry. I didn't introduce you. This is . . ." Machiko caught herself. "Attila. Oscar Attila, my assistant and personal secretary."

Obviously not feeling like getting up again, Daniels assayed a brief salute. "Howdy there, Mr. Attila." Ned nodded as well. Machiko noticed that the handsome man seemed to be retracting even further into some private space. Daniels seemed to have plenty of scars on his exterior, but Sanchez seemed to have his own as well, albeit on his interior.

It made her wonder about him. He seemed to resonate on some level that intrigued her. The fact that he was merely polite to her, taking no other particular interest in her except as the woman who was going to command him, pricked her ego slightly—and made her wonder why.

She made a mental note to have a talk with him sometime during this visit. Obviously she wouldn't get much from him now, especially with Daniels ingenuously clogging the airwaves.

Still, with the man so freely dispensing information, she figured she should probably tap what she could.

And, as always, men talked more when they had a bootful.

"You know, Dick," she said, smiling, "I once knew a guy who reminded me of you."

"Oh. How so?"

"Big. Brave. Strong and obviously a man of the universe, as it were. I admired that man a lot."

Daniels responded with a cocky grin and a pleased

twinkle of the eye. The approval he'd so desperately wanted was his, offered on a satin pillow.

"One big difference."

Double take. "Oh? What?"

"He drank a lot more beer. And a lot faster. He'd have that beer done by now."

"Sheeee—it," said Daniels. "I'm just sippin', to be polite."

The gauntlet clearly thrown down, Daniels smirked. Refilled his mug. Upended.

The remainder of the liquid, at least a pint and a half by Machiko's estimation, slid past his big, bobbing Adam's apple, very little indeed slopping over his lips and rolling down his cheeks, or snorting up his nose.

Daniels clapped down the large mug, red-faced but satisfied. "There you go."

"I am truly impressed." She was indeed. Within moments the man's face was noticeably redder. "My other friend didn't drink *that* fast."

Another burp interrupted the conversation.

Machiko sipped her own drink, pursing her lips thoughtfully . . . and then thought, What the hell, let's go for it.

"We seem to be alone," she gestured around inclusively. "We can talk now. We seem to be a bunch of pretty powerful troubleshooters. What seems to be the trouble?"

Daniels blinked a little blearily, accepting the next cup from Attila. "Crap. The bastard didn't tell you?"

"Let's just say I'm more interested in what he told you."

"Fuckin' *bugs*. That's what the trouble is. That's the biggest trouble I've heard of on *all* these planets." Daniels developed a slightly gray pallor. "Fuckin' bugs. Don't know how the hell they got here. Only with bugs, you never do, do you?"

"And that's the *only* trouble?"

"Far as I know. . . . Oh, shit—well, there's the hunters, the rich assholes who think they know which end
of a gun the bullet or whatever come out of. Evanston
knows he's going to have some accidents, which is
why he sets 'em up with training and insurance, even
though right now he's not legally bound for nothin'.
Nope, there's plenty enough trouble not to buy any, I'll
tell you."

"No sign of other kinds of 'iffy' activity? Any other
kind of trouble?"

Daniels, for the first time, looked concerned. "Hey,
lady. Aren't the bugs enough? Shee—it. I've been in all
kinds of action. And bugs are the worse."

"But you're willing to face them again," said
Machiko.

"For the money we're getting, and the treatment?
Not really." The affable look was still gone, replaced
by a startlingly sober expression for one getting into
a drunk. "Look, this ain't just for the money. I guess
the truth is, Evanston's offerin' me a home. A goddamned family. This pirate looked at forty a long time
ago, and it's about time to commit to a goddamned
bar stool. Eh, Ned?" He elbowed his companion, his
good nature again suffusing his face.

Ned just shrugged. "We all have our reasons."

"That's damned right. And I'd like to know if yours
are any different."

"Evanston got me out of the Company."

Daniels raised his eyebrows. "Really?"

The lug seemed honestly interested. Machiko found
herself relaxing even more.

"I don't know about family, I don't know about
home. . . . What I do know is that this is better than
pushing papers. Would you agree?"

There wasn't a fighting person who wouldn't agree
with that. No reason that Machiko had to hide anything with these guys.

'Sure," said Daniels. "But, hell, I got my fighting experience in the Marines, and Ned here's been after the bugs all his life. Where'd you get your experience?"

"Well, I'm a trained martial-arts expert, and I did time in officer's school—and I dealt with the bugs on a planet called Ryushi," said Machiko.

Daniels's mouth dropped. "Damn! Isn't that the planet where nearly everybody got wiped—"

"Not this body."

Daniels said nothing. He seemed to be trying to grope with something, like coughing up some other memory he had on the subject. He didn't seem to be successful, so he just took another chug of beer instead.

A flicker of interest grew in Ned Sanchez's eyes.

There was a knock on the door. "Hey. Guys. We hear noise. What's going on in there? A party?" The voice was thin, whiny, and annoying.

Daniels slapped his face. "Jeez, it's Lou MacCraken. He can smell fun a kilometer away and then comes to ruin it for everyone. Don't let him in, Ms. Noguchi."

"Is he one of the troubleshooters?"

"Yep. And if there's no trouble, he'll attract it."

"Then I should meet him."

She told Attila to open the door. A tall, gangly man came in with a big wide smile and a long nose. He had a shorter, curly-haired Neopolitan sort with him, who already had a bulb of beer in his hand. Introductions were made. MacCraken's friend's name was Mishka Marino.

"Glad to meet you," said Machiko. "Would you like a beer?"

"No. I don't drink," said MacCraken, eyes shining with a kind of goofy glee. "Give Marino something, though. He drinks."

"Only with one hand, Lou."

"That's so he can grab the guys. And the gals. Right, Marino? Better watch out, Ms. Noguchi. You're his type. You're all his type."

Marino rolled his eyes as MacCraken cackled a
high-pitched laugh.

Machiko cringed a bit and looked over to Daniels
as though to say, You're right; where did Evanston get
this geek?

Still, this manic guy was entertaining if you didn't
take him too seriously, and the conversation pro-
gressed. With the right questions Machiko drew out
some little essentials about Evanstonville and
Livermoreland that only a few days' stay could have
obtained.

For one thing, not only had Evanston hired a great
many workers and started up a colonist movement to
this planet, he had somehow tapped the resources of
the corporation in terms of expertise, just as he had
done with Machiko. There were apparently a good
many "four eyes" here—a Marine bit of slang for technicians and scientists. Many of them, Daniels said,
worked in the factory and really didn't mix much with
the rest of the community.

Machiko tried to milk them all for more information about that factory but came up totally dry. These
guys hadn't even gotten *close* to the thing, nor were
they particularly interested in doing so. They were obviously thrilled with their jobs, not so much because
of the bugs, who obtained the unhealthy respect they
deserved, but because of the environment here and
the perks involved.

They talked about the other people who'd been selected. All seemed to have similar backgrounds: soldiers of fortune mostly, experience with bugs, a
mercenary bent with an inclination to settle down in
a place that had its share of thrills and excitement.
Evanston must have promised them a place in his
structure here, just as soon as the little problem was
gone. Guides. Battle technicians. Simulators. Whatever. This was just their kind of place, no question—a

paradise for men with a trade in violence, who hankered for some peace of mind.

"I look forward to meeting the others," said Machiko finally.

"Should I round them up?" asked Lou eagerly, excess energy radiating from him.

"Uh—no. No, I confess that—ah—Mr. Attila and I are a bit tired. And I, alas, have had my share of beer already. Tomorrow. Formally. It's been great meeting you guys informally, but let's just call it a day, all right?"

"Sounds good to me," said Daniels, getting up and scratching his butt.

"One last question, though," said Machiko. "It would seem that the bugs would be perfect hunting material, the ultimate experience. Do you think maybe Evanston planned to use them this way, and they got out of control?"

Daniels raised an eyebrow. "With all respect, ma'am, anyone who hunts bugs for sport has either got to be crazy, suicidal—or maybe just a little buglike themselves."

From the mouths of lumbering bruisers, thought Machiko.

They bade their adieus and filed out to find whatever other fun they could.

Ned Sanchez was the last one.

"Mr. Sanchez," said Machiko, putting a hand on his arm.

"Ned would be fine," he said easily, his dark eyes unreadable.

"You don't talk much. I get the feeling you might know more about this operation than the others."

His face remained expressionless. "I get the feeling you know more than all of us combined."

She shrugged and let him go.

But the parting seemed incomplete. She wanted to know more of what this man knew. She wanted to know more about Ned Sanchez, period.

11

You've been holding out on me," said Attila above the whir of the blades.

"Oh?" She adjusted her headset so she could hear him properly. "How so?"

"You never told me you could fly a copter."

She shrugged. "The way they make these things these days, it only takes a couple of engram imprints, some virt/real lessons, and then some hands-on." She smiled at him. "I bet we could just plug a new program into you and you could do it, too. Fact, I bet you could do it right now." She pushed a button. The steering wheel came off and she handed it to him.

He looked alarmed for a moment, and then he handed it back. "Ha ha ha. It's on automatic, isn't it?"

"Glad to see I haven't lost my sense of humor?" she said.

"Actually, I'm glad you haven't lost control of this craft!" Even though he didn't have the right sort of circulatory system, it was clear that Attila was white-knuckling the ride. She didn't blame him at all. She was swooping around a bit too much. Well, she'd keep the grav copter on a steady keel for a while.

It was the afternoon of the day after they had arrived on this world, and already they were out looking for trouble.

Machiko had requisitioned the vehicle that morning. Evanston had advised against looking over the terrain quite yet, but he'd been too busy catching up on other affairs to give her any real orders, so she'd talked him into at least letting her take a look at the surrounding environs, to get a feel for the lie of the land.

The other troubleshooters were out on maneuvers. She and Attila had joined them briefly. She'd met them but hadn't said much. They were pretty much as Daniels had said: worn mercenaries, looking for a home. She'd given them the usual patter: good to meet you, let's get this job done and done right, blah blah blah. Fortunately, her enthusiasm was real. All this was *so* much better than tapping input into a computer and riding herd on corporate mining nonsense.

And the possibility that she'd be dead next week, acid rotting out her brain? All the sweeter, because of the sharpened sense of life that she felt now.

They were in tree territory . . . alien trees, a kind of deciduous rain forest with large patches of plains and rivers. Wild, wild, with herds of native creatures glimpsed here and there and bright, vivid colors poking through the general green and brown.

"I wonder what kind of ecologists Evanston hired," said Attila.

"You think he's thought that far ahead?"

"Oh, yes, he would have to. There's no need to

terraform this place, but its life-forms are complex enough to take great consideration, especially if he's introducing new species."

"He's probably got a lot more on his mind now than just that."

"Probably. Nonetheless, he was talking about settling this whole planet—"

"He's most likely not too worried, since he's only settling a continent at a time. This one he figures he can mess up."

"A shame. It looks quite nice the way it is."

"I think that's the idea. A whole island continent for hunters to joyously plunder, free from restrictions and rules."

"Paradise."

"Or hell."

"Depends on your point of view."

Machiko thought for a while as the verdant land swept under the rotors and body of the copter.

"Til, something's going on here, something more than Evanston's told us about," she said finally.

Attila nodded. "I think we should talk about that. Put the pieces together . . ."

"I'm almost afraid to."

"Why?"

"I don't know."

"Sure you do. It's that gift-horse phenomenon."

"Yeah. But still—it's better than where I came from."

Attila sniffed. "We'll see about that."

"What, you want to go back?"

"I didn't say that. I'm just performing my function."

"What? Being a goddamned stick in the mud?"

"No. Being someone you can bounce ideas off of. Still, I'm entitled to my opinions, right?"

"I can think of a few other things to bounce off of you at this moment."

"You'd be so lonely without me." He smiled. Needling was such a gentle revenge. Machiko knew that deep down in his masochistic heart, Attila was rather enjoying it. Truth was, he was probably just wondering if he'd have to actually transform all that theory he was brimming with into practicality—and if the wise sage would get reduced to rubble in the process.

"Well, nothing untoward so far on sensors. You wouldn't have noticed anything, would you, with your special little nodes?"

"A great many things, but nothing that sends needles into the red."

"We'll just bank and take a look at the northwest quadrant awhile and then go back, okay?"

Attila nodded. "Fair enough."

The android didn't seem in a real hurry to get back to the fun and games of Evanstonville; he was just clearly not thrilled with being aloft, flying over unknown territory.

The wild land swept below them, a verdant carpet of mysterious life. Machiko perused it in silence. Such a *huge* area. How could they possibly hope to find any sign, any clue of what was going on there in just a quick field trip?

Nonetheless, they did.

She was about to call it a day when Attila spoke up. "I hate to admit this, but I see something."

"Where?"

He gave her the navigational reading, and she checked it on her scope.

Activity in a clearing.

Small things.

Big thing.

"Whoa!" she said, pulling up short and hovering for a moment. She thought about it and then lowered to a position still within sight of the scene, but far enough away not to attract undue attention. Then she punched up sensor screens and thumbed her telescopic step-ups.

"It's some kind of big lizard being attacked by smaller creatures."

Attila nodded. "I can't tell what kind, and I can't see what the creatures are."

"I have a suspicion. And if they're what I think they are, I don't want to go hovering around in that area." She pointed down to another adjacent plain. "I've got to have a look, though."

"I was afraid of that," said Attila. "Can't we just zip over and take some pictures?"

She shook her head. "If they're what I think they are, they'll know we know about them, and I'm not sure that's good."

"Better to be safe than sorry."

"And what is knowledge and the value of surveillance and intelligence?"

"Power," Attila said in a small voice.

"Exactly."

They landed.

"I want you to stay here," she said.

"Look, I may act truculent, but my job is to be by your side."

"I appreciate that, Attila. However, I need you here to keep the engines going in case we need a speedy takeoff."

"Perhaps I should go and reconnoiter and *you* can stay here."

"What? And let me miss all the fun? Besides, you're the reluctant one, aren't you?"

"Perhaps I am the careful one."

"Precisely. And I appreciate that. Sometimes, though, there are things that have to be done. And, Attila, this is something I have to do. This could be the key to everything."

"You could get yourself killed, too."

She shrugged. "Obviously. I also could have fallen out of my bureaucratic chair back on Dullworld and broken my neck. Now keep things revved up here. I won't be long."

She grabbed the camera, a blaster, and a weapons belt and hopped out of the copter, giving the rotors a wide berth. Quickly she loped up the grassy knoll separating the fields and then skulked through a large copse of trees. She was glad the copter was quiet; if the subjects of her quest here were as involved as she thought they were, they wouldn't have noticed the copter at its distance. She supposed they should have gotten just close enough to get a make on them and split. However, something deep inside her wanted some action, wanted to get closer. Was she being reckless? She thought not. There was something more down here than could be recorded through a telescopic lens.

And she had to see it for herself.

She made her way through the trees and underbrush, finally coming out through a glen to a perch above the clearing. Halfway through she began to hear the sounds of a most peculiar battle. Roars and snarls and cries. She could smell blood and conflict in the air.

She looked out.

Standing on its hind legs in the slight valley below, lunging and slashing at its attackers, was a thirty-foot-tall beast with a tail the size of a large tree, teeth and claws the size of butcher knives.

The attackers were ten yautja.

They could have been members of her old pack. But, then, Predators had no particularly variable fashion consciousness. They pretty much all wore the same kinds of clothing and armor. They were using spears and other manual weapons do deal with the creature, although a couple stood in the background with plasma pushers. This was a baiting game, clearly, not particularly in the realm of honorable.

She'd somehow expected to see Predators here and was glad that her hunches were paying off. It was good to have that knowledge. However, the beast provided the biggest surprise.

She'd never seen it before. She recognized it from books.

It was a tyrannosaurus rex.

So *that* was one of the things that the big DNA factory had been up to. It made a lot of sense. She'd heard that the biotechnology was available to bring back monsters of the past not just from old DNA, but from actually *building* DNA patterns according to specifics. She had just never seen it in use before.

Hard to imagine it done on a more dramatic level.

This was a ferocious beast, carnivorous savagery gleaming in its beady eyes. Blood rivuleted from cuts in its side and front, and a spear poked from its neck. However, all those pricks and nicks seemed only to have enraged it further.

The Predators appeared to be actually on the verge of retreating—or of using their stronger weapons. Clearly, they had bitten off more than they could chew.

She took out some binocs to have a closer look. Ranged it over the warriors . . .

And stopped on one.

Oh, God.

Shorty.

She tried to correct the focus, but it was sharp as a pin. A little bigger, a little more battered, but all the armor and other visuals aligned—this was the Predator who hated her.

Too bad she couldn't have killed him when she had the chance.

What was more, he seemed to be gesturing and carrying on as though he were in charge, orchestrating this odd exercise against the dinosaur. And not having a very good time, from the looks of it.

They were going to have to kill the beast, no question, and then immolate it or something; presumably the Hunters were operating secretly here, just as they always had on populated planets, and they wouldn't want their presence known. Should Evanston find one of his T-rexes dead from a spear wound (or blaster burns), he'd certainly have a better take on the mysterious things happening on his world.

Her mind was spinning with conjecture and speculation.

So much so, that she hardly heard the sound of the leaves rustling, the snapping of a twig.

Nonetheless, something deeper alerted her: a rising of her hackles, a deeper instinctual alarm.

She turned and saw the Hunter behind the tree.

Instantly, she realized how lucky she'd been. Doubtless, if they'd realized they would have had to deal with intelligent prey, they would have worn their cloaks. This bastard might have sneaked right up on her—

But then again, after living with them, after working with them, she rather doubted it.

Anyway, it gave her warning. The fact that he wasn't there to make friends was immediately apparent. He had his own blaster and was raising it to fire.

She was fast with her own, but not fast enough.

Nonetheless, at the same time, she *was* able to jump back and away. The edge of the jagged spout of energy caught the bore of her own weapon, and she let it go. It slammed against a tree and exploded. She rode the force, tumbling down a hill. Leaping to her feet, she used the momentum of her fall to give her a head start.

By the time the Predator swung around to shoot at her again, she was well away, running through a batch of tree boles.

She weaved helter-skelter.

Dodged.

Bark exploded next to her. She could feel the burn of the weapon's blast but did not take a moment to look back. She dived behind the bole of another tree, careful not to allow the vines growing at its base to impede her. Just down the glade, sunlight poured through an opening that she'd come through to get her view of the proceedings on the other side of the hill. If she could get through there, she'd have a clear run for the copter. Attila, seeing her coming, would be ready to take off immediately, and they'd have a chance. . . .

She leaped down the hill.

Ran into the clearing.

All the while behind her she heard the sounds of crashing pursuit.

She wondered if she should stop and make her stand. She had a pistol, and she could hide behind a tree. If worst came to worst, she could use the knife in her boot. The Hunter had a blaster, and even if they got off the ground, theoretically he could take a successful shot and destroy them both.

One of Machiko's talents was for quick, good decisions. Had she still been running with the pack, had she still been in that honor-is-everything frame of mind, doubtless she would have spun around and attacked her attacker.

However, her gut instinct was that her best hope for survival was to run for the copter.

Besides, life was just getting *good*.

She broke through into the clearing, began running for her life. Machiko noted to herself that next time she went on one of these little jaunts, she was going to bring along a radio unit. She just hadn't intended to leave the copter—this was supposed to be only a quick reconnaissance. Anyway, she had to live now with the realization that she couldn't contact Attila.

Which was unfortunate, in light of the fact that when she stormed down that ridge pell-mell, there was no sign of copter *or* Attila.

She hardly paused. She kept on running. Across the clearing were more woods and cover. If she could make that, there was a chance.

The thought pounded in her head, though:

What happened to Attila?

A blast ripped a fiery divot just to her right side. She zigzagged, dodging any other burst. In doing so she caught sight of the Predator, pounding into the sunlight, armed and ready for anything. Hardly a sight fiercer in the universe, and this was no ground on which to fight the bastard.

Her lungs aching, she hurled herself toward her objective.

She expected to feel the blast of a bolt in her back at any moment. *No*, she thought. *No*, came the voice of the warrior in her.

Better to meet death head-on.

Challenge.

She wouldn't make it to the other side of the clearing. This guy would be too good a shot. She had to rely on something she knew well—

The warrior's ego.

Standing in the open, seemingly unarmed, she doubted the Predator would kill her.

Not without allowing her a fight.

Unless, of course, things had changed, which didn't seem likely.

She was just in the act of turning when she heard an explosion.

Her instinct slammed her down onto the ground immediately, but her peripheral vision caught the action.

The top of the Hunter's body simply blew apart in a gale of fire and blood. Shards of armor and limbs and skull and bone went every which way, as if a ripe metal pumpkin had just exploded.

The remainder of the body teetered, fell.

Machiko hit the dirt, rolled. The taste of rich loam and blood was in her mouth, but she hardly noticed.

A familiar whooshing . . .

A dark form swooped down toward her. . . .

She raised her pistol but then lowered it.

The grav copter lowered itself, drew even with her. The door flapped open.

She didn't need an invitation.

She jumped, catching hold of the ladder and quickly pulling herself up and over the lip of the door. In a flash she was into the passenger seat, the door closed behind her.

Attila pulled the vehicle up and over the tops of the trees, heading back for Evanstonville.

"Are you all right?" he asked, hands steady on the controls.

"Yes . . . yes." She shook her head and shot a look back at the biological wreckage. "How—?"

"I hadn't realized it before, Machiko, but this cop- ter seems to be very well armed. That little exhibition, for example, was the result of a first-rate rocket launcher."

She took a deep breath. They'd already jumped a goodly distance. Some of the adrenaline was seeping out of her, replaced by surprise.

"Attila, I didn't know you could fly a copter."

"An unexplored area of my programming. When I detected the fracas in the woods, I assumed you would return, most likely pursued. I thought it would be best to reach a firing point at which I would be able to deal with a maximum of pursuers."

"Good choice. I thought you'd *left* me."

The self-satisfied look on Attila's face melted. "Machiko. I would never do such a thing."

"No. No, of course not. I'm sorry. Thanks. Good move. Now let's get back to home base."

"To confront Livermore Evanston on this matter?"

"No. We've got to give the situation some thought first." She remembered then to buckle her harness. "The Hunters are doing their bug thing—but why here?"

It seems obvious to me," said Attila the Hun, lying on the bed in a relaxed state.

Machiko Noguchi stopped her pacing. She looked at her android warily. Since that little flying stunt a couple hours before, she was seeing him in an entirely different light.

She knew he'd had a "life" before she'd bought him. She didn't know about the programs that still existed inside him. What other residues of past talents, past memories, existed? Attila insisted that he had no memory of being able to do what he did—at the time his sensors detected trouble, something had just kicked in, and he'd had access.

This was something they would have to explore.

For now, though, there were other matters to attend to.

"I'm glad. Would you care to enlighten me?" she said, hands on hips.

"You'll have to pardon me, but I'm merely operating on what you tell me about the Hunters—your tales of your experiences with them."

"Yes, yes, go on."

"Well, it strikes me that they've got a fairly simple game plan. They like to find likely opponents, likely places to perform their rituals of honor. And, frankly, think about it—Blior is perfect. If their lives are the feral art they consider them, then for Predators this must be a masterpiece planet."

"A what?" Machiko asked.

"Masterpiece planet. It sounds as if Ryushi was being used as a training ground for young Hunters."

She nodded. "Blooding."

"That was their apprentice work, then. Whatever the word has come to mean since then, a 'masterpiece' used to be the article a craftsperson made to earn his or her master status. Blior is the place Hunters may earn 'master' status, in effect."

She nodded. "Yes, well, that's pretty obvious. But go on for a moment. Any other thoughts?"

"Yes. The reason it's a masterpiece planet is that there's nothing the Predators like to Hunt better than other hunters. . . . It's the ultimate challenge, right?"

"That's right. Unlike our race, they won't Hunt 'innocent' things—except possibly food."

"A noble breed." Sardonic twist of phrasing. "Anyway, somehow they discovered the operations on Blior, and they saw what a perfect place to Hunt it would be."

"But why bring on the bugs as well?"

"A little twist, a little spice. Who can say? Perhaps this was a world where they'd already Hunted bugs before, and they were just returning."

She shook her head. "No, I don't think so. If there were bugs on this planet before, there would have been a spillage. That's one of the problems when the Preds play with the things—they get loose and start breeding."

"Sloppy sorts."

"Let's just say that their sense of honor is a bit tunnel-visioned."

"So they're here—and they know now that we know they're here."

"I think that's what the lawyer was so excited about. And unless my guess is wrong, Evanston's got a suspicion as well."

"More than a suspicion. I mean, he has physical evidence!"

"Yes."

"He somehow seems to know you're associated with them."

"I don't think he knows as much as he strongly suspects."

"It stands to reason . . . after what happened. . . ."

She let out a breath, shook her head. "The pieces still just aren't there—"

"Seems pretty pat to me," said Attila. "He's got problems with anomalous intelligent creatures as well as the bugs—and he's just trying to get this project off the ground. Can you imagine the bad publicity if word gets back to civilization? Why, this business venture would be a total bust! Who would want to go hunting on a world where the hunters are the victims? I dare say that Evanston is a rich man, but no matter how rich he is, I'm sure that he couldn't afford a failure on this magnitude." Attila nodded. "A man like Livermore Evanston takes time to go get you to help, you know it's got to be this magnitude of importance."

"That does work . . . logically . . . but there's another level."

"Something intuitive?"

"Yes ... that T-rex ..."

"Not a curious resurrection. ... Ideal, if you think of it. ... What with the taste for hunting as it is, I would think that resurrected dinosaurs would be perfect for hunting."

"Yes, of course. I'm talking, though, about the level of sophistication a biolab needs to create the size and scope of a tyrannosaurus rex!"

"You're saying that it could create a lot more. ... Well, isn't that the idea? To create fantastical and wonderful creatures for rich people to shoot?"

"You're not getting the point. What *else* can it create? Why is Evanston being so secretive? Why won't he let us look at the inside of that big biolab factory?"

"*He* hasn't refused—just his underlings."

"Well, then, I guess that's the next bit on our agenda, isn't it? We're going to have to ask."

"And if he won't let us see what's inside?"

She smiled. "Then we'll have to find out on our own, won't we? And we'll know that something intriguing *is* there."

"Of course. I'll take you through the factory tomorrow morning, if you like," said Livermore Evanston, absently tapping ash from his cigar. "There are more serious matters that have to be dealt with immediately, though." The large man leaned over his intercom, hit a button. "Would you send in Brookings and Zorski, please?"

Machiko had to work hard to maintain a blank expression. This wasn't exactly what she'd expected. Attila was going to give her a great big "I told you so" when she let go of this bit of news.

Evanston was sitting in a comfortable ergonomic chair, in a comfortable smoking jacket. His perch in his office building gave him a panoramic view of most of the beautiful, growing expanse of this fabulous settlement that would soon be one of the more wondrous cities in the universe.

Evanston did not look his usual happy and confident self.

The teak-paneled door opened. A man and a woman entered. One Machiko recognized: the man who had come up to them and talked to Evanston on their arrival. The woman, though, was a different matter entirely. She looked like the kind of corporate sharpshooter that Machiko was supposed to have been. A Company woman from sleek black hair to perfectly manicured fingers.

Introductions were made and remade.

Abner Brookings. Lawyer. Meet . . .

Chelsea Zorski. Head of operations. Meet . . .

Hello, Machiko. I hope you can help us.

Good to meet you. I did some of the background work to dig you up. You can just call me Chet.

"Sit down. Have a drink. Tea or coffee or harder stuff, I don't care. It's time not just to think-tank this situation . . . it's time to take action."

They all looked like drinking people. However, they all passed over the ample supply of liquor squatting atop a corner cabinet like a model of a city of multicolored skyscrapers.

Instead they all went for coffee.

Black.

When it was steaming and aromatic before them, as Machiko took the first few acrid sips, she studied this woman Chet Zorski.

First and foremost, she was a corporate shark. Machiko could *smell* that as she walked in. It was in her perfume and shampoo, her very breath. The shine of her eyes, the flash of her perfect teeth. The tailored hang of her clothing. These people could have been made in biolab factories, for all she knew; they had the perfection of premodeling about them.

Zorski had a cleft chin, a square jaw, a nose as perfectly angular as could possibly be desired. Bright-blue eyes. Wide cheekbones. A shock of black hair. Bland stuff in general, but the congruence gave her a sharp and feral look, and the flashing of teeth made her look bright and hungry beneath the smoothness.

"We hope you're well situated," said Evanston.

"Yes."

"You've met your people," said Zorski. "Had a little dustup with one, I hear."

"Good for morale."

"Absolutely. So . . . what do you think of them?"

"Motley, but they'll do."

Zorski beamed a little at that. "Good. I thought you'd be able to look past the rough edges. I looked for a lot of special qualities in these men. Experience being paramount."

"Experience with the bugs, you mean."

Zorski looked at Evanston as though for permission.

Evanston nodded.

"Yes. The bugs."

"Look, there're some things we've got to talk about—"

"Yes. It's time to level with you, Noguchi."

She was taken aback. There was no longer confidence and control in Livermore Evanston's face. He looked, in fact, a bit at a loss, a bit desperate.

Machiko sat back in her chair, maintaining her calm, hard facade. "I'm listening."

"It's not just the bugs." Evanston turned to Abner Brookings. "Please, Abner . . . tell Ms. Noguchi what happened the other day." He swiveled to deliver a sincere stare at Machiko. "With this caveat. As my employee, you are directed *not* to discuss this with any of our other employees or guests. It's of a quite sensitive nature."

"What about my people? And my assistant?"

"Only if absolutely necessary for the men. However, your assistant is an android and clearly secure."

"I appreciate that."

"Go ahead, Abner. It's your show."

"Thank you. Ms. Noguchi, I'm one of the head lawyers for Mr. Evanston. A highly trusted employee. There are a lot of legal things that have to be worked out for this new world, of course, in its interface with the rest of galactic civilization. That's my job. However, I also fancy myself a bit of a hunter. And so I take a bit of a vacation here from time to time. I was on just such an expedition a few days ago. And that's when this awful incident happened."

Machiko listened as Brookings told his story.

A safari.

Invisible attackers.

Death.

Himself, the only survivor.

When he was finished, a silence fell upon the meeting.

"Mr. Brookings was given a thorough evaluation by psychtechs afterward. It would appear, Ms. Noguchi," said Evanston somberly, "that indeed we are *not* the only hunters on Blior. Indeed, these other Hunters— presumably alien, since there are no extant civilizations on this planet—are the source of the bug problem as well."

He looked significantly at Chet Zorski.

"Yes, Machiko. And as you might have suspected, that's one of the reasons you were selected. We believe you know who these creatures are—and how to deal with them."

She looked at them all, one by one. She said nothing. Stare for stare. They looked away.

"I should emphasize," said Zorski, "that we are not prying into your past, your background. We do not want a confession here. We are just asking for knowledge . . . and for help. . . ."

"And for you to do your job," added Evanston.

"Or bail out and take off, as our agreement states?" Machiko asked.

Evanston frowned. "That's up to you."

"No, wait . . . ," objected Brookings. "I worked up the language in that contract. There's a clause—"

"Yes," snapped Evanston. "A clause that I took out."

"It's not as if she can really go anywhere you don't want to take her," said the lawyer in a cold voice.

"Look, Brookings, I want—*need*—the best we can get from this talented woman. I told you—no goddamn legal tricks." He snorted. "Like the law has that much value out here."

"That's the idea. It's elastic. That's why I'm here," said the lawyer. "To help you form it into the shape that is best for you."

"Look, if I want to get out of this place, there are other ways than going up," said Machiko.

"Gentlepeople, *gentlepeople*," said Zorski, a conciliatory smile on her face. "Please. I don't think you need to worry about Ms. Noguchi's enthusiasm for this particular project. You see, I chose her very well. I think we have a fascinated, very enthusiastic leader on our hands now . . . don't we, Ms. Noguchi?"

"Yes. Damn you." She couldn't help but smile.

Brookings shook his head. "I don't understand. This is going to be dangerous. I assure you . . . what I went through . . . These bastards are dangerous."

"Please, let's just say I have the feeling these aliens are old allies, old enemies of our employee," said Zorski. "And besides, she's *so* much better off than she was before, under the shackles of the Company. . . ."

"Don't worry. I'm here to do a job and I intend to do it, and do it as well as I can."

Livermore Evanston visibly relaxed. "You can bet I'm glad to hear that, my dear. We *need* you."

"Okay. Now you level with me. What more do you know about these Hunting aliens?"

"Much less than you do, clearly," said Brookings.

Machiko looked from face to face.

All were unreadable.

"Well, I guess I should be grateful for what I've gotten out of you gentlemen. Now, thank you for your coffee. Maybe I should get my force whipped into shape so we can do something about scouting out this situation. Hmmm. Meantime, I'll look forward to that tour of the biofactory tomorrow."

"Why are you so interested in what's going on there?" said Brookings.

"It's just in her nature," said Zorski. "Extreme curiosity."

"No, I really think we're due an answer," insisted Brookings.

She didn't think she should tell the whole story, since she was sure they weren't spilling all their beans.

"We were doing recon. Something came up while I was checking the area."

"You just let her look around?" demanded Brookings.

"Yes. I gave her permission personally," said Zorski. "And after getting the okay from His Nibs here." She pointed playfully toward Evanston.

"Well, I appreciate that—but let me tell you, I saw something very troubling. . . ."

"Don't leave us dangling so," said Brookings sarcastically.

"I saw a dinosaur." She gave the creep the glare he deserved. "A tyrannosaurus rex, to be specific."

"Ah," said Zorski. "The T-rex."

"Not surprising. A big creature," said Evanston.

Brookings looked a bit taken aback. "But . . . those things are extinct!"

"Precisely," said Machiko. "Which means that biolab is doing some pretty heavy-duty stuff."

"Wow—that's truly *big* game!" said Brookings, looking a little disconcerted, but at the same time excited at the prospect of actually bagging a *dinosaur*.

"Yes. As I told you, we want to make things interesting for our guests," said Evanston.

"Of course. I understand. You did explain that. . . . I only thought that you might be manufacturing creatures of interest to these mysterious Hunting aliens, these Predators, as it were."

Evanston was all smiles again. "Of course. I'd never thought of that. And you'd be the person to distinguish that, wouldn't you? Excellent. As I said, I'll give you the tour myself, to be as much help as possible. . . ."

"Tomorrow morning?"

"That's right. Tomorrow, right after you get back from your maneuver, Machiko?"

"What? I haven't even gone through any training with these guys!" said Machiko. Suddenly this business with the biolab factory wasn't a primary concern.

"You'll do it on the fly," said Evanston. "Because tomorrow my hired mercenaries are going out to scout the area where Brookings and his band were attacked."

Chet Zorski pulled out a map.

13

akuub, Straight Spear, stared down into the holding pen of the yautja starship. There a *kainde amedha* stalked its prey. The *bisor*, a small doglike mammal from the surface of this Hunter's World, whined and barked as it scampered as far as it could go into the corner. The Hard Meat, a youngster not yet a good Hunter's challenge, crept forward infinitely slowly, drool from its secondary jaws slathering the floor, savoring its approach and kill as much as it would doubtless savor the juices of its food.

Bakuub, however, brooded upon other matters than this life-and-death drama below.

Something was happening in the *ooman* settlement. Something of great gravity and importance. The yautja named Bakuub could feel the electricity crack-

ling through the atmosphere of this planet, and he felt
entirely ill at ease.

He had sifted through the remains of the *ooman*
Hunting party they had killed, through their supplies
and weapons, but the detritus contained no clue as to
what was being concocted by their leaders.

The encounter with the female *ooman* while Hunting the big creature they had discovered, that was just
as troubling as the creature itself, a monster that was
not native to this planet. The *oomans* had seen the
yautja. The *oomans* had killed one of their number.
How? Lar'nix'va, though he struggled hard not to
show it, was clearly troubled. Bakuub had heard tales
of the female *ooman* Dahdtoudie, whom Lar'nix'va
had fought with. Surely this was not the same one. . . .

Bakuub had wanted to do some kind of detailed
exploration of transmissions and emanations from
that settlement, utilizing what little of that sort of
equipment they owned. The other packs Hunting now
on this world had been notified, but they did not seem
as concerned as he. And he, alas, was not the Leader
here. Lar'nix'va was the Leader, and Lar'nix'va was a
fool.

Bakuub could see straight through the *tarei'hsan*
offal. A yautja like Lar'nix'va did not have the best in-
tentions of his people at heart. A yautja like Lar'nix'va
cared not for True Glory, merely for his own stupid
ambitions. Normally this would not be troublesome,
for fools such as he were eventually found out and
dealt with, hoisted on their own petards. But in this
ticklish situation, with much at stake, leadership by
such a fool could be dangerous for the yautja's cause.

Bakuub would have to monitor the situation carefully. True, tendencies toward personal ambition were
rife among the yautja. That, after all, was a part of
their nature. Ego was a genetic as well as a cultural
development in the True Dominators. Ambitious fools
tended to get themselves killed at an early stage of

warriorhood; however, an occasional hothead would advance to Leadership and make a mulch of things—a situation not considered particularly bad, but, rather, a challenge—part of the OverPath's progress. But at a ticklish time like this, such Leadership was not opportune and could cause a great deal of trouble.

Below, Bakuub could smell the terror and urine of the prey mammal as it cowered. The Hard Meat slunk forward, lizard-insect evil in its every smooth movement. The acid smell rose from below, amid the offal and straw scents. Soon it would mix with the harsh copper smell of mammalian blood.

Bakuub had personally seen that the others of the flotilla were alerted to the potential problem. The Leaders of the other packs had all shown concern and stated that they would join them in their efforts if needed. However, they were presently in the midst of their own particular Hunts, be they sport or blooding rites, and had to see to that.

Yes, Bakuub thought. But this was much more of a problem than anyone else realized. When Ki'vik'non had been killed by a weapon-holding *kainde amedha*, that had been bad enough. The implications were enormous. That such a creature existed meant a new and dangerous enemy for the People. Challenges were challenges, and to be cherished—however, just as the arrival of the Soft Meat amid the stars was more than a mere challenge, so was the advent of this super Hard Meat.

It was a threat.

Suddenly a wave of hatred passed through Bakuub.

For the Soft Meat, certainly.

But also for the Hard Meat.

Hatred was not unusual in a yautja, but generally reserved for another of their species. Hatred for the Hunted usually meant fear.

Hatred flowed through Bakuub's veins.

The Hard Meat's secondary jaws were extending.

Its claws and extensors held the *bisor* firmly. The progress of the creature's dinner was painstaking and deadly.

Bakuub reached forward, hit a button. The entry lid of the cage slipped back. Even as it did, Bakuub reached behind his back, pulled out his spear, aimed.

With one swift motion of his trained arm, Bakuub sent the javelin downward with blinding speed. The razor tip met with the back of the *kainde amedha*'s head, driving down with such force that the upper carapace was pierced as well.

Bakuub had judged well. It was for good reason that he had taken pains to study the anatomy of the Hard Meat. He had judged his blow not only so that the nexus of nerves in the thing's helmetlike head would be destroyed, but also so that there would be a minimum of its acid blood spilled.

The Hard Meat let go its prey. Shrieking, it reached back for the spear, but it was far too late for that. The angle had been perfect, an angle that was never presented in normal combat, and the blow had been swift and sure.

The creature shuddered and staggered.

Its limbs twisted and shivered like dying snakes.

With a final horrible scream the *kainde amedha* flopped to the floor of the holding pen, writhing out the last of its life in hisses.

Stillness descended upon the holding pen. Bakuub reached out and thumbed another button.

The outer door opened and a small ramp extended. A breath of outside sailed in, rich with green life and sunshine.

"Go now," said Bakuub to the *bisor*. "Live. And the life you have now will be the purer and more cherished for your terror here."

The *bisor* paused for only a moment. Then it inched around the side, eyeing the fallen Hard Meat as though it expected the creature to rise at any moment, and ran down the ramp to the outside.

Bakuub closed the door. Just as well. The Hard Meat would pose a distraction, anyway, to the true task at hand. He would tell Lar'nix'va that the thing had attempted escape. And if the fool challenged him—well, then, the fool would die that much sooner, and all to the good.

14

"Tell me again why we had to leave the omniterrain bus," said Attila, looking around warily, his sensors doubtless high.

"This is *a maneuver*, chum," said Dick Daniels, his gun tilted slightly toward the ground, but obviously ready. "We're just lookin' over territory. I don't think we're going to run into anything much."

"This *is* the place where the sporting safari ran into the Hunters," said Machiko. "We're just having a look, checking out the lie of the land. And operating as a unit for the first time. Which reminds me." She clicked on her wrist radio. "Unit? How are we doing?"

The answers ticked off one by one from the twenty-member team. They'd spread out in a wing formation, covering this open area of ground. Machiko could see them all, but she figured that as long as you

146

had technology, you should use it. Besides, she wanted to make sure the stuff still worked.

The sun had just lifted off the horizon, and mists were rising up like moody chromatic wraiths from vines and the *yanga* trees. The air smelled ripe and yeasty with a damp chill soon to be burned off by the sun, but enough to give early risers a shiver or two. Machiko still had the taste of good coffee in her mouth. She savored it, as did the rest of the men. As Daniels had said, "At least the food and the drink are good on this gig."

Food, in fact, seemed to be on everyone's mind.

"So what's for lunch?" said Lou MacCraken, still yammering away as usual.

"Shit on a shingle," snarled Truck Tankerslee, a grotty short toad of a man with a foul mouth, a foul mind, but the record for the most bugs obliterated of the lot of them.

"Yeah," said Nick Gillespie. "Question is, is it *good* shit?"

"I don't know," said Machiko, trying to keep in the jocular mood of the bunch. "You want me to call back to the bus and check?"

"Good idea," said Marino, squinting into the dark below the mists. "I got a feeling that looking forward to something's a good idea on this particular mission."

Machiko shrugged and looked over to Sanchez, on her right side. "What do you think, Ned?"

He smiled at her. "Better to think about beans 'n' franks than lurking Death. I say go for it."

"Yeah," said Daniels. "We got guys back on the bus. Might as well have 'em do something other than sit around with their thumbs up their butts."

"Well, I should hope they're not preparing the food," sniffed Attila.

"Right. And I should hope that it's something better than beans or creamed chipped beef," grumbled Daniels.

"Let's check." She tapped out the numbers, spoke into the radio node sticking in front of her face.

"Yo. Michaels?"

A bit of static in her ear. Then: "Got you."

"How's it look there on the bus?"

"Still all bozos here." Pause. " 'Bout the same as before. You guys just left minutes ago."

"Well, you know the saying. An army travels on its stomach. So we were just wondering here—what's for lunch?"

Lane Michaels laughed. "You mean that big ice chest they sent with us? I been wondering about that myself. Maybe I better get that lawyer in to work on it."

Machiko laughed. "You do that. Get him to do *something* other than cower in the back."

Abner Brookings was turning out to be something less than the Great White Hunter he fancied himself. He hadn't wanted to come along on this mission, but Evanston had ordered him to, so he could pinpoint for the group the exact location. Brookings at least had the gift of a quick and smooth tongue, and he'd persuaded Machiko to allow him to hang back as consultant rather than directly participate in the maneuvers. His "inexperience," he claimed, might hamper the operation. But, please, don't tell old man Evanston. In return he promised to "have another look" at Machiko's contract and "provide her with free legal help." The ashen pallor of his face informed her that this was no act. Although he had a gun, it was clear that his enthusiasm for weapons had waned somewhat.

Just as well, really. Amateurs and guns generally didn't mix.

"I am not cowering at all," declared Brookings's voice abruptly. "I am available for consultation. And I am performing valuable help in guarding your means of transportation back."

There wasn't a trace of irony in the man's voice, which ingratiated him to her not a wit. "That's very kind of you. We do appreciate that effort.... Now, could you both check that storage box?"

There was a moment of silence, followed by thumping and opening sounds.

Michaels came back on-line. "Hmmm. Lots of cheese. Fruit. A nice ham. Crusty bread. Looks mighty tasty. I think I'll make myself a sandwich right now."

"I think you'd better consult with Mr. Lawyer there on the legal implications before you do that," said Machiko, laughing. "But I think you'll have a few disgruntled comrades as well."

"Oh. Yeah. Guess that wouldn't go down too well." Dumb voice, with fake realization.

"Right. Just stay on call, both of you. We're getting into the area where you said you were attacked, Brookings."

. "Good. Keep your line open. I'll do what I can from here."

Just because she was actually glad he hadn't come along didn't mean she couldn't rib him about the subject. Besides, the other guys were in on the joke. It kept things light in the face of some pretty heavy-duty danger.

In fact, they were entering some heavier growth, just as Brookings had described. Without focusing Machiko could almost imagine herself on some African veld, approaching forest. However, there were no earthly leaves that looked quite like the ones that dangled in the breeze, glistening with jewellike dew.

"Anything, Til?"

"Nope. No signs of bodies."

She didn't really expect any. When working covertly like this, the yautja tended to take their grisly trophies and dispose of the bodies cleanly. Still, you never knew, and she actually approved of Evanston's suggestion. She wasn't thrilled with the idea of com-

ing up against a pack of the Hunters so soon, but she
honestly didn't expect any such contact.

Too, it was good to work with these people. On the
way out they had been an unruly lot, joking and curs-
ing and laughing. Now, though, they were falling into
line like a practiced crack unit. Zorski had chosen
well.

"Just a minute," said Attila. "I'm picking up something. . . ."

Machiko's stomach lurched a moment, that familiar
surge of fear. However, the adrenaline kick that followed evened her out, even thrilled her. This was
what she'd been seeking—this moment of on-edge
aliveness.

"Anything specific?"

"Odd. It's about sixty yards over there, among the
bush. Residual traces of burning . . . carbon ash . . .
acid . . . biologic residue."

"We'd better go check it out then, eh?"

"Yeah. That would be a good idea," said Daniels.
"Ned and I will take point, if you like."

"No, just back us up. Attila knows how to use the
sensor unit." The android had an instrument sensor
pack to account for his talents, but in truth he was relying mostly upon his internal nodes.

"Sure. Go ahead. Ned, you'd better go with them,
though."

"Right." The dark eyes remained expressionless, absolutely free of fear or nervousness. There was, however, a flicker of something in them now, a crinkle of a
smile, as though Sanchez was grateful to help out.

Machiko felt an unfamiliar warmth in her heart at
the sign. The guy liked her, wanted to watch out for
her. An instinctual man-woman thing. Not that she
needed it; she'd watched her own ass for a long time,
but it warmed her cockles. Maybe, just *maybe*, she
wouldn't mind warming his.

There might be some *other* perks to this job.

"All right," she said. "Let's do it."

The three of them, weapons at the ready, moved ahead into the area that Attila had indicated. They walked through weeds and brush, and the sweet smell of bright flowers. The mist was gone now, and the sun was fully launched, chasing away most of the shadows. They passed through a stand of trees into another clearing, cautiously. Immediately Machiko's nostrils flared; a harsh acrid smell assaulted them.

"Damn. No wonder your sensors beeped. What *is* that?"

Burned shell?

Burned insulation?

Burned blood?

All of them.

"Over there," said Attila.

"Right. I can see it," said Sanchez.

Machiko could see it too, poking above a clump of grass. Some kind of greasy, blackened pile.

"Something dead," she said.

"Yeah, but no flies," said Sanchez.

"Correct. Presumably this planet has other decompositional agents."

"I don't know. Even a bacterium couldn't grow in *that*," said Sanchez.

Machiko stepped up to it. At first it looked like the remains of some kind of garbage-heap fire, but then she started to discern identifying details.

"Looks like the burned remains of a bug. That would explain the acrid odor. Burned acid."

Machiko found a stick and poked around.

"I detect metal and plastic and glass as well—" said Attila.

Machiko poked some more. Overturned fused glass and blackened circuitry.

"Analysis?"

"Too far gone to tell," said Attila.

"Looks like somebody threw some equipment on

top of a bug body, doused it with incendiary chemicals, and then torched it," said Sanchez. "But why?"

"Some sort of cover-up?"

"What—by the alien Hunters? To hide their presence?" said Attila.

"That must be it."

"On top of a bug and equipment?"

"I don't know. Maybe they were hiding the equipment too. Maybe it was just convenient. Maybe we should take back a specimen—"

A yelp over the radio, echoed by a real-life vocalization beyond the tree.

Then:

"Noguchi. You'd better get back here." Daniels's voice.

"Right. Come on, guys."

It could be the Predators. She steeled herself. She wasn't particularly ready for them today.

But, then, was *anyone* ever ready for them?

They ran back. She expected to hear the sounds of battle at any second, the sizzle of blasters through the air, the booms of explosions.

Instead she saw merely that the party had moved closer together, and weapons aimed toward a clump of bush.

She ran up to Daniels.

"What's going on?"

"Something's in there."

"Could be some kind of animal."

The bushes shook. Something stood up, staggered out.

Weapons raised.

"No. Hold your fire."

The figure stumbled into a clearing. Blood. Torn clothing.

A woman.

She gripped a gun but made no effort to use it. She just staggered forward.

"Stay back," said Machiko.

The woman stopped. Fell to her knees.

"Thank God," she said. "Thank God you've come for me."

"It's one of the damned guests," said Daniels. "She's survived somehow."

"How come you didn't go back?"

The woman shook her head dizzily. "Don't ... know ... unconscious ..."

"Well, don't just sit around gawking," said Machiko. "Give the lady some water. She's probably dehydrated."

Water was administered, and then a name was obtained.

"Petra Piezki," said Machiko over the radio. "Ring any bells, Brookings?"

"I don't believe it. . . . I thought she was dead. There was this—"

"Whatever. We're bringing her in. She needs medical attention. You want to break out the first-aid kit?"

"Of course."

Piezki drank some water. With the help of a man to either side of her, she was able to walk.

"Piezki. What did you see out there?" Machiko asked her.

"Monsters. Killers." Then her head slumped, eyes dimming, as though to escape.

"Let's get her some help. And then we'll think about looking around some more."

Actually, Machiko had pretty much found what she wanted to find. She'd tested the mettle of her people and was satisfied that she had a crack troop.

Anything else would be pushing things too far.

They'd probably stretched their luck far enough, and when you dealt with the Predators, luck was a commodity you didn't play games with.

15

You bastard. You left me!"

"Piezki! I thought you were dead."

"That's a lie! You left me out there to die!"

Before Machiko could do anything to prevent it, the seemingly weak Piezki lurched from her slumped position at the campsite and lunged across toward Abner Brookings. Her thick hands clamped around Brookings's neck, and she began to throttle the lawyer, shaking him violently.

"You left me! You left me!"

Brookings's eyes bugged. The surprise of the attack had caught him off guard, but he was not a defenseless or weak man. With one great heave he pulled Petra Piezki off her feet and then slammed her into the metal side of the ground crawler.

Piezki's hands lost their grip. Her eyes rolled up. She slid down the side of the bus, unconscious.

"Oh, great," said Machiko. "She's going to tell us all about what she saw now."

Brookings loosened his collar. He was gasping. "You saw it. Self-defense. She was trying to kill me!"

"Apparently with good reason, if you left her to die!"

"I swear, we were both running. . . . I thought she was a goner. If I thought I could have helped, I would have."

"She's all right," reported Sanchez, looking up from the unconscious body.

"Save the real story for later," said Machiko. "Let's get her back to Evanston. We've got a report to make."

Machiko sat down beside Sanchez. Their vehicle was bumping its way back home, and the man's dark eyes were directed toward the passing landscape.

"Nice planet," said Machiko.

"I've seen more beautiful, I've seen more dangerous, I've seen not-nice planets I liked better," he said, not looking at her.

"I get the feeling you've been on your share."

He shrugged. "After you fight the bugs awhile, you get sort of empty inside. You need to go away for a while, or you just get a bad case of interior rot."

"So why are you back in the bug-battle saddle?"

He looked at her. "Money."

"A guy like you could earn money other ways."

"I did. Not enough. Let's just say this was an offer I could have refused but would have been an idiot to."

"I think I know what you mean. But there's more to you than just money, isn't there, Sanchez?"

He looked at her. "Is there?"

"You fight bugs for a while, you get a sense of no-

bility, don't you? Like you're doing something important. I bet you haven't been doing anything really important for a while."

"Combating an intergalactic blight. Yeah, I guess it
makes you feel like something more than a pile of
shit."

For the first time something tremulous and deep
crept into his intonation, something beyond sardonic
monotone.

She thought about this for a moment.

"We may have more in common than our brilliant
and wonderful personalities," Machiko said finally.
"Maybe I should buy you a beer tonight and we can
talk about it."

He looked at her.

"Sure. Can't hurt."

"A nice beer generally helps." She looked up and
saw that they were approaching Evanstonville. "And
something tells me after today we're both going to
need one . . . even though I generally don't drink the
stuff."

"Ms. Piezki. How are you feeling?"

"Better."

"Ms. Piezki, I can't tell you how sorry we are about
what happened," said Livermore Evanston in his most
charming and millifluous tones. "Nonetheless, you
were aware of the danger involved. It was in your
contract with us. And you are an employee."

Piezki eyed them, daggers gleaming in her eyes.
She said nothing, but the threat was there: I'm going
to nail you if I can.

Lawyers, thought Machiko Noguchi.

What a lovely, lovely bunch.

Take Brookings, for example. The bastard was
sulking in a corner, clearly not wanting to be there,
but waiting for the debriefing.

Chet Zorski was there, looking awake and aware and concerned, leaning on her chair and studying the patient, clearly taking mental notes.

And, of course, there was old Evanston himself, solid but hovering. He'd come immediately to this treatment room when he'd heard there'd been another adviser located.

"May I suggest you settle that matter later?" said Machiko. "What we need now is information. Ms. Piezki, we've pretty much heard your colleague's story about what happened on that safari. Would you care to give your version?"

Piezki coughed.

"Are you all right?" asked the medtech who'd cleaned the woman's cuts and applied the bandages.

"Yeah. Little pain in the chest. Catch in the throat. Glass of water." The medtech got her one, and Piezki drank it all down. "Yeah. Better. Thanks."

She told her story.

It was almost exactly the same story that Brookings had told, save for one significant strand of facts.

The hunt. The hunters. The quarry. The invisible hunters. Massacre. The run . . . loss of memory . . .

The change of detail was that Brookings's valor had not quite been as much in evidence as he'd claimed.

"What happened when you tripped?"

"Can't remember," she said, shaking her head. "Something dark. I remember screaming and hearing my own muffled screams . . . and that was it." She put her hand to her chest. "Nurse, do you have something that will settle my stomach? I seem to have developed a really terrible case of heartburn."

The woman looked uncomfortable, but nothing that made Machiko immediately alarmed.

Something bothered her, though.

"And you were in the same location for about a day and a half—most of it unconscious."

"I remember bashing about in the brush, but that was it. I'm just glad I'm"—she accepted a glass of fizzing stuff with a thank-you—"alive." Drank.

"They let her live," said Evanston. "How curious."

"Perhaps they didn't know about her," suggested Zorski. "If she was out in the bushes, they just must have moved on."

A possibility. If she'd run far enough away, they wouldn't have detected her heat-image, thought Machiko.

Then again, there were bugs in the area ... and that was what bothered her.

"Brookings. Did you see anything attack this woman?" she demanded suddenly.

Brookings shook his head. "No. Like I said, I thought that she'd been killed. Truly."

Muffled screams? Something over her head? Why hadn't she thought about this before?

"Brookings, this is very important. Is that the absolute truth? Because if it's not, this woman could be in danger from—"

"Absolute truth," said Brookings, looking as though butter wouldn't melt in his mouth.

Suddenly a surprised look came over Piezki's face. Her face twisted.

"Ms. Piezki," said the tech. "Are you all right?"

Piezki belched.

She took a breath and smiled. . . . "Oh. That's much better." Relief was obvious on the woman's face.

Machiko relaxed.

Piezki fell off her chair.

She writhed and screamed, and a sudden bubble bloomed on her chest.

"Get back!" cried Machiko.

Too late.

Before any of them, frozen with surprise, could do a thing, the bubble burst. Like a gory jack-in-the-box, flaps of bone and flesh lifted off, and suddenly a wormlike thing stood up in the middle of Piezki's chest. Blood sprayed around the room like a crazy water sprinkler.

They were all splattered with it.

Petra Piezki got one look at the creature she'd given crimson breech birth to, and then her head fell back, holding Death in its eyes.

The wormthing chittered at them and started sliding out.

"Stand back!" cried Machiko. She pulled out her gun from its holster and fired at the creature.

It slapped off to one side and skittered away.

The two slugs slammed into Piezki's body, kicking up divots of shattered ribs and gouts of flesh and blood.

Machiko tracked the running, slithering thing. No question. Bug-larvae time.

If she knew one thing, she knew she had to clip its wings before it flew into ductwork or down the hall to hide in some broom closet. She was grateful she'd had pistol practice.

Now, though, she'd have to prove she could use it in the clinch.

The thing was at the door. Closed. It slithered quickly toward shadow.

Machiko squeezed off three shots.

The first missed.

The second bit off a chunk of flesh on the tail.

The third rammed directly into the head, exploding the ugly, bloody mass into an uglier, bloodier mass. The thing flipped over and commenced spasming, somehow still straining for escape.

Machiko calmly walked over and put another bullet in it.

The acid blood smoked as it ate away at the floor.

"Better get some neutralizing agents in here, Zorski."

Zorski got on the phone.

Machiko put her gun back in her holster.

Too bad Attila couldn't have seen that. He would have been proud of her.

She turned and walked over to where Abner Brookings stood, bloodied and horrified.

She tapped his chest. "Hello. Hello. Anyone in there?"

"No. No, I wasn't infected. Don't cut me open. . . . I swear."

She looked at him in disgust. "I was talking about your heart."

Recovering, Evanston had somehow found a towel and was wiping off the blood. "Nurse. Have that body taken out of here and destroyed immediately."

"The problem hits a little closer to home, Evanston."

Evanston nodded. "Yes. That's why I hired you and the others."

"An excellent choice, all of us."

"You worked well this morning?" His words were strained.

"Very well."

"Good. I'm sure you're going to be busy very soon."

"Fine. That's what we're here for." She found a towel herself and began to get rid of some of the blood. Funny, it didn't really bother her. After the business on Ryushi, after her time with the pack, after helping those miners, she'd experienced plenty of blood, much of it hers.

A detail.

"That tour of the genetic biolab," said Machiko. "I really should have a look. There may be infection—"

Evanston shook his head. "I can't—I'm in no state now for any kind of silly tour."

"This evening, then?"

"No. No, I'm sorry."

"Well, tomorrow."

"Tomorrow I want you to go out again and do what

I hired you to do, Noguchi." His voice was firm. "I will advise my scientists and workers to look for infiltration into their systems. When things are down to a mild roar here, I'll be happy to show you the place myself."

"Surely someone else can—"

"Have you forgotten? I am your employer. I make the rules. Now leave me be. I have"—he shook his head sadly—"to take a shower and start coordinating precautions against these things." He put a chubby hand on her shoulder. "Thanks for the good work here, though. And the quick thinking."

"Good thing you let me wear a sidearm," she said. "Better if you'd let me see that biolab."

"No," he said firmly, and began walking away. "That's impossible."

She looked down at the body of Petra Piezki, eyes wide-open and face frozen in a rictus of terror.

She could sense it now.

Something was very wrong here, and it wasn't just the yautja, it wasn't just the *kainde amedha*.

16

They were having that beer.

"Too bad about Piezki," said Sanchez.

"Yeah." She took a long, hard gulp. Grimaced. She didn't particularly like it, but sharing a beer with someone seemed important now. "I should have called it."

"Me too."

"We can't get everything right."

He drank again and there was silence.

"I guess there have been times with both of us when everything has been wrong, hasn't there?" said Machiko.

"You know, Noguchi, you're just too damn perceptive for your own good."

"That beer looks gone. You want another one?"

"Helps limber the tongue, doesn't it?"

"Sometimes."

She went and got two fresh brews. Opened his. Set it before him.

The beer was good and cold, a dark, yeasty ale. No label. Brewed here.

They sipped in silence for a moment.

"You know," the man said after a while, "back where I come from, when a woman takes a fella back to her room, orders the assistant out, pours him a couple beers, and starts talking personal stuff, the man might think she was trying to seduce him."

"So what do you think, Ned Sanchez?"

He shrugged. "I'd say you're not the most feminine creature that's crossed my path. But, you know, you're probably one that I could respect in the morning—so to speak."

She smiled tartly. "Bullshit. I can tell when a man fancies me, Sanchez."

"Sounds like you can tell when you fancy a man, too."

"The hard head takes a little cracking—" She looked away. "I'm sorry. It's just been a while since I've felt that way, I guess. Never mind. Sorry to be so forward. Probably turns you off."

His hand suddenly took hers. Although it was a rough hand, it was warm, and it had a firmness and a purpose to it.

"No. Not at all. I guess I'm just used to being the pursuer."

"Want to start over?"

"No. I'm fine with the way it is." He took another drink.

He slowly and solidly got up.

Pulled her to her feet.

Brought himself up against her.

She could feel herself melting against him. His arms went around her, and for once her mind could just drift away into nothingness and release. The next thing she knew she was kissing him, and it was warm and right.

When they came up for breath, he said, "I take it back."

"Take what back?"

"The crack about your not being feminine. You're entirely female."

"I'd hardly get respect bug-killing in a dress."

"No."

"We might both be dead tomorrow."

"But we're not dead now."

Later, in the afterglow of a particularly satisfactory biological act, coated with an intriguing amount of pheromones and a kind of odd connection she'd never quite felt before, Machiko found herself speechless.

"You know, I guess I should count my lucky perks," Ned Sanchez said finally.

She put a finger to his lips. "Shh. Let me savor this."

"It's been a long time since you've had a man."

"No. It's been a long time since there's been any feeling involved."

"Ah. I think I'll need some silence to think about that one."

He took it.

She closed her eyes and just lay there a moment. God knew what was ahead of her, but she knew what was here now, and she accepted it gratefully.

Eventually, he spoke.

"Maybe I should tell you something, Machiko."

"Maybe you shouldn't."

"No, I think it would be a good idea."

"If you like. I'm not digging anything out of you."

"No. And that's why I'm telling." He closed his eyes,

took a breath. "What I said about quitting the bug-killing business?"

"Yes."

"It wasn't really the total truth. You see, I had this buddy. Let's call him Joe. Joe and me ... well, we killed a lot of bugs."

She was going to say something smart-ass but realized it wasn't the time or the place. She smelled an intensity, a seriousness about him now. The only appropriate response seemed to be just to listen.

After a moment to put the story together right, Ned Sanchez said, "You know, I could tell you a long, long story."

"If you like."

"No. I'm going to make it short."

"Fine."

"Joe and me, we went into a hive. We made a couple of mistakes, some big mistakes. Joe didn't come out. I did. Sometimes I think it should have been the other way around."

"I understand."

"Do you? Do you really?" He snorted. "Well, maybe you can tell me, but when I heard about another chance to prove myself, I guess I was just fed up with all the guilt that had been building up inside me. So I signed on."

"It wasn't just for the money, then."

"No, I guess not."

She nodded. "I can relate. I felt that in you, Ned. Maybe that's why I was attracted to you."

"Hmm? What—you've got a story, too?"

She told him about her father. About the family shame. About how she was trying, in her own small way, to alleviate that shame.

She told him about Ryushi, her first colony world, and how she had failed it. People had survived, and she was responsible for that; but the colony was gone.

All in simple, concise terms.

"What say we promise each other something, okay, Machiko?" he said, cupping her face in his hands.

"What's that?"

"Let's live long enough to tell the long version of our stories."

"That's going to take a long time."

"Then we're going to have to live a long time, aren't we?"

He kissed her, and that was the only reply that was necessary.

"You slept with him, didn't you?" said Attila the Hun.

She was changing her clothes. Ned had gone to eat dinner with the rest of the men, but she couldn't bring herself to go with him. Superstition or something. Maybe they'd be able to smell the sex or something. Anyway, for some reason she had no appetite.

"I did," she said.

Attila plopped down in a chair, folded his arms. "Great. Just great. Now when you dump him, we're going to have a heartbroken soldier on our hands."

"What did Lao Tzu say about heartbroken soldiers?"

"Unreliable." He sniffed affectedly.

"I didn't say I was going to dump him."

He gave her a surprised look. "Well, did you ask him to help us break into the biolab and have that look you so desperately and foolishly want?"

"No."

"No? Why not?"

Looked at him. "I just didn't."

"Look, I thought the whole idea of getting to know this guy was that if he liked you, he'd help us."

"No. That wasn't the whole idea."

"Okay, okay," Attila said peevishly. "You had the hots for him."

"I liked him. I saw something there. And you know what, Til? It *is* there."

"Wonderful. I'm happy for you. There's a there there. But you didn't ask him to help us."

"Look. It's our suspicion. It's our problem."

"He's a hireling, too. It's *his* problem if we find anything we don't want to find. Which makes me wonder now if we should even bother. I mean, clearly you're not that concerned."

"Look, Til. I'm sorry I've upset you. Are you jealous?"

"What! Nothing of the sort. I hope you had a very good time. May you both be very happy together. Et cetera, et cetera."

"I just don't want Ned to get involved at this point. . . . Okay, okay, I don't want him to get into trouble. *We* get into trouble, that's different. We're at a higher level. We're more likely to take the heat without a burn. Sanchez, though—they can boot his ass out of here, no money, no nothing."

"Okay. It's your decision. Maybe it's for the best."

She nodded. "Thank you." She put her dinner plate to one side. "So, Attila. Your little recon—how did it go? Are we even going to be able to take a stab at this crazy mission?"

He finally smiled.

"While you were so amorously whiling away your time, ducks, I simply waltzed into the biolab factory."

Her mouth dropped. "So then we don't even have to break in! You've done it."

"Hardly. I certainly wish. No, the truth is that apparently much of the factory is under very loose security. And why not? This is a small settlement. There is no crime here."

"So how did you get in?"

"I just walked in, saying I wanted to look around.

They said fine, sir—there are just certain areas that are off limits. Certainly, I said. I understand completely. I took a little tour."

"And?"

"And it seems to be just what Evanston claims it is—a biolab. Cloning factory. Lions and tigers and bears. Exotic alien animals. Simple enough."

"But."

"I'm glad you inserted your but there. It's a big but."

"Hey. I like it."

He smiled. "But a cute one, as Mr. Sanchez will no doubt attest. No, Machiko, there are large areas simply off limits—and I saw most of what was necessary to be a fully functioning biolab."

"So the question is, what else is there?"

"Precisely."

"Any sensor input?"

"Nothing much. I need to get closer."

"So how do we get in tonight? How do we get closer when we do get in?"

"To the first question"—he pulled two badges from his pocket and put them on the table—"I stole these and altered them, complete with fake retinal and DNA patterns. These will get us in. As for the rest—well, with my sensors and a good laser toolbox—"

"Good job."

"You didn't even ask this Sanchez guy if he'd ever been a burglar."

She frowned at him. "That subject is closed, Attila."

"Okay, okay."

"And you had no problem? They didn't ask you what you were doing there?" she said, looking for potential foul-ups.

"No. Security seemed amazingly lax on the outside. I daresay that Evanston and company are worried about other things. However, beyond the main part of the lab—behind those closed doors . . . they are definitely hiding something that they don't want us to see."

"Well, that just makes me want to see it all the more."

"I confess, despite my less-than-warriorlike attitude for this entire adventure, I too would like to have a look."

"Tonight, then, a little private exercise of our own," said Machiko.

17

Attila had done his job well.

Not only had he counterfeited those badges, but he'd managed to sneak into a supply closet and procure two of the biolab uniforms. They actually fit well, too.

"The deal is this," said Machiko Noguchi as they strode past the open outer gates of the factory, past security operatives, the setting sun of Norn at their backs, the brisk cool smell of evening settling down on the still lushness of this cultivated frontier settlement. "We get caught inside the perimeter, we tell them we're authorized by Evanston."

"And if we make it through to the other part, but get caught then?"

"We run. We go back to the barracks and grab beer

cans. I didn't want to involve Ned in this actual operation—but I don't feel bad having him back us up."

"I suggest that we just not get caught. And most certainly not use weapons."

"I like to have one on hand, if possible. They let me wear one here, and it put me in good stead with that bug this morning."

Attila had prepared tiny stasis generators to cancel out any weapons-detection device, and again Machiko was impressed and grateful for his varied talents hidden in that plain-looking shell.

For all her martial-arts abilities, Machiko felt far more comfortable with a sidearm. The news that she'd be able to wear one on this mission was certainly welcome.

They walked past the posted guard with just a flash of their fake IDs. Security officers were not as numerous as Machiko had expected. Much of the security was automated. Shifts were apparently changing, and stragglers from the midshift were just making their way home. They appeared to be normal workers, looking forward to dinner and a beer. The shift that they were infiltrating, on the other hand, had far fewer workers, who were clearly far less industrious. The few people they encountered did not seem at all upset about the pair of new employees in their ranks. The departments in the biolab were diverse enough that they probably assumed Machiko and Attila were headed for sections other than theirs.

And of course, they were totally correct.

Attila had briefed her on the layout of the biofactory in descriptive enough terms that Machiko was able to wend her way knowledgeably through it, acting as though she had a definite mission, not goggling about like the first-timer she was. Nonetheless, she allowed Attila to lead slightly and used her peripheral vision to take note of the stations and activity around her.

Tanks.

There were tanks of stainless steel and glass, connected by tubing all around, with conduits and flanges and wheels. There were lab stations and racks of chemicals and equipment—the usual panoply of functioning scientific research and production. The smell of flame and harsh elements clung to the air, wafting in currents of warm and cold. Wisps of steam and frost escaped from doors and hatches opening and closing, and altogether the effect was of some well-scrubbed, sterile satanic kitchen.

Walking by one of the glass-enclosed tanks, Machiko caught a glimpse of something through the glass paneling—something caught in milky liquid.

A half-formed beast with great claws and sharp teeth, slowly forming in a nutrient bath.

A lion? Some alien critter. A Hunter being aborn for Hunting? Hard to say, but it certainly was pretty much as Evanston had described it, at least so far.

"There's a whole wing over there," whispered Attila, discreetly pointing toward the north, "devoted to cages, many of them empty so far."

"The beasts to be set free and hunted."

"Precisely."

"Nothing here to cause alarm to my perspective," she said as they went to a drink dispenser and pretended to fish for credit vouchers.

"That's just it. According to my data catalog, these vast rooms have got everything they need for a fully functioning biolab factory."

"So?"

"So much of the operations of such are patented secrets and usually kept secreted away. However, they're out here for all to see."

"Which means—?"

"Think about it."

It didn't take long.

"Which means *what* the hell have they got locked away, if they're allowing most people to see all of *this*?"

"Exactly."

She looked around again. She heard the murmurings and burblings of bubbling beakers, the slurpings and drippings of liquid, the tapping of retreating footsteps. It all smelled mysterious and acrid, like the entranceway to some chemical amusement-park ride.

Only they had no ticket for the next part.

"So, what now?"

"Down this hallway here."

They waited until there was no one around.

This time there was no pretense of who was leading and who was following.

Attila went first.

They moved down a corridor that eventually bent to the south. Doors lined either side.

"Storage rooms," Attila explained.

"Open and innocuous."

"As far as I can tell." The hallway was totally deserted. "This, though, was what I was telling you about—down here at the end of the hall."

Another slant to the hall, and they were there.

Machiko was taken aback.

At the end of the hall was a round, vaultlike door of hard, shiny alloy. It was more than apparently *extremely* locked.

"What—is this the *gold* supply here?"

"Looks like it, doesn't it?"

"What do your sensors perceive?"

"It's an alloy they can't get past."

"Hmmm. But you think we can pick this lock?"

"Oh, yes. It's an electronic locking device, and I made sure to bring a probe." He held up a long metal device.

"Looks like a coat hanger."

"I'm sure it could be used as such. In any case, by inserting it into this aperture here"—he did just that—"I can change polarities and reroute electrical flows in such a way as to cancel out the necessity for codes and thus gain access."

"In other words, we can get through."

"Precisely."

She looked around. "Nobody coming?"

"No."

"Problem is, there could be someone inside."

"True—however, shifts are changing, and an entry would be presumed to be authorized. We can take a quick look. I can store data through visual and auditory means, as well as my usual sensory panoply. Thus we can nip in and then duck out, without causing undue notice."

"Sounds good to me."

She was happy there wasn't much security there; but then again, why should there be? It wasn't as though an intelligence agency was necessary in Livermoreland; it was much too far removed from anything. The security forces seemed more interested in their war re-creations than in actually patrolling the colony. Evanston's people must have reasoned that these simple precautions would do.

For Machiko they would have done quite nicely.

However, they hadn't reckoned on having a talented android picking their locks.

Attila did his stuff, slipping his device in. Machiko heard a few clicks and whirs and then watched Attila's concerned expression change to one of relief.

"There we go. That should be it."

He stood and pulled a latch.

The door opened.

Machiko leaped to action, helping Attila pull the hatchway open with the minimum of noise. It eased back as though it had just been oiled.

Machiko peered into the next room.

It was a large chamber that stretched off into the distance. Along its upper sides were catwalks and pulleys and waldos. Racks of laboratory equipment hung below these. The lighting was quite low, the dominant colors being deep reds and lambent yellows.

Burblings.

The acrid smell was even heavier here, and there was a new scent to the air: something dreadful, something familiar, and yet Machiko could not precisely place it.

In the distance was the quiet sound of voices, yet this part of the long chamber seemed absolutely deserted.

Ahead of them were the familiar tanks, only these seemed noticeably larger. From the two intruders' angle, however, there seemed to be no viewports into the contents.

Machiko quietly pointed this out. "Could be that what they're brewing in there, they don't want us to know about."

"I was thinking the exact same thing. Just a moment here." Attila placed a small piece of metal between door and doorjamb. "This way we can exit quickly, I think, which may prove most fortuitous."

Machiko was in a hurry, but she took the precaution of moving as quietly and warily as possible, as they made their way around the tank.

There *was* a porthole on the other side, and she was able to peer through the murky liquid, and into the contents.

"Oh, my God," Machiko said, and though she was not particularly religious, it was as close to a prayer as she ever got.

Back in Boring-World, with so much time on her hands, Machiko Noguchi had done a great deal of reading. Fortunately, the Company had been considerate enough to vest its mining world with an excellent library of varied files on their Comp-Access.

One of the books she'd read was a large picture book concerning the history of human freaks, and there had been some horrifying anomalies indeed, from Siamese twins and pinheads, to geeks and other abnormalities of human and bestial natures.

However, nothing in the book could match the horror of what Machiko stared at now through the glass, through the milky nutrient bath.

At first it just seemed another beast, some hapless genetic code from some far-flung alien clime that had been appropriated for hunting purposes by Evanston's henchmen.

Claws.

Teeth.

Mandibles.

However, as she looked closer, she saw other things in the brew.

A shell that would become chitin.

Legs.

Arms.

And at the ends of those arms, digits.

Digits with opposable thumbs.

The result was obscene beyond belief. A combination with aesthetics from hell, but doubtless incredibly deadly.

Machiko took a sharp intake of breath.

"What is it?" asked Attila. "Besides really, really ugly."

"You can't tell?"

Of course he couldn't, she immediately told herself.

He hadn't had experience of the things. He hadn't gone through what she'd gone through. He wouldn't appreciate either species, much less the juxtaposition.

And then the realization hit her, so hard that she was stunned.

She would have invoked a deity's name again, only something had stopped her vocal cords.

"Well? Communication would be helpful," he said sharply.

"It's . . . it's the most incredible warrior ever designed . . . and Jesus, Attila . . ." She pointed. "Look . . . behind the neck there. Is that what I think it is?"

He peered closer. "My goodness. It does look like some sort of electrical neurotransmitter link-ups."

"As in cyborgs . . ."

"As in cyborgs, precisely."

She tapped the window, pointing. "Attila. What you're looking at is . . . well, apparently, and I don't

know how—but these crazies have been able to warp
the genetic code of the bugs ... and add their own
twists."

"What—to create some kind of ultimate target for
guests to hunt?"

She shook her head vehemently. "No, that couldn't
be. One of these ... linked up to Buddha knows what
... could tear apart a bunch of hunters. It could
outhunt, outkill anything. ... Hard Meat with brains
and weapons!"

"Some sort of bug/yautja hybrid?"

"Thank God, *no*. Just an *improvement* on the
bugs." She snapped her fingers. "What's the root of
any army, Attila?"

"Warriors, of course. Soldiers."

"Smart bugs. Incredible, resilient ... well, put some
of these down and breed them on a world and
you'd—"

"Why, you'd dominate the world!"

"Yes, and through the computer interface of cyborg
connection ..."

"Of course. You'd be able to *control* those warriors!"

They stood for a moment in silence, staring at the
oxygen bubbles forming around the growing creatures
and then floating up to the surface. A mad mélange.

"But *why*?" she murmured.

"Power, presumably," said Attila. "Why else?
Evanston doesn't want just a world. He wants
worlds."

"*That* was what we saw out there—one of these
creatures. It wasn't a pile of different creatures and
some machinery. It was a *single* creature ... somehow on the loose. That had somehow been killed."

"By the yautja?"

"I guess so. That would make sense ... but who
knows?"

Thoughts were twisting and turning inside her

head. She wasn't sure what she had expected to find inside this part of the biolab factory ... but it certainly hadn't been this.

"What now?"

"Are you taking all this in?"

"Yes."

"Sufficient data?"

"Yes."

"Then now we get the hell out of here and figure out the next step. Now we—"

Inside the tank the creature's eyes opened.

A bug with eyes!

The head of the thing was a terrible and ungainly amalgam of the banana-insect helmet of a bug and the chromium sheen of complex cyborg implants. But the eyes looked just as sharp and intelligent as any that Machiko had ever seen in a warrior's head.

Despite herself, she jumped.

"Damn. It's looking at us."

Attila said, "Time to depart, indeed. In fact, I hope it's not too—"

A siren started to sound.

"Late."

"Go! Go!"

They tore away, heading back toward the vault door they had entered. They were just pulling it open when the security men rounded the corner about thirty yards away.

"Halt!"

Yeah, right, thought Machiko. *Or you'll shoot.*

They didn't halt, of course. They dived through the opening and began running, Machiko hoping against hope that they hadn't been recognized. This would certainly take some explaining. . . . Well, Mr. Evanston . . . I was just looking for the ladies' room. . . .

They were out into the main section of the biolab and still running when the other troop of security came around the other corner, cutting them off.

They dived behind another tank, not pausing for a moment, but scurrying away like pursued rats in a maze.

"Alternative exit?" said Machiko.

"Yes. Follow me."

Attila ran down another aisle, the end of which was a door. With absolutely no ceremony or precaution, he banged against that door, pushing on the latch simultaneously . . . hurling himself into the outside.

Machiko followed.

They were out on permacrete now, in some sort of empty parking lot. Beyond was a perimeter fence, and beyond that a gate yawned open invitingly.

They ran for it.

"Stop," screamed someone from behind them.

"Run ahead of me," said Attila, positioning himself between her and their pursuers. "I can take bullets a lot better than you can."

"Thanks," she puffed.

There were explosions behind them, and the whizzing of fired ammunition to their sides and over their heads.

Something blasted to the left. An incendiary impact nearly tore them off their feet.

"What the hell are they shooting at us?" said Machiko.

"Nothing good, I promise you. Hurry, we're almost through the gate."

She put on a burst of speed, her attention fixed on her goal.

Another explosion, immediately behind her.

This time she was lifted off her feet. With a combination of instinct and training, she rolled with it, coming to rest with a minimum of scrapes and bounces.

"Come on," she called to Attila. "Let's go—"

"That would be very hard," said Attila, ahead of her.

She looked around.

Attila's headless body lay behind her, front down, back and chest section a burnt mangle, oozing fluid.

Some kind of bazooka shell had hit him, exploded, and now the android was in tatters.

"Til!" she cried. *"Til!"*

"Quiet! Over here!"

Still in front of her.

She looked toward where the voice originated from, astonished. There, lying in the gutter, upended, was Attila the Hun's head.

Mouth moving.

"Well don't just stand there, Machiko. Pick me up and let's get the hell *out* of here!"

She got past her astonishment.

Her reflexes went to work.

She dodged over, picked up the head, tucked it under her arm, and started to run.

Another spray of bullets swept past her.

"Over there—that car. That's our only hope," said Attila.

She raced over. It was a four-wheeler, open.

She hopped in. There was no key, and no time to hot-wire it.

"Stick me up to the ignition," said the head.

Not thinking, just obeying, Machiko did just that.

Something whipped from Attila's head, slotting into the ignition.

The car kicked to life.

"Now go," said Attila. "Go!"

She put the car into gear. Bullets whanged into the side.

She pushed on the accelerator and got the hell out of there, Attila's head hanging like a bizarre key chain from the ignition.

She zoomed off into the night, headlights flicking on.

Off and away, escaping.

But to where? crashed the thought inside her head. To *where*?

19

Dawn crept up warily on the horizon.

By its new, thin light Machiko Noguchi cupped her hand and dipped it into the river.

She drank.

The water was cool and sweet.

She'd tasted it early, by the light of two moons, and it had tasted even better then.

She looked up into the sky, as though expecting company at any moment. Nothing. No thropters or skimmers or any of the other number of airborne vehicles that could be pursuing them.

She sighed and stood up. Her back was stiff, but otherwise the couple hours' rest had been fine. She walked back up to where the four-wheel-drive vehicle was sequestered, in a bowerlike assemblage of river-

side and trees. Here it was neatly hidden from sight
. . . but, then, who knew if there were other ways of
detecting it?

With no other place to go, she headed out to the
wilderness.

She couldn't exactly hop on a starship and race off
for the safety of light-years-distant planets. She
couldn't barge into the barracks and holler for help
from men who didn't really know her from Eve and
who were being paid royally for their loyalty. The
thought that she should somehow contact Ned
Sanchez crossed her mind; however, she nixed it immediately. No way would that work now.

No. She had just one hope.

With what she knew now, there was another
chance.

With her added understanding it was a slim possibility but one that she had to take. Oh, she supposed
she could have simply allowed herself to be caught.
Evanston most likely would not indulge in simple
Death; her talents and abilities were too valuable. No,
most likely he'd just do a selective mem-wipe. Of
course, some of her personality might get pulled up
by the roots in the process, but hey, that was too bad.
Make her a little more docile and less likely to poke
her nose where it didn't belong.

She went back to the car.

In the passenger seat was the head.

"How ya doin', short stuff?"

"S'all right."

Attila winked at her.

She remembered her shock and grief at his seeming
demise.

However, as interesting and valuable as the android's body was, it would seem that his actual consciousness circuits were in his head, and apparently
capable of operation for quite a while on their own

batteries. For his part Attila seemed oddly resigned to his new state, merely glad to be still in existence.

"What do you think? Shall we keep going in this thing?"

"If speed is what you want, then we should. However, it would be risky."

"Yeah. They're bound to have copters out looking for us now."

"Not necessarily. Wouldn't that be admitting that there was some secret they were keeping?"

"No. All Evanston has to do is claim we were snoopers for some rival company. I'm sure he's well within legal rights to seek us out and kill us."

"Or he can cover up."

"So the question remains."

She thought about the issue for a moment.

Decided.

"They must be watching. They know we're here." She looked ahead. "That clearing there. That will do."

"And if it doesn't?"

"Then we'll get back in the car and raise such a ruckus, they'll find us."

"I'm glad you know what we're doing. I certainly don't. But I'll be glad to back you up."

"All I can say is that I'm just glad you're still around, Attila—in whatever form."

His mouth managed to form a smile. "Thanks."

She put on the backpack she'd found in the car, and then she tucked Attila under her arm and set off.

"Looks like it's going to be a nice day," said Attila.

"Yes," she said.

She marched.

It took ten minutes to get to the clearing. She strode across it, toward the trees that ridged the other side.

"What now?" said Attila.

"Watch. Listen."

She set him on a nearby rock with a good vantage point.

She placed herself into a stance.

She raised her hands to her mouth.

She made the Call.

A high ululation carried over the trees, punctuated by a gruff, low-pitched snarl.

She let it unwind for a full ten seconds, then allowed its echo to settle into the leaves.

"You learned that from the Hunters?" said Attila.

"Yes. Now, be quiet. This is going to be very delicate."

"If it happens at all."

"Yes."

She waited some minutes, listening.

There was no direct answer. However, her honed instincts detected something in the distance.

Something coming.

She felt her adrenaline rising. She felt the old machinery clicking into place. Machiko Noguchi let loose again the *ka'rik'na*, the summoning, and the *mesh'in'ga*, the battle-dreamtime, folded over her. She was able to access areas of her mind that had been retreating from her human state.

Yes.

They *were* coming.

The question was, would she have time to explain what had happened? Would these creatures remember her betrayal? If so, then she had just one slim chance, and she inwardly prepared herself to take advantage of that chance.

One moment the glade in which they stood was empty save for them.

The next, a warrior materialized, shutting off his invisibility device.

She did not recognize him. She spoke immediately, using a few simple phrases she remembered from the abrupt, barking language of the yautja.

"I am one with you. I come to fight with you. I am a Blooded One."

She had made sure before that her locks were well pulled away from the singed marking on her forehead, the marking that Broken Tusk had given her, the marking of bug acid mixed with yautja blood. This had saved her before and would give them pause now.

The warrior was dressed in armor and helmet and stood in a battle-crouch.

He advanced slightly, to have a look.

Grunted with surprise.

Called back to companions as yet not visible.

Seeing she was not armed, he stood up and addressed her.

"Prepare to die."

She had warned Attila to expect this, and when it happened, to keep quiet, no matter what. Even though he wouldn't understand the word, he would doubtless distinguish the doom in the intonation.

However, this was to be expected. It was a kind of rough greeting as well as a challenge. A test, if you will, and easy enough to pass.

"Should I die, it will be in battle. I have many trophies. My honor will last while my bones last."

The Predator grunted.

He approached her.

He was a regular-sized creature, which is to say much taller, much bigger than she. Although with one swipe of the blades on his wrist he could cut her down at any time, she stood stock-still. One hint of fear, one tremble, could be her undoing. She stood, chin outthrust in a stance of honor as he walked around her.

With a sudden clang the blade erupted.

The creature jabbed.

The alien steel stopped just inches from her eyes.

He said something quickly, only snatches of which she understood.

". . . death . . . dismemberment . . . skull . . . wall . . . treachery . . ."

It didn't sound good.

She said three words.

Honor.

Courage.

Danger to the megapack (or words to that effect).

The blades lowered.

"Danger?"

"Hard Meat. Soft Meat take Hard Meat." She tapped her cranium, indicating her brain. "Dangerous warrior now."

The creature shook his dreadlocks with a great moaning growl.

"We must stop," said Machiko.

The Hunter stepped back.

"Trick," he snarled.

However, if he really believed this was a trick, then her guts would be hanging from the trees now, and her white, shining skull would be inside the guy's net bag.

"No," she said.

An easy word, even in yautja parlay.

The Hunter growled up some word from the back of his throat, spat it out. He backed up, bristling. From a belt he drew a knife. He raised it to the skies, and a call ripped through the air.

Machiko, however, was not afraid.

Machiko knew the meaning of the gesture, if not the precise meaning of the word.

It was a summons.

The bushes ridging the glade rustled as though some sudden selective wind had passed through them.

Like some sort of photographic special effects in a 3-D movie, spectral figures began to take shape, walking from the bushes, fading into reality.

Ten of them.

From a blur to solid, fierce reality.

The pack.

They stood, some holding spears, others holding burners. The fact that they had more than just spears and knives meant that they were now involved in more than just a Hunt.

They stood as a unit, staring at Machiko, their eyes burning into her soul.

She stared back, defiantly, proudly. It was as though she could feel the sign on her brow pulsing, its burning flame a signal to them.

This one is Worthy.

She is a Hunter.

She has been Blooded.

She stood her ground and called a greeting of comrades.

"I need your help in a great battle," she said. "I have come to tell you of something you should know."

Suddenly, though, another wavering, and another smaller spectral figure emerged from the bushes.

Took form.

Became.

"We know," said the new arrival. "You are Traitor."

Machiko's heart froze.

Lar'nix'va.

The Hunter she had come to call Shorty.

20

Shorty.

Lar'nix'va.

No question about it, even though he wore his armor and a helmet, she recognized the diminutive form.

He was no longer the youth he had been; he had grown in muscle if not in height. There was a Napoleonic swagger to his step, and arrogance to his stance.

Not only was it Shorty, but from all signs he seemed to be the Leader of this group.

"No," she said. "No traitor. Warrior!"

Damn!

In this kind of situation she wished she had more than just a few words, a few honor-filled postures to use. She could explain everything in detail. Instead, she just had to rely on imperatives and single emphatic words to get her meaning across.

"Kill her," said Shorty.

There was no time, it would seem, even if she had the words she needed.

She had one slim glimmer of hope, one trump card, and even as weapons were raised, she took a step forward and held up a hand.

"No. I *challenge*. I defend honor. Battle."

This caused a great commotion among the yautja. They jabbered among themselves for a moment and then stepped back as one, away from their Leader.

Shorty grunted.

He raised his spear.

Threw it.

The thing throbbed to a halt in the dirt at Machiko's feet. Without hesitation Machiko picked it up. Brandished it.

Shorty called to a second, and immediately there was a spear in his hand.

He took a significant step forward.

The duel was on.

Machiko had gambled on this. She knew that if she threw down the gauntlet, it would have to be picked up. Such was the code of yautja. Honor was all. Courage had to be met with courage, and life itself was not so important as the valiant and brave departure of life.

If she could best the Leader of this pack, then she could get them to listen. And she felt that if she could get them to listen, *really* listen, then she could get them to join with her in an assault; then possibly this horror being perpetrated by this rich maniac might be prevented, curtailed, stopped.

First, though, she had to defeat her old nemesis, the Hunter she called Shorty.

And defeating a Hunter in this kind of situation meant one thing.

A fight to the death.

Shorty feinted, then stepped back two steps.

He made a series of snorting sounds that was the equivalent of yautja laughter. Did a little shuffling dance, then mimed her usual initial attack moves.

Damn!

He'd seen her fight, of course. He knew that she knew some fancy steps, knew some sort of odd physical/mental laws generally dubbed "martial arts."

If she tried anything ordinary on him, this genius of combat, this Predator would know exactly what was going to happen and would be a couple of steps ahead of her.

Besides that, all she had in terms of weapons was this short spear. Shorty had his spear, along with his personal arsenal, to say nothing of his armor and helmet.

The Hunter concept of "even-steven" was rough indeed.

Shit.

"Well, you bastard," she said. "Thank God I've got some new moves."

She attacked.

If anything, she was in better shape now, more limber and agile, and she put it all to the test in just under two seconds. She feinted, flipped, rolled, jabbed, retreated, rolled, ran, fell, and then thrust upward toward the place she knew was the most vulnerable.

The moves clearly surprised Shorty.

Nonetheless, he wasn't quite in the spot where he was supposed to be, so the point of her spear only glanced off the side of his armor.

With a snort he brought his own spear down toward her.

Mistake.

She dodged the thrust, grasped the shaft by its base, and twisted the torque of her body in such a

way as to capitalize on the momentum he had gener-
ated.

Her legs went up, and she executed a perfect flip.

The force of his fall on his back broke his grasp on
his spear, and suddenly she had two weapons.

She used her original immediately, trying to push
the head under the armpit of the armor.

Shorty wrenched away.

His wrist knives flipped out as he rolled to another
fighting stance. He crouched and regarded her, doubtless with more caution and respect now.

"Bitch," he snarled. Or a word to that effect.

Well, maybe not respect.

She bounced on the balls of her feet, agile and
ready, warming up and prepared for the next onslaught, the next maneuver.

They circled each other warily. She could hear him
breathing harshly behind his mask. She could hear his
mandibles working with hate and frustration. Shorty
had despised her. Now he loathed her even more, and
he had the chance to finish this particular warrior's
tale. Oh, how much the little bastard longed to rip her
spine out. Oh, how proudly would he display her
bleached Soft Meat skull, finally removed of the coun-
terfeit blooding scar that had tormented him so!

Yeah, buddy, she thought.

Come and get it, you asshole.

Two spears were not the ideal pairing of instruments.

In fact, she would have preferred a good hard
knife. However, Machiko knew she had to make do
with what she had. Although a thought occurred to
her. . . .

The spear shafts were made of wood. She dropped
the blade of one quickly to the ground, then stepped
down, hard, upon it.

Snap.

She now had a knife.

She picked it up just as Shorty lunged.

With no wasted motion she leaped, rolled, and came up several feet clear of his attack. Seeing an opening, she whacked him across his buttocks with the broad side of the spear.

No damage, but doubtless it hurt his pride.

She laughed and called him the Hunter equivalent of "jackass."

He roared around and came for her. The move was expected, but it was so fast that she had to meet him head-on. She narrowly avoided the slash of his blades as she sidestepped him. She thumped the knife against the back of his head.

When she came away, she saw the blood on it. A nasty yellow-green.

She displayed it for the others.

"First blood!" she called.

Anything to put this killing machine off balance.

Maybe too off balance. Before she could recover from his last lunge, he lunged again.

This time she didn't have time to dance away.

Shorty whacked into her, and suddenly they were rolling around on the ground. Not exactly the optimum position in which to exercise her knowledge of martial arts.

Now it wasn't even street fighting.

It was dirt struggle.

Had he been a normal-sized Hunter, surely his strength would have overwhelmed her immediately. Fortunately, he was not, and she was able to keep those deadly razor-sharp blades away. Nonetheless, when they finished their roll, he was on top, bearing down, albeit without his mask, which had somehow gotten loosed in the ruckus.

His eyes glared evilly, and his mandibles crawled like crab spiders descending upon their prey. His blood seeped from behind his head, dripping at her.

"Know that I have killed you." He said the ritual

words and brought the blade down toward her neck, struggling against the grip of her right hand.

It was like an unfair arm-wrestling match. Shorty had the right angle for all the power. Sweat popped out on her brow.

Her other hand. It had the knife. If she could just have a moment, she might be able to use it, now that the helmet was gone.

The clicking mandibles came down.

The burning eyes . . .

The blades . . .

Inches from her eyes and—

There was a hissing sound.

A wisp of smoke.

Machiko watched, astonished, as a tiny hole was punched in the side of Shorty's temple.

His force bearing down on her was abruptly diminished, and she did not wait around to question her opportunity but pulled the spearhead up, around, and stabbed with all her might at this oblique angle.

The edge of the spearhead thrust up into the soft juncture of chin and neck, below the mandibles.

Up, *hard* up, through arteries and brain tissue.

Shorty's eyes flamed and looked down with surprise at the warrior he thought he had bested.

Blood spurted from his neck.

The lights in the eyes struggled to stay lit. They went out, hatred still glaring, denying that Death was coming.

The muscles relaxed, and the Leader of the Hunters dropped upon her.

She pushed him off.

Got to her feet.

Pulled the makeshift knife from his throat, ripping out corded vein and artery and muscle in a swift coup de grâce.

Not necessary, but an effective touch.

She brandished the gory weapon, the defeated's

blood runneling down the blade onto her hand and her shirt.

"Victor! To me, glory!"

She didn't know many phrases in the yautja language, but she knew the most effective and necessary ones.

The Hunters raised their own weapons. Not to retaliate, but as a gesture of acceptance and respect.

She stood there a moment, taking her due for the victory, a foot squarely on top of the defeated Shorty.

Well, you bastard, she thought. *Payback time.*

However, most of her mind was preoccupied with trying to figure out what had happened. The other Hunters clearly hadn't noticed the hole burning into their Leader.

The question was, Where had it come from?

She calculated its direction of origin.

Took a quick look.

And was astonished.

There, looking out at her from the open bag in which he had been transported, was Attila the Hun.

The android winked at her.

What the hell was going on?

21

Livermore Evanston watched the creature through the thick glass wall. No matter how long he stared at the things, he could never get enough of them. His geneticists told him the same thing was true about the study of their genetic code, and they had similar adjectives to employ.

Fiendishly clever.

The bug had been drugged by a gas, and the mist of the stuff still clung to the chitin of its ventral section. This one happened to be a genetic parent to the altered replicants down in the tanks. There had been another bug, another batch, but for some reason those had not worked out so well. In fact, one had managed to escape with a gun, of all things. It had long since disappeared, but Evanston had been gratified to learn of its discovery. Apparently the other mysterious alien life-form that visited this planet had killed it, which was just as well.

The bug's helmetlike head stirred. It's secondary jaws were extended, and Evanston marveled at the hard black of its teeth and jaws. The creatures, his scientists had reported, had the approximate intelligence of dogs. Alas, however, unlike dogs, they could not be trained. When Evanston had bought his first bug, obtained on Ryushi after the calamitous infection there, he'd seen its potential immediately, but the genetic work on it had taken years and an incredible amount of money. Evanston had seen immediately that this work could not be done with the Company's knowledge. Evanstonville was already in the works, and so it was a natural choice to establish his bug project there.

He'd searched for a cornerstone of Conquest, and these cybernetic warriors, surely, were it.

Cybernetics: that was the key, and Livermore Evanston had seen possibilities, if not the actual biotechnical details, immediately. Breed the things for higher intelligence, to be connected to hyperneuraltech transducers and synaptic shunts. Stick on machines, wire up the correct programs for radio control, design armor and weapons.

Result: efficient, almost unstoppable warriors of the future.

An army with which to conquer worlds.

In school was where Livermore Evanston had dreamed of conquest. Not military school, but business school. It had been his hobby. He'd played computer war-games. He'd fought all the great battles, from Waterloo to Gettysburg, from the Battle of the Bulge to the Battle of the Millennium. And as his ties with the Company grew, he began to see the potential for his dreams of absolutely boundless power.

The Company had little vision. They were bean counters. Evanston, however, saw the potential. Economic might was just the springboard. With the energy of scientific breakthroughs, all the way from faster starships to this marvelous genetic razzle-dazzle, the proper kind of mind could unlock the keys to the universe.

Livermore Evanston knew human history.

Humankind was destined for this kind of conquest.

If he didn't spearhead this effort through the means at hand, then surely some other great mind would. If not this century, then next. The stars were in reach, but the stars had to be *grasped*.

The history books were open and there was a gaping blank there.

If he didn't write "Livermore Evanston" in them, large, then someone else would.

And maybe too late.

These new races ... they were frightening, and they had to be nipped in the bud: get them before they got humanity.

What better way to kill them—and use the best, most terrifying qualities of one of them in the process—than to combine them into one easily controlled being?

It had been a stroke of genius that had been his genetic engineers', not his, but he'd hopped onto it quickly and immediately implemented it into the growth of Evanstonville.

He thought, however, that he'd have more *time*.

Oh, well. He was not a stupid man. From the time he was a little boy, under the tutelage of robots and virtually ignored by his parents, he'd seen life as a playing field of diverging possibilities.

If something went wrong, you tried another tactic.

It was unfortunate about Noguchi. His hope for her had been that she would not only command his mercenaries in their efforts to control escaped bugs, but that she'd seek out and destroy this other race that had visited Livermoreland. It had been with his discovery of oddments of alien armor and clothing upon settling this planet that he'd realized that Evanstonville would need a significant security force, proper fences, and armament. He knew on a gut level that she'd dealt with the monsters before and had betrayed them. After a few years of employ he would gradually introduce the Augmented Warriors, and she would train them, and finally, perhaps, she would even become one of his right-hand generals.

Alas, it was not to be.

She was out in the wild, probably doomed. If the bugs didn't get her, then the things she'd betrayed surely would. She didn't have her android buddy to help her now, either. The idiot's body was off on one of the scientists' tables. He'd have it dissected and analyzed later. Right now there were other things to deal with.

As Evanston looked at the creature behind the glass, a recurring vision suddenly rose before him. He saw himself in a proud battleship in space, commanding a flotilla of vessels. From planet to planet would these vessels step, and upon each one, should it not surrender, should he need ground troops, he had only to let loose these creatures, controlled from afar—

Let loose the Dogs of War.

And then he could remake human civilization according to the ideas he knew were correct.

His personal comm button sounded. He sighed. There were many things to deal with before that time, but oh, when it came, it would be glorious; it would put all other human visions of conquest to shame.

Suddenly, without warning, as he was about to answer the comm, the bug leaped.

Leaped at Evanston.

It smashed into the reinforced glass, snarling and shrieking. It was as though it knew the purposes for which its species was being used.

Evanston flinched, but he did not move. He pressed a button that would summon more gas down upon it and quiet the thing.

Then he answered his comm.

22

What the hell is going on?" Machiko demanded.

"I mentioned before that I was equipped with other 'gifts.' I merely placed some new programming into effect, accessing new weapons," said the head. "I should explore my circuitry. It really is something that I should analyze."

"Would you do that? It's not that I'm ungrateful. It's just that *I really would like to know what the hell is going on!*"

She spoke the words in a terse, urgent voice.

This android—what the hell was he? Truly?

She needed to know, and she needed to know right away. There was nothing in the manual about laser-beam support, that was for sure. But, then, he could project holographs. Why not deadlier light?

They were off by a tree. She had taken the break
while the Hunters were conferring among themselves.
Clearly, she had bought her life by defeating Shorty.
She'd tried, as best she could, with the few words she
knew, with gestures and mime, to present them with
the facts. They did not seem to understand entirely,
but they were picking up something of what she was
trying to communicate.

Now a representative was coming out.

He was much bigger than Shorty; she just hoped
that she didn't have to fight him.

"You are accepted," she thought the creature said.
"However, we do not understand what you are trying
to say."

Or something like that.

A few more words.

The Hunt.

A state of Oddness.

Bad Hard Meat.

Well, at least they accepted the fact that indeed
something was rotten in Blior. Nonetheless, there was
still the same uneasiness with them that she'd felt at
the beginning of her jaunt with that other pack. Despite her blooding from Broken Tusk, from Dachande,
she was still an alien to these creatures and likely
would always be.

Nonetheless, she was reasonably safe now.

She had allies.

Her whole life, in falling apart, had tilted onto the
edge again. . . .

And that, she found now as she looked on these
creatures and this world with new eyes, was where
she liked it.

"Machiko," said the head, still within the confines
of its carrying bag, "I believe I've come up with something."

"Look, Til. I appreciate your help, I really do. But
I'm the one who's going to have to deal with these

guys, okay? Maybe you'd better let me muddle through it on my own."

"They don't seem to be thoroughly accepting."

"That's something that I've had to deal with before . . . and something I'm going to work on now."

"I hate to tell you this, Machiko. I can understand them, and they're giving you about two hours before they decide to kill you again."

She did a double take. "What . . . ? You *understand* them?" She was flabbergasted. "Some newfound program?" Disbelief. Sarcasm.

"Yes," said Attila.

"A program that allows us to speak in the Hunter language?"

"Yes."

"Where the hell did you get that? Why didn't you *tell* me about it?"

"I didn't know. I was not programmed to explore programs, and you never asked me to. You see, in many ways I *am* merely a machine. Actually, the program seems to be some sort of Universal Translator. From the information you've given me and what I picked up from listening in on the Hunters as they've spoken, I've been able to pick up deep structure and words. These are not complex creatures, I think. Their language is not complicated."

"No. I mean, yes. I mean . . . Attila, anything *else* you're going to spring on me?"

"I don't know. Perhaps you'd better bring me over to them?"

"A head? Oh, they're going to like that a lot. A talking head."

"Just call me exactly what I am. Your assistant. A kind of robotic Swiss Army knife."

The Hunters had stopped talking.

They were now staring over at them.

She had to do *something*, that was for sure.

"Okay, okay. Let me introduce you to the crew."

She grabbed him up and took him over.

She pointed at him and said simply, "Attila."

"Attila," barked back one of the Hunters, his expression unreadable.

"Yes. Attila." She held him up. "Okay, Attila. Do your stuff."

Immediately the android began speaking slowly but clearly. Machiko understood some of the words, but the way they were connected was different.

The yautja, however, listened with obviously surprised attention.

Well into the explanation, though, she could see they were increasingly reacting with gestures of rage and challenge. Not toward her or Attila. Clearly to the information they were being presented.

Finally, after a pause, Attila asked them a simple question that Machiko understood clearly:

"Do you know how this could have happened?"

The Hunters conferred among themselves.

A spokesman stepped forward eventually and said, "Yes."

Then he told them his tale.

Machiko listened to it later from Attila as she sat down by a tree, eating the cooked Meat and drinking the water that the Hunters had given her.

It was like old times. The rancid smells of the creatures, the ripe, yeasty taste of their favored meat, the sound of their harsh, grating, challenging language.

One big difference.

She had herself a translator now.

Only what *else* did she have on her hands, buried inside that inscrutable lump of circuitry that was Attila the Hun's head?

Only time would tell. She was paying damned close attention.

"It does tie together," said Attila. The android head

was propped on a rock with a view of everything, and
an ear cocked toward the conversations of the Hunters, in order to pick up new odds and ends of language to communicate better later. "The oddments of
Predator uniform we discovered on Evanston's
ship—"

"Yes, of course. That figures in with the knowledge
they have of the yautja. I'm not sure how that ties in
with augmented *kainde amedha*. Question is, Where
did they get them?"

"The answer is simple enough. Something we
should probably have realized from the outset."

"Okay. I'm all ears."

"This planet has been in use by the Predators for a
long time. For Hunting purposes. Not just bugs, either,
but other beasts. And apparently there haven't been
the slipups that would have created a bug world either. . . ."

"But the bugs are no strangers here."

"Precisely. As for the Hunters, though—apparently,
some years before Evanston and company arrived, the
Hunters crashed a ship here. All aboard were killed,
and the ship was considered a monument to their
lives. The Hunters left for a while, as is their wont.
When they returned to this world, they discovered an
entirely new situation. This continent had been settled. And the monument to their dead had been plun-
dered and taken apart. Alas, there were apparently
preserved bodies of bugs there too.

"The Hunters bided their time. They watched and
waited—and, of course, Hunted. Eventually, they
came to realize what we'd speculated. They realized
that Evanston was turning this into a hunters' planet:
a perfect place for them, an ideal situation in which to
operate. They could prey on hunters, their favorite
source of amusement, a perfect way to derive honor
and excitement from kills."

"And they killed that augmented bug we found?"

"Yes. But not before it killed their leader with a gun. Seems to have been an escapee. Crazy and out of control.

"So we can assume that this brand of bugs—let's call them the 'Buggers'—is not quite perfected yet. The Hunters spoke in rather intuitive terms—no concrete evidence."

"However, they did not take this news well."

"No. They are incensed. They spoke of revenge, destruction, terror—trophies. They see great honor in store for themselves here. . . ."

"And the eradication of a threat to the galaxy," Machiko added.

"Yes. They see themselves as the biggest threat to the galaxy, and that's apparently the way they want to keep it."

She nodded. "Yes. The yautja, the way I know and love them. The biggest badasses on the galactic block."

"No great intellect here," Attila observed. "However, I didn't care to point that out."

"And they've agreed to help us."

"Yes. We need to formulate a plan that we can present to them."

"We'll get to that in one moment," Machiko said. "What we need to talk about now, though, old chum, is this progressive improvement in your abilities."

"I thought we'd get around to that."

"When I purchased you, you were guaranteed to have been wiped and then programmed to my specifications. Apparently this is not the case. The question is—who are you, Attila? And are you my friend, still . . . or an enemy?"

A chagrined look passed over the face of the android. "A friend. A dear friend, of course, Machiko."

"An enemy would say the same. What was it your beloved *Art of War* author said about spies being the most important part of winning a war? It would seem that you, my friend, are the spy. The question is, what war am I in?"

"You must realize, this is all new to me. This programming has just kicked in. However, I will try to explain." He sighed, an odd affectation for a creature without lungs. "There is more to human civilization than the Company. . . ."

"Yes. Of course. Like Evanston."

"Evanston? Livermore Evanston has deep ties to the Company. Who do you think has allowed him to grow and prosper? He is not independent. He is a puppet. And, in an ancillary sense, so is the program."

"The Hunter's World?"

"Masquerading the preparation of new warriors to confront threats, to destroy civilizations that stand in the way of the Company's galactic conquest. Why do you think it was so easy for Evanston to get you out of your contract? Because the Company felt you were needed here."

"Okay. Assuming all this is true—where the hell did you come from?"

"Machiko, when you returned from your lark with the Hunter Pack, do you think that your work for the miners on that world was not noted?" Attila asked.

"Of course it was noted. That's what saved my butt. Otherwise the Company would have crucified me."

"As I was saying, there is more to present-day human civilization than just the Company. There are people, groups of independent thinkers within the Company itself—and without, of course—who do not agree with its policies and philosophies for the future of humankind."

"Subversive groups?"

"Yes. And there is a selective group, linking these loose and very different people. . . . I will not burden you with their true name. Call them X Group."

"Okay. X Group. Now what the hell does X Group want with Machiko Noguchi?"

"Your maverick tendencies were noted, as well as your loyalty to the human race. More important, your ties with this mysterious race of Hunters were noted. X Group realized that you had been noted by the Company as well—or at least by significant members therein. When you made inquiries concerning a training assistant, an android companion, that information was noted—and one was especially programmed for you."

"Namely you."

"Programmed to help you should just this kind of situation become reality. But also, ultimately, to contact you and induct you into its cause."

"Wonderful. And I'm supposed to believe this garbage?" Machiko asked.

"Believe what you like. Right now I have sourced all my latent abilities and am here to help you do what you know in your heart is right: Stop this awful menace to humanity, to civilizations everywhere."

"The Buggers, you mean," she said, mulling the notion over. "Yes, you know, Attila, I must admit: I can't think of something more worth stopping. And as much as I hate working for some secret subversive group . . . the present cause seems just and right . . . and about my only recourse now."

"So you trust me, then?"

"You've really given me no cause not to, have you? Except perhaps hiding oodles of information from me."

"That information was hidden from me as well," Attila pointed out.

"Yeah. So you say." Machiko looked back at the group of Predators. "What other resources do we have besides these boys?"

"This is not the only group. All told, they say they number fifty."

"Hmm. Still not a whole lot. There are only fifteen mercenaries, true, but there are hundreds of armed security forces in Evanstonville. And I'm certain that now that they know I know what's happening there, they are going to be on the cautious side."

"They haven't searched for you."

"No. And probably wisely," Machiko said. "Where am I going to go? No place but back, eventually. The question is, When? The sooner the better." She shook her head. "The damnable thing is, some of the other mercenaries, if they knew what was going on, would help me."

"Like dearest Ned?"

"Ah, that personality of yours remains sparkling, despite the new programs."

"Twinkle twinkle."

"Yes. Ned Sanchez would help."

"He's in this for the money, just like the others."

"Yes, but there's more to it, too. You can only take cynicism so far."

"You're absolutely sure about this?"

"Yes." She shook her head. "How can I communicate with him, though?"

"If you could communicate with Sanchez, do you really think he'd help us? Because, believe me, we need all the help we can get, brilliant warriors or no. I've got the feeling that even as we speak, Evanston and Zorski are putting all their trumps in a row, just in case."

"Yes. Yes, I'm certain."

The android head said, "Fine. Because we have a trick up our sleeve as well. And I can play it tonight."

"Is it a trump?"

The head smiled. "Oh, and more. That is, if it works."

23

Leader!

Bakuub was the Leader now.

As he stood in the stark control room of his ship, he gloried in his new position exactly one second, allowing the pride and thrill to swell in his chest.

Enough.

There was important work to be done.

Bakuub turned to the communications controller.

"Open the lines to all fellows in the vicinity. Be sure it is on a wavelength not monitored by the *oomans*."

"Yes, Leader."

Leader!

There were moments of static, and then slowly the acknowledgments of contact began to come in.

Finally, when full communication was engaged, Bakuub began.

"Lar'nix'va is dead. I am the new Leader of this pack." He paused for that information to be assimilated. "The *oomans* in the settlement have begun a dangerous program transforming Hard Meat into warriors. It must be destroyed. We shall need to join together for a ground assault upon their program, under my direction."

Questions poured in. Defiance. Disbelief. Tactical advice.

"The evidence was presented earlier. We cannot utilize our ships. The airways above the settlement are secured by weapons we cannot match. However, we have allies within the compound." He paused for a moment and his mandibles clicked dramatically, like the clashing of daggers. "It shall be a Hunt of Great Honor, Great Glory, I promise you."

Growls and snarls of enthusiasm.

This was language that the yautja packs understood.

24

The sun set.

All day long Machiko Noguchi, expecting some sort of attack at any moment, had watched it rise in the sky, then slip down through the afternoon. She requested a scout be set up. The yautja had assented. Silent and inconspicuous surveillance, after all, was one of their specialties.

However, there was no sign of active pursuit.

According to the relay of information, another scout had seen a couple of copters trolling through the air, but this was absolutely casual compared to the kind of military manuevers that she was expecting.

There was nothing more, though, and it made her a little nervous.

When the last of the sunlight slipped down over the

edge of this beautiful world, the new Leader of the
yautja, the warrior named Bakuub, came to them. He
informed them that the warriors were ready and that
they would prefer to do battle as soon as possible.

"Please, Attila. Explain to him that the preparations
are not quite ready."

Attila had acquired a much larger vocabulary that
day, and by now he was able to speak with greater fa-
cility and diplomacy. Nonetheless, it did not take
much understanding of his language to realize that
Bakuub was not happy at the news.

The warriors were straining at the bit. They hun-
gered for action. They longed to avenge this slight
upon the sanctity of their place in the universe.

Eventually, Bakuub went away, but only after a
great deal of reassurance that soon they'd be on their
way to scoop up many trophies.

They had collected, all told, fifty Predators for the
attack. This was not as many as Machiko would have
liked, but at least it represented several packs.
Against this kind of opposition, they certainly would
need more than a pack, no matter how excellent their
battle skills were.

"Look, I don't know how long we're going to be
able to stall these guys," said Machiko. "What's going
on back at Evanstonville?"

Even though she'd had some sleep during the day,
she felt tired. Unusually tired and ill at ease, and
eager to get at this thing herself. They'd spent half the
night planning it with the help of Ned Sanchez and
the three others he had corralled to take part in the
rebellion. She'd been surprised that he'd been able to
get so many. Dick Daniels hadn't been difficult. From
the very beginning the man had not liked this particular setup. "Fishy to the extreme" were the words
he'd used. It was Daniels, though, who'd seen the op-
portunistic value of a rebellion such as this. "Shit. You
knock out this crappy genetic-lab operation, you

whack the bosses—you're in charge. You got the spaceships, you got the whole friggin' world. I've *always* wanted a world to myself."

Machiko had pointed out that this was not at all their goal—that they simply wanted to stop the obscene and dangerous genetic engineering. She hadn't mentioned the Company subversives. They had a big hump to get over. If they got over it, they'd figure out the rest later. However, it was the "even more riches" line that Daniels used on MacCraken and Marino, and Machiko was glad he had, because it worked. Not that Lou and Jim were not appalled at the truth of what was happening here—they were simply mercenaries, with a taste for loot and adventure. It had taken a very long time, through the medium of Attila's burned body, to explain the situation, to convince them. Finally, what it came down to was cold, hard cash. Nonetheless, their roles in the rebellion could be minimal, though vital. She and Sanchez, along with the horde of yautja, could deal with the principal part of the operation. But they were going to need some serious help in getting to that point alive.

"What's going on back in Evanstonville?" said the head of Attila the Hun. "Just about the same thing as when you asked ten minutes ago."

"Yes, but when do you think we can be ready?"

"You're going to have to ask Sanchez yourself, because I certainly don't know."

"But where *is* Sanchez?"

"Out getting ready, I suppose—"

"Look, I know it takes a great deal of effort, but could you please tune back in and see if he's gotten back to Operations Headquarters?"

"Operations Headquarters" was a tool shack behind the garage which they were using for a base.

"All right, all right. Hold your horses."

The light in Attila's eyes momentarily dimmed as he made the necessary interneural connections.

They brightened again.

"There. I'm through. You can speak," said the android.

"He's back?"

"Yes."

Machiko leaned closer to Attila's head, which served as her microphone in these communications.

"Sanchez?"

"Yes, Machiko." His voice sounded weary.

"How's it going?"

"Well."

"Good. What time tonight can we make the raid?"

There was a pause. "Look, Machiko. I'm not so sure that tonight's the right time."

"What! Why not?"

"Zorski called in all the troops. They're patrolling. Armed to the teeth. It's like they're expecting you or something. It's hard to coordinate this because they've got us out there too."

"You mean it's impossible."

"I didn't say that. It's just that—well, we were up most of last night, and we're pretty damned tired."

She thought about this. Not good. On the other hand, she had the pack of Preds in fighting trim and ready to go. Nothing worse than a huffy, impatient pack—and there were numerous packs here. Hell, they'd start fighting with each other!

"Look, I can sympathize. I'm tired, you're tired. But you've got stims, right?"

"Sure."

She sighed. "Then you're going to have to use them, because it's gotta be tonight."

Another pause.

"Okay. You're the boss here. I guess I'm going to have to go with what you say, Noguchi."

"When can you have the setup ready?"

"No earlier than midnight."

"Midnight's a little too dead-on. Let's make it a half hour later."

"You got it."

She was half expecting more complaints. When she got a positive answer, she was taken aback, but relieved.

"As planned?"

"As planned."

"Fine. We'll count on you. And you know what to do if there's any problem."

"Twist this body's right hand off."

"Yes, but only in an emergency. I think it's going to be as hard to get back on as the head."

She switched off.

"You *had* to remind me," said Attila.

"Look, pal. You had better hope we get you and your erstwhile body into the same room together eventually," said Machiko.

"Oh, that's all right. I've always been rather cerebral anyway."

"Attila?"

"Yes."

"Heads up."

She tossed him in the air like a basketball, caught him on the way down.

"You're the kind of gal who tries a poor android's soul, Machiko."

She grinned, feeling a little better.

"Thanks. I'm starting to appreciate better that you've got a pretty special one, Attila."

"One favor, then, Machiko—that is, if we get through all this?"

"Yes?"

"Can I get a new name? I think I'm going to want to disassociate myself totally from this war business."

She looked over at the group of yautja, fencing and sparring and exercising in the glow of their lanterns beneath the cover of their bower.

She took a deep breath.

"I think I know exactly what you mean," said Machiko Noguchi.

At midnight they met at the base behind the garage.

Sanchez.

Daniels.

MacCraken.

Marino.

Ostensibly, they had turned in for the night in their rooms at the barracks, pleading exhaustion after a long day's work. As mercenaries, they were not under any particularly strict military pattern, cut off from the rest of the security forces, especially now that their leader had gone rogue. However, Sanchez had figured that it would be best for the operation if anyone in even vague authority believed that they were presently visiting slumberland and not planning outright and total mutiny.

Sanchez drew in a lungful of smoke from his cigarette. "All right," he said. "Are we all clear on our orders? Have we all got the equipment we need?"

"You bet," said Lou MacCraken, holding up his compact but quite effective incendiary device. It had been programmed personally by Sanchez for maximum pyrotechnics, maximum noise. "Gee, I always wanted to blow something up."

"You want mine, too?" said Marino, looking down with extreme misgivings at his own device.

Since Sanchez doubted these two soldiers' abilities the most, he'd given them the simplest things to do.

All they had to accomplish was a simple jaunt to an area on the southern perimeter of the settlement, farthest from the biogenetics lab. Here they would set their bombs by the force-field emplacements. They would blast away the perimeter barrier with maximum effect, leaving a gaping hole in the preliminary defenses.

Many troops would then disperse to meet with presumed attackers.

However, they would find nothing.

Meantime, Sanchez and Daniels would go to the appropriate section of the perimeter fence itself and turn that off quietly and discreetly. Fortunately, Dick Daniels had the circflow experience to accomplish this, without a great deal of trouble. "You just gotta know which fuse to fry," he'd explained. Even Attila had agreed this was the proper tactic.

At that point Machiko would lead the Predators to the lab.

The rest would come naturally.

She'd instructed them as to the lab's layout. They'd be equipped with plasma blasters, not just sharp weapons.

It seemed to Sanchez a bit of a suicide mission on the part of the aliens. He just knew they couldn't accomplish this on their own.

"You haven't seen these guys working as a group before," Machiko had said, adding that it would probably be best if all four just stayed out of the way and came to clean things up when it was over.

All four seemed to think this was a marvelous notion.

"What about the other guys?" said Lou.

"They're getting paid for fighting. They're going to earn their money," said Dick Daniels. "If all goes well, they'll survive, and Evanston and the others won't—or will be taken prisoner. At which point we'll be the ones who will offer the fighters money. And they'll be our mercenaries."

"Which means, as our own bosses, we're just going to have to pay ourselves double, right?" said Marino cheerfully.

"Hey. Just don't fry your goddamn chickens till they're hatched," Daniels said.

"Yeah, something like that." Ned Sanchez got up. He started to distribute the weapons and ammo and equipment he'd swiped from the nearby magazine.

"Everybody know what they've got to do?"

They all knew.

"Everybody got your comms on the prearranged frequency?"

Namely, one that Zorski's men would be able to pick up, accidentally or on purpose. Daniels had done the handiwork on that one, the sly fellow.

"Good," said Sanchez. "We've got a new job to do, and I'm here to tell you it feels a lot better than the one we were stuck in before. Now, let's go do it and live to tell the story over some beers."

They charged out into the night.

Time?"

"One half hour after midnight."

Machiko Noguchi looked around at the Hunters gathered impatiently behind the car. They looked startling in the dim moonlight, like primitive gods sprung up from ashes of past bonfires, wild and slavering for revenge. The night smelled of blood and horror, and her heart beat with adrenaline and with purpose.

"Bakuub?"

She gestured in a questioning challenge method, a kind of stirring motion meant to bring up a fellow's blood, charge him with kinship and all the finer points of bonded honor.

"We hunger for it!" proclaimed the Leader of the Predators, his snarling voice muffled through his mask. He pounded his hand blaster on his armor. A

stream of words came out that Machiko did not quite
recognize.

"Destruction to the outrage and the perpetrators of
this abomination," Attila interpreted.

"My sentiments exactly," returned Machiko.

She thumbed a switch on the car's control panel.
The motor throbbed to life. Her senses were so keen
now, she instantly smelled the engine discharge.

"All right," she said. "All we have to do now is wait
for the diversion."

They waited.

This waiting seemed to be a bit of a strain upon the
Predators. They had ceased their warming maneuvers
and now stood tall and still against the night, ready
for the Hunt, but Machiko could sense their impatience, their bloodlust. They would as soon charge the
settlement now, diversion or no diversion, but their
patience and obedience to their new Leader held
them in check.

The same patience of lions, hanging back in the
bushes, waiting for the proper time to lunge and give
chase to a herd of antelope.

Problem was, this time the herd of antelope was
heavily armed!

"What time is it?"

"Two and a half minutes late," answered Attila.

"What the hell is taking them?"

"There's no way to tell. They're all out—I hope
doing their jobs."

Another moment passed.

"Dammit," said Machiko. "This is what we get for
using a damned body as a radio. There's no way to
carry it around with you."

"A relay system could have been concocted, but it
would have been difficult to regulate. No, Machiko.
Have confidence. You have chosen your allies well.
They are good soldiers."

Machiko looked yearningly toward the settlement.

Its taller buildings were in its center, and they gleamed in the moonlight, the smaller outlying buildings huddled around them like children gathered around parents. The genetic factory was one of the farther buildings to the northwest, but it was to the west that the attack party was skulking; this was the portion of the fence that Daniels claimed could be most easily deactivated.

Then, as though in answer to her mental commands, the diversion began.

The bright flare of an incredibly incandescent explosion leaped up from the far side of the settlement, like a knife in the sky.

Moments later another separate explosion of radiance, slightly more amber and jagged, shot up—a rocket flare, without the rocket.

Yes!

Machiko called out, "Advance!" raising her hand at the same time: the agreed-upon semaphore.

They moved out.

"Oh, ye of little faith," said Attila.

As though in agreement the thunderous sound of the initial explosion finally reached them. The second echoed soon after, even louder.

"Ah!" said Machiko. "That should get their attention. That should bring their forces to that side. Meanwhile, we go in through the side closer to the factory."

There were two Predators lying on top of the roof riding shotgun, and the added weight slowed the vehicle down somewhat. However, as fast as the Predators were, they still clearly struggled to keep up. They did not complain. The fighting frenzy was upon them, and they had plenty of strength and energy to draw upon.

Less than a kilometer separated the fence and the factory.

When they reached the perimeter, Machiko noticed a shimmer.

Her heart leaped into her throat.

What—were the force fences still up?

What had happened to Sanchez, goddammit?

However, as they got closer, she could see that a section of the fence was down, and two figures were gesturing at them.

Sanchez and Daniels, waving guns.

"Come on, come on!" Daniels yelled. "There's a damned good chance, diversion or no diversion, they've spotted you on sensors."

"I thought you took care of that," said Machiko.

"I did. You just never know."

The two opened the back door and hopped into the backseat while the car was still moving.

"Hey! I thought you two were going to stay out of this part. I thought that was the agreement."

"Hell with it," said Sanchez. "You go, we go."

"Yeah," said Daniels. "Anyway, I want to see what they've got in there before you and your weird aliens blow it all up."

Machiko had about one moment of consternation and concern, which instantly changed to appreciation and a kind of hard, flinty, steely love. A comradely love born of brethren in arms.

"Okay, it's your butts. Off we go—"

"The Alien Mobile!" said Daniels.

Sanchez said nothing. He just got his gun out as Machiko hauled ass toward the factory.

"So there you are," said Daniels, leaning his brawny visage over the seat and regarding Attila's head, snuggly fitted between two boxes so that it wouldn't roll around. "I must say, it's been damned strange working with that headless body of yours, buddy."

"You think it's been strange for you? You're not the one who's counting on Machiko Noguchi for transportation. I am *not* the dependent sort."

"You've been a godsend, I'll tell you that. What else can this android body of yours do?"

"That's something that I am finding constantly surprising," answered the android head.

"Well, for the record, in contrast to these hunting behemoths I find myself surrounded by, you're Mr. Normal." Daniels looked around. "Hey! Where the hell'd they go?"

"They've put their invisibility devices on. If you look at them peripherally, you'll notice a blurring of their form as the light bends around them."

"Jeez. Yeah. You're right. These are some high-tech whizzes for such barbarian-brains."

"Who knows where they got it?" said Machiko, shrugging. "Maybe they stole it. Maybe they have scientists."

"Heads up," said Ned Sanchez. "Factory dead ahead—and it looks like, for all our efforts, they still have a welcoming party."

Livermore Evanston was expecting something like this.

Nonetheless, when it came, it came more spectacularly than he'd expected. . . .

And from *inside* the compound.

His instruments told him that.

He'd anticipated an attack sometime this evening, and so, after taking a long nap, enjoying a steam bath and a first-rate therapeutic message, he'd camped out here, in his state-of-the art war room.

Even though Blior was situated in the middle of nowhere, he'd always been aware of its military future, and so one of the first things he'd constructed, in the basement of his central fortress, was a personal bunker, linked to the topside world by the most sophisticated sensor and communication system possible. Here he was safe and snug from any kind of attack, shielded behind firm layers of permacrete and steel. At his fingertips was a wealth of weapons.

Still, for all its shimmering completeness, Livermore Evanston hadn't expected to be using it this soon.

Nervously, he snacked on his own special blend of spiced, salted nuts for the energy and stamina he felt he was going to need, even though he'd packed in a full dinner that night, supplemented by vitamins and tonics, minus his usual doses of alcohol. Cigar fumes hung about him now as he stared out his screen, watching as the light of the explosions reached for the nighttime sky.

"Damn," he said. "They're breaking into the south perimeter."

"We're dispatching forces to deal with it, sir," said Zorski, via radio.

"Yes, of course. But watch out," said Evanston after the computer analysis floated up on the screen. "Those blasts came from within the fence."

"Saboteurs?"

"Got to be."

"Damn."

"Look," Evanston said, "there's no reason to leave the principal thing we're worried about unguarded. Just put out an exploratory force to see if there's really anything coming in. It can always be reinforced if necessary."

"Evanston. We've got people out here—civilians. Guests."

"Give them guns. Tell them it's a part of the show we're experimenting with—and just might get out of hand. If they're not security, just have them shoot at anything that looks like a monster or Machiko Noguchi from the window."

"Yes, sir," said Zorski. "But don't you think you're being a little too glib?"

"I wouldn't be glib, Zorski, if I didn't think that this wasn't something we could deal with."

"That's a fine thing to say when you're tucked in safe and tight where you are."

"Ah—do I detect a hint of insubordination? May I remind you, Zorski, that you're one of the architects of this great plan, and every bit as enmeshed as I?"

"Frankly, I wish I was enmeshed down there with you right now."

"Zorski, Zorski." He might have been saying "Tsk, tsk." "Rewards demand risks. This has never been a sure or safe enterprise. And yet its rewards will be astronomical."

Zorski sighed. "Right. No time to bicker."

"Time to fight. Time to solve problems. I'll be here, the voice of experience, monitoring, controlling the vital elements that need controlling. And believe you me, Zorski. If worst comes to worst, I'll be out there with a blaster pack strapped to my back."

"Yeah. Right. I'll believe that when I see it."

Communication ceased.

Evanston turned back to his equipment, glittering and shining competently.

He just wished he actually felt as confident as he sounded.

Anyway, there were far more effective measures that could be taken than strapping a weapon on himself.

The thought made him smile.

He almost hoped it would come to those measures. The results could solve a great deal of testing.

Humming an aria to himself, his hands began to tap emphatically across controls.

26

Lights.

They blazed on with unexpected brilliance.

It was as though a batch of stars had suddenly settled down upon the sides and top of the building that held the biolab factory and then blazed their light in shafts toward the approaching troops.

Machiko Noguchi had been in raiding parties before with the yautja, of course, but she'd never been in an actual planned military maneuver against an armed opponent.

She was running this one by the seat of her pants.

So she was surprised that the exactly correct thing sprang to her lips, even as fire began to rip through the newly brightened night.

She pointed. "Kill lights!"

The result was immediate, and shockingly effective.

The alien rifles went off almost as one, hurling plasma and laser beams with pinpoint accuracy. Most of the lights were eliminated. Crash of plasglass. Trickle-tinkle down the sloping sides of the factory.

"Okay, we're out of here," said Daniels.

"You know what to do," said Sanchez to Machiko.

"You bet."

The two mercenaries leaped from the car and began to fire at the gaggle of security forces.

A couple of them went down immediately.

The rest returned fire, but it was clear that they were not highly trained. They should have had some sort of cover—instead they were out in the open, behaving like total idiots.

Machiko wasn't really surprised at this. It was Attila who had pointed out that there hadn't been any military operations on Blior in decades, and many soldiers simply were not trained in the basics. It certainly wasn't just a matter of standing in the open, firing at the attacker.

Machiko didn't complain, though.

Certainly, she was also surprised at the Predators.

They behaved like a crack unit, working together seamlessly. Like a bunch of well-trained Trojans. These guys had a military background, no question. It wasn't just Hunting. Was it in their traditions, their training—or their genes?

Her job, however, was not to dawdle about and gawk.

As driver of the car, she had specific goals.

She watched as the intense fire of the attackers cut a swath through the defenders. The security forces wisely beat a retreat, leaving an opening just the right size for her.

She checked her safety harness, then grabbed Attila and stuffed him tightly between her legs.

"I suppose I should get a thrill out of this," said his muffled voice from between her thighs.

"Just get set for a different kind of thrill," she said.

She gunned the accelerator.

The skimmer skipped ahead with the last reserves of its power. Machiko kept low, and it was a good thing. Bullets splattered through the side windows, raining her with glass.

She kept on, though, aiming for her objective.

When she and Attila had run their reconnaissance, the first thing they'd done was to scope out the exterior of the building. From her memory of that survey, Machiko had calculated which of the doors into the main hall would be the weakest.

It was toward that door that she streaked now.

She guided the car as best she could, angling it just so—and then braced for the crash.

It came, just as expected, but with a fury and violence that could never be prepared for.

Upon impact the crashfoam grew, and just in time.

The windshield shattered, and the front of the skimmer crumpled.

So did the door ahead of her.

This portion of the factory had not been built to withstand assault and was not reinforced. The four-wheeler smashed through. One door was torn off its hinges. The other smashed down onto the ground beyond.

Braking was not necessary.

The skimmer smashed into a cement stanchion-and-girder arrangement a few yards in, bringing it to a halt.

"Damned good job if I say so myself," said Machiko.

She grabbed Attila's head by its hair in one hand, and with her gun in the other, kicked open the door and hopped out.

Next stop: those tanks, and their hellish contents.

*　　*　　*

Livermore Evanston watched on his screen as Machiko Noguchi's car smashed through the door into the main portion of the biolab factory.

Livermore Evanston was not eating.

"More troops," he said. "Get me some more troops into this breach," he shouted.

"I'm working on it," said Zorski. Her voice seemed to have lost its composure.

Breaking into the factory was not difficult, and was expected.

However, the suddenness of the breakthrough was *not* expected.

There had been no time to maneuver more troops around.

Noguchi and this strange army were acting like kamikazes, not soldiers. They seemed to have absolutely no regard for their own lives, which was not something that Evanston had anticipated. It broke all the rules he knew of common sense, all he'd studied about war in school.

Livermore Evanston swiveled in his chair.

He examined his options.

"Surround the building with any available troops, Zorski. But don't go inside. I've got other options available."

Eyes canting up to take in the action as the hordes of invisible Predators swarmed through the opening that the skimmer had just bashed into the factory, Evanston bided his time above the proper controls. He could see the disturbances their devices made in the air, some imprints in the ground vaguely determining their numbers.

He bided his time until the alien warriors would be unable to escape.

And if, for some reason, they could—

Well, the rest of his soldiers would be waiting out there for them.

No.

Things were not that bad at all!

Machiko watched as the horde moved in, cleanly and efficiently, weapons cocked and ready for action.

Bakuub stepped up to her.

"That's the entrance, down at the other end of the building," she said, pointing.

Bakuub got the gist of the message and gestured accordingly toward his companions.

They started advancing upon their objective.

"This is most satisfying," said Attila amid the sound and fury coming from outside.

"I don't know," said Machiko. "It's almost too easy."

"Nothing is easy in war. You take your victories where you find them."

"Did you warn them about possible traps?"

"They already anticipate such. According to Bakuub their motto is something like 'Take things as they come.' "

"Yes," said Machiko. "I know that all too well. Well, come on. We might as well get into the action."

She stuffed the head into the strap pocket that she'd prepared especially for him, cocked her gun, and then began to advance warily.

Attila's head swung on her side like some bizarre baby.

A voice called out from behind her. "Machiko."

She turned around.

It was Sanchez.

"Sanchez. What's the situation outside?"

"Glad you're okay."

"Oh, I used to wreck my cars all the time. I'm real good at it. Too bad I don't have insurance now, though."

"I don't think anyone's going to sue. Daniels is out there guarding the back, and a good thing. I'm going to have to join him soon. All the Hunters seem to feel the party's in here."

"Yeah. They tend to be like that."

"No complaint. They seem to know their stuff. Better than the security forces. They've made like pea soup and split."

"Now you get talkative!"

"It's the excitement."

"Okay, they're probably just regrouping. I want you and Daniels to get in here and guard our backs. What about MacCraken and Marino?"

"On the lam after the fireworks."

"Fine. No reason to stick their heads in where they might get them blown off. They've done their jobs, even though a little late." She patted him on the butt. "Go on out there, hero. It's good to fight with you."

"Thanks." He skipped on out, calling for Daniels.

"How touching," said Attila.

"Give me a different time, a different place, peace, and a bed, and you'll see some touchy-feely."

"Please, don't subject me."

"Then be nice." She turned around to see what kind of progress the Predators were making.

They had slowed a good deal, cautiously making their way toward the entrance of the sealed-off lab that Machiko had pointed out.

Suddenly a booming voice blasted from ceiling speakers.

"Welcome, marauders," proclaimed the amplified tones of Livermore Evanston. "Welcome, Machiko Noguchi. Welcome to a lovely trap!"

27

The yautja stopped. Raised their weapons as though to blast at the voice. They restrained themselves, however.

And then continued on their way.

"I would sincerely advise against that action!" suggested the voice imperiously.

The Predators ignored him, heading for the door.

"Noguchi! Warn them. They must stop, or they will be sorry!"

"I don't think that these folks have that particular word in their vocabulary, Evanston."

"You know, darling, you never even gave us the time to talk. I could have explained a great deal, and we could have had an even more mutually beneficial alliance."

"Gee, you know, that might have been a real

possibility—if you hadn't blown up my partner and tried to kill me!"

"That wasn't me. That was my security system, which you should have known would be in place and programmed to take defensive measures." Evanston's voice reeked with self-righteousness.

"I don't think, you lying monster, we would have had much to talk about, anyway."

"You may have made too many assumptions about my program, Machiko. It is for the best interests of humanity! You want to stop us from achieving our destiny?"

"If it's doing something stupid and dangerous and plain insane like what you're doing in there—then yes!"

"You are a traitor!"

"Okay, so arrest me. Lynch me. Whatever you want, Evanston—but first you have to get through my friends here."

The Predators were already pounding and blasting at the entrance doors to the secret lab.

As they worked, a green mist began to plume from the doors, folding in upon them and through the chamber.

Laughter drifted and echoed down from the speakers.

"You're a fool, Noguchi. You'll soon be surrounded by the well-trained security forces you managed to divert. What do you hope to accomplish?"

"Destroy this abomination!"

"Well, haven't we become the torch-bearing villager approaching the castle of Frankenstein? Perhaps if you'd attempted this a month ago, you might have had more success. Unfortunately for you, what you saw in the lab is only the process."

The sound of gears.

The sound of doors opening.

"We've had plenty of excellent results."

The sound of boots clopping toward them from the other side of the chamber.

Figures moved through the mist.

Emerged.

Machiko gasped.

"Oh, dear," said Attila, peering out of his little hammock.

"May I introduce you to our new warriors," said the voice of Livermore Evanston. "We have twenty up and on-line. I think they'll do very nicely. Aren't they stunning? They'll do humanity proud."

A clank.

A creak of chitin and armor and equipment.

The familiar, stomach-wrenching smell of acid.

"And now we shall deal with invading vermin, eh?" said Evanston.

The new arrivals attacked.

There was a booming of speakers and voices inside, but Ned Sanchez couldn't make out much from where he and Dick Daniels were entrenched behind a permacrete outbuilding, guarding the flanks of the operation.

"They're not coming in," said Daniels. "The bastards are just forming up out there, waiting for something."

There had been a few who'd rushed in, but Sanchez and Daniels had toasted them properly, and they'd scurried back to douse their tails in buckets of water or whatever.

Otherwise, they weren't doing anything.

"They're not shelling 'cause they don't want to hurt the building, if they can avoid it."

"Or what's *in* the building."

"I don't like the looks of it. We should be in there and out by now. It's going to take a lot to get through those guys!"

"We got in because we've got some pretty fierce fighters on our side. Take my word for it. Machiko knows her stuff."

"She was one of the survivors on Ryushi. I just hope that's not the case here," said Daniels.

"What? You want to have your cake and eat it?"

"You bet."

"Me too."

There was some sort of commotion within.

A seepage of mist.

"Somethin' sure as hell stinks in there," said Daniels. He made a face. "Literally."

"Yeah." Sanchez glanced uneasily toward the security forces, hunkered behind their vehicles.

"Look, you better get your butt in there and see what the hell is going on," said Daniels. "I'll keep the army guessing."

Another clatter. The sounds of blasting from within.

"Yeah. Right. Thanks."

Sanchez patted his fellow on the arm and then made a quick dash for the opening of the building.

No one shot at him.

As he entered, he immediately felt a raw blast of intuition.

Something was very wrong.

He saw, first, Machiko Noguchi, standing tall but with a somewhat cowed expression on her face. The face dangling below her—Attila's—appeared equally upset.

He turned in the direction of what they were facing, and saw the problem immediately.

"Jesus!" he said.

Though there was absolutely nothing holy about what he was looking at.

"Exactly," spat Machiko.

A trapdoor had opened in her chest, and her heart had fallen through.

"We've got more than we bargained for, I think," said Attila. "I just hope your boys are as good as you say."

What they had witnessed growing in that bubbling nutrient tank only hinted at the true monstrosities that glowered over them now, outfitted fully for killing and destruction.

They were the Buggers.

Bigger than normal bugs, they towered over the Predators, armored and outfitted with cyborg exoskeletons and extensions, with several arms, all holding weapons of various kinds, from blasters to spears and knives.

Nor were they all identical.

Some leaned more toward Queenhood, drool dripping down from their razor-sharp fangs, claws curiously tangled with weapons in awkward grips.

Some looked almost exactly like normal Hard Meat, from claws to shells to fang-ended head-tubings. However, metallic extensions wrapped around these: focusing oculars.

These Bugs could *see*.

All, however, moved stiffly, without the fluidity of their counterparts.

These were not tested models, Machiko realized.

These were creatures that had just been put on duty today, and hastily at that.

This was their first testing.

And *that* was their one hope.

With this realization Machiko called out to Bakuub.

The Predator immediately began to strike back toward them.

Machiko communicated her perceptions quickly to Attila.

"Tell him. Tell him there's hope—but his people must fight quickly and agilely."

Attila did so immediately and fluidly, also adding his own particular strategic insights.

The Predator traipsed back to his crew, speaking rapidly and gesturing.

The group split up.

"Thank you, Evanston," cried out Machiko Noguchi. "We don't have to go in there to destroy them now!"

She lifted her blaster and fired at the closest one.

It was a good shot.

She hadn't fired to kill. She had a good angle on what appeared to be an opening: an uncovered portion of the frontmost monster's leg.

The blast caught the thing in the knee joint. It emitted a high-pitched squawking and tumbled in the path of the others in a squabble of limbs and armor.

Like formation fighters, the Predators split and began to attack.

The monsters seemed taken by surprise at the fall of the foremost. Nonetheless, they aimed their guns and began to fire as well.

A Predator was caught full in the chest and bashed across a table like a toy, crashing out of sight. However, a moment later it popped back up like a burned jack-in-the-box and charged again, firing at its adversary.

The Buggers were more impressive physically than kinetically; however, they were not without power and cunning in battle. Nonetheless, there was a feeling of inexperience and confusion to their monstrous visages, a tentativeness to the movements.

And why not? They were, after all, fresh out of the vat, so to speak, armed with artificial memory and directed from afar.

The Hunter in Machiko sensed this.

She intuited that the Predators sensed this as well. She could see hand motions and clipped commands. Clumps of them broke apart, re-formed differently.

The fallen Bugger rolled away, and the others hurled past, eager to tear apart their prey. They were met with cross blasts from unexpected angles. For a moment their ranks held, but then, when two of their number literally blew up under the blaster onslaught, they retreated. These close quarters were not what they were programmed to fight in. And whoever was commanding them wasn't doing the proper job.

Nonetheless, it was a bloody, nasty melee.

Inexperienced though they might be, the Buggers were still fighting machines, and they fought with a fearsome coldness that held the worst and the deadliest of both races.

Nonetheless, the Predators were fighting machines as well, and fighting machines that now, in a contest not just for honor but for survival, fought with a single will and absolutely incandescent genius.

Machiko had never seen the like.

Nor, apparently, had Ned Sanchez.

He stood there, gawking.

"Get down," order Machiko, taking her own advice and parking herself behind a high-backed lab table.

"Shouldn't we help?"

"We'll just get ourselves killed now."

Anyway, Sanchez would. She'd run with a pack before and could probably meld her instincts into the group mix. Sanchez couldn't; he would probably get caught in the buzz saw of action and get ripped to pieces.

He got down as well, though he peered out at the action with great interest.

"My God, I've never seen anything like this. Talk about berserkers."

The Predators were fighting with a grace and precision that bordered on ballet. They somehow knew just the right moments to dodge, just the right moments to fire, just the right moments to advance.

They were defeating the enemy, an enemy programmed only for victory.

"Evanston bungled *this* project," said Machiko. "He

didn't realize how *stupid* the bugs are, and that's programmed into these creatures as well."

"What—you're saying they were no threat?" said Sanchez. "That we're doing this for nothing?"

"Oh, no. He could certainly make refinements, I'm sure. Nonetheless, fearsome and nasty as they are, they don't have the thousands of years of practice that the yautja have."

"Would someone please tell me what's happening?" said Attila.

"We're winning," said Machiko. "As far as I can tell."

From the looks of things, there were five of the twenty hybrids down, and only a couple of Predators. The Buggers were backing up toward the exit they had come from.

This retreat could not have come from their genetic programming. Retreat was a human notion. Evanston must be backing them away, hoping to re-form.

And then something odd happened.

"Dammit!" said Evanston.

Sweat was dripping from his brow.

Frantically, he engaged override programs for the team of xenos he'd sent in to kill the marauders. They had to retreat, re-form, and then attack again.

They would defeat these bastards. They had to. The computer had predicted a 95 percent probability of victory for just these conditions. He was going to have to run strategy variations and then—

A blue arc of electricity snapped from the panel.

Static power frizzled through his hair, making it stand on end.

The screens blacked out for a moment, then zapped back to normal.

What they showed on the screen, though, wasn't normal.

His creations were moving of their own volition.

Those that remained operational were not merely retreating, but scattering in all directions at a speed that he had not anticipated.

Evanston hit the control override button.

There was no response.

The control signals had shorted out. This was all happening too soon. There had been inadequate preparation time, dammit!

The things were free!

He snapped on the troop-radio comm-link.

"Zorski."

"Yes, sir."

"Red alert. There's a problem here at central. I've lost control of the creatures."

"Which creatures, sir. The bugs? These Hunter things? You want to settle down and stop shouting?"

"No, Zorski. The goddamn project. I've lost control of the project."

"That's just peachy keen."

"We've no choice. We're going to have to abort. Destroy everything. Get away from the lab. I'll give you thirty seconds, then I'm going to blow the whole thing," said Evanston.

"Yes, sir," said Zorski.

Livermore Evanston knew exactly what his creatures would do.

Rampage and destroy.

Indiscriminately.

At this point Livermore Evanston realized he had little reason to feel as confident as he had about the future of this project.

He'd have to scrap it and start over.

Fortunately, he'd be able to eliminate a number of his problems with it.

His fierce little smile returned as he groped for the keyboards and began to tap in the code for the program he would need.

At the top of the Buggers' shoulders sprouted the metallic squibs and squiggles that constituted the upward portion of their cyborg attachments.

A shiver of sparks and power spouted from these, like fairy dust spraying over their heads. They spasmed for a moment—and then they bolted.

"Dammit!" cried Sanchez. "One of those big bastards is heading this way."

Machiko had noticed, and she was up and ready.

Because the retreat had been so regulated before, despite their quick reflexes, the change in the Buggers surprised the Hunters. Several of the Buggers simply whipped through one flank, managing to injure one of the smaller warriors in the process. They were moving with a speed that Machiko had never before witnessed in another species. There was a frenzy, an insanity to their movements that was unnatural.

She could feel it in the air.

"They're *nuts*!" said Sanchez. He readied his gun to fire, drawing bead.

"He's lost control," said Machiko. "Totally lost control!"

She suddenly realized something else.

"No," she said. "Don't—"

"What?"

Before he could fire, Machiko jumped on him. She pushed his blaster rifle away, pushed him down behind a lab cabinet.

"What the hell—"

"Let it pass," she said. "It's not after you. It just wants to get out of here."

Even as she spoke, the creature hurled itself past, all aclatter, toward the door.

Machiko looked up.

All the Buggers were thundering away, not interested, it would seem, in fighting the yautja—except if one got in the way. In that case it was the Predator who was in trouble.

The Predators seemed as surprised as Machiko, and for the most part allowed the Buggers to race out into the night.

"We've got to get out of here!" said Machiko.

"Why?"

"What—do you think it's a trap?" said Attila.

"That's a definite possibility—what I think, though, is that Evanston has lost control and he's panicking right now—and he's going to just cut his losses and try to cut us in the process."

"How?"

"Blow this whole place up." She didn't wait to explain more. "Attila, I want you to tell the Hunters in no uncertain terms to *get out* of here. Right away."

Attila did not quibble.

Machiko lifted his head, and in a loud, commanding voice he made the announcement in the Predator language.

The Hunters turned to Bakuub for confirmation.

Bakuub made a definite gesture.

Out of here!

Machiko and Sanchez ran.

They ran through the door, out to where Daniels was stationed.

"What the devil is going on? Those monsters—" said the man, still behind cover. "Look!"

He pointed.

The Buggers had run straight for the security troops.

They were tearing them apart wildly, savagely, pausing in their flight to rend and mutilate. Splatters and mists of blood rose, and blasters churned with bright fire, limning the beasts in mad berserker carnage.

The Hunters started to stream out of the place.

"Trust me," said Sanchez, grabbing Daniels by the arm. "We've got to make a run for it. Now."

Daniels nodded. Unquestioningly, he followed as Machiko raced ahead, guiding them to the safe side of the insanity.

She could feel the urgency boring down upon her.

Got to get away from here.

Away.

Her breath was strained and heavy in her lungs. She could feel the deadliness in the atmosphere—

Livermore Evanston groped, found the button.

Pressed it.

Spoke the voice commands, modulated on his tones alone.

Better luck next time, he thought.

*   *   *

The biofactory exploded.

The blast emerged from the very center, like a vortex of pure energy, ripping apart every board and girder in its flash-quick pathway.

The force of the explosion slapped across Machiko's back like a hard hand, picking her up and throwing her a full two meters, trying to pluck Attila's head from her grasp.

She held on.

She held on and hit the ground, rolling and clinging to her consciousness.

Around her she could see, peripherally, the equally devastating effect that it had on the others. Several Predators who had not quite gotten out of the building were just pieces of flesh and bone and armor now, spread in clumps of gore. The others had been tossed a greater distance than Machiko had, some into unconsciousness.

Most, however, survived.

Most got to their feet immediately.

She could see them now, taking stock of things as a great wave of fire ripped and tore through what little remained of the factory.

The force of the blast had knocked over the security soldiers. Some were running for their lives now. Some were being wasted by the hybrids, who were buzzing through them like bloody chain saws, senseless slaughtering.

"Attila?" she called.

"Still here. Getting used to this."

"Sanchez? Daniels?"

" 'Fraid Dick got himself pretty well konked out. But I'm still here," Sanchez said.

"He'll be all right. Leave him for now. Probably he'll be safer there."

She could see Bakuub rallying his troops.

"They sure haven't quit. They're going after the hybrids."

"More power to them."

Even as he spoke, blaster fire began again, faded in the light from the fire.

"What do we do?"

"We take advantage of the chaos," said Machiko, "and we find the people who are responsible for this carnage. That might be the only way to stop it."

She pulled on his sleeve and then headed for the control headquarters, leaving behind the screams and the heat.

29

They found Chet Zorski in the main headquarters.

She'd had security guards around the building, but it took only a show of the firepower of Machiko's team and an explanation of what they were about ("We've got to stop these monsters—help us and we all might survive") for the security force to capitulate.

As for Zorski, she folded like a bad poker hand.

"It's out of control." She addressed Machiko calmly, but with her eyes wide with fear as she left her office. "We need your help to stop it. Have you got command of the Predators?"

"No, but we can work with them."

"We can establish some kind of truce and understanding?"

"Yes. But they'll want those superbug creatures destroyed."

"It's a bargain. They've gone nuts. I told Evanston it was too soon to use them."

"Where *is* Evanston?"

"He's got a control bunker. Down in the basement."

"Take us there."

"That's a bit difficult. He's got it pretty well sealed off. I don't think he's liking what he's seeing on his monitors."

"You've seen it?"

"You bet I've seen it. Between the bugs and the genetic progeny that we concocted, this settlement is going to get sliced up pretty badly."

"It doesn't have to be that way. Let me talk to him," said Machiko. "That is, if there's still a communication line down to him."

"Oh, yes, there certainly is. And it's glowing cherry-red now, believe me."

The group was quickly conducted into the room.

The monitors hanging from the wall depicted different scenes from the settlement, all showing a similar theme:

Violence.

Explosions against the night sky limned the struggle of man versus alien . . . versus beast.

The technicians all stayed in their seats, their hands on their heads without that gesture of surrender being requested. They, like most of the people there (with the exception of the mercenaries) looked as though they'd never had any experience with this kind of thing, much less the proper training. They were just colonists. Soft, noted Machiko, like most colonists.

Well, with what was coming out from under galactic stones lately, they were all going to have to get hard, fast.

That, of course, was why Evanston—and doubtless

the Company he was associated with—wanted creatures like those they were breeding.

Humanity, in its present stage, just didn't have the hard edge to spearhead deep into the heart of the stars.

Now, though, they were discovering that it took a lot more than a genetic mix to deal with the Unknown.

The Unknown was buried deep in the heart of that very mix.

"Punch me through to Evanston—immediately."

"Sure."

Zorski reached over for a comm-mike, handed it to Machiko, then caught sight of what she was carrying in her bag.

"God. It's the android," she said with an audible gulp.

"Hello, there!" said Attila.

"Just keep them covered, Ned," Machiko said, and clicked on the mike. "Evanston. Livermore Evanston. Do you read me? I need to talk to you, man. I need to talk to you *now*."

Silence.

She turned to Zorski. "Are you sure this line is open?"

Zorski leaned over and punched a button. Consulted a readout. "Yes."

"Evanston. Talk to me, dammit. You've got people out there getting killed!"

A voice, slightly shaking with stress, broke through the speakers.

"Yes, and who's killing them? Those damned creatures that you've led here. It's you, Noguchi! *You!*"

"Let's take a step into reality, you bastard. You know what's gone wrong. Don't deny it. There's no time for that now. No time for philosophizing."

"What do you want?"

"Something went wrong with the control on those things."

"Yes."

"There's got to be an override on them—right? A button you can push. You're no dummy, Evanston. You foresaw the possibility that you might not be able to control them. You had to have foreseen the need to destroy the things. Individually."

"What if there is?"

"Use it. Kill them, and we can make a truce. I can talk to my alien companions. You and your settlement will be spared. They just want the creatures destroyed. They are an insult to their sense of honor!"

"No! They are *mine*, and they contain the work and wisdom of decades! This eventuality *was* foreseen—there are independent programs in the creatures that will make them seek shelter. That's what they are going for now—shelter. When they are safe, they will turn off and be malleable—to the proper parties, of course."

"Bullshit. You'll blow them now, you bastard!"

"No. Plain and simple, no, Noguchi—and there's no way you can make me. I'm sitting tight here. Don't worry—everything's going to work out fine for me. For you, though—I honestly don't think so. . . ."

"Machiko!" cried Sanchez.

The mercenary pushed her aside, bringing his gun around. A flash of energy ripped into his side, knocking him back and into her gun arm.

The smell of singed flesh.

A yell.

Sanchez was down.

Standing just meters away was Zorski, holding a gun.

She looked terrified, but triumphant.

"Okay, you bitch. The ball's in *our* court now!"

30

Machiko did not even think; she just acted automatically.

The smoking, unconscious body of Ned Sanchez had fallen upon her own gun, but she had access to the sling that held the head of Attila the Hun. She allowed it to roll away to the side.

"Don't shoot!" she said.

"Oh, don't worry," said Zorski, still looking terrified, but a little more under control. "I think that Evanston has other plans for you."

"Good job, Zorski. That's why I was talking to her, to distract them," came Evanston's sneering voice. "Now I think we might be able to accomplish a few things."

"How many of your Hunter friends were still alive

after the blast?" Zorski demanded. "We need to know—ungh."

The grunt was due to the pencil-thin beam of light that streamed from the floor, connected with Zorski's forehead, and drilled a neat hole through her brain.

A wisp of smoke flew up from the cauterized wound.

Zorksi's gun dropped with a clatter.

Zorski dropped.

Dead.

Machiko was up in a moment, covering the technicians.

"One wrong move, and you're all on the floor," She looked over at Attila's head. His forehead still had the laser device peeking through. "Good job, Til."

"Ready for anything. Good placement. Excellent tactic."

She checked Ned. Still breathing. Burned some, but he'd make it.

She grabbed the mike.

"You heard that, you saw it," she wailed. "Now, Evanston, get your fat ass up here before we have to *blow* it up here!"

There was no reply.

There was no reply in the main headquarters from the lower bunker, because that bunker had been abandoned.

Plan B was in effect.

No sooner had he seen Zorski go down, his last hope, than Livermore Evanston grabbed his own gun and pack of necessary supplies, jumped, and lit out the emergency-exit tube, stuffing a handgun into his belt, just in case.

He'd foreseen the possibility of having to get out of his bunker. That was a little military lesson that the luminary Adolf Hitler had neglected in planning his

escape, and since Evanston had studied all the great
leaders, it was natural that he'd wanted to avoid their
mistakes.

He'd made enough of his own.

After slipping his rotund self inside and strapping
in, he pulled the glass top of the car down, pressed
the release button. The car pneumatically responded,
rocketing down the tube. The rush was amusement-
park-ride quick, zooming through the darkness, zooming under the complex, and then suddenly rising at a
rate that pushed him back in the seat with G-force.

Then he hit.

Springs and belts cushioned the impact, but still
Evanston almost lost his breath.

The door whooshed open.

No time to waste.

There was but one hope for escape, and it was beyond that door. He struggled up and hurried there,
grabbing the handle and pulling it open.

Night air rushed in, smelling of burned flesh and
other less savory things.

Evanston didn't notice. His attention was on the
sleek vehicle below the ramp above which he was
now perched. The limo. And there was a figure inside,
slouched down so as not to draw any attention from
anything that might emerge from the violence that
flamed just a few hundred meters away.

Evanston puffed down toward it.

The light of flames streaked across the door as he
opened it.

"Good job."

"Thank heavens it's you," said Abner Brookings.
"We're getting out of here."

"Yes. For now." Evanston got in, slammed the door,
and motioned for the lawyer to get away from there.
"My ship. We'll get out of here for now. But when I get
back—there's going to be payback. Believe me."

The limo rushed through the night.

*   *   *

"Where's he going?" said Machiko. Not fooling around: Her gun was pointed right under the nostril of the chief technician.

A drop of sweat slipped down the man's smooth brow. "There's an escape tube from the bunker. He'll have a car waiting. I'd say he's given up. He's always got his spaceyacht ready. He's capable of piloting it himself. He's out of here."

She looked down at the head of Attila.

"Any thoughts on this?"

The thing lumbered out of the night.

"Jesus," said Brookings.

Evanston recognized it. It was too fast. It would catch them. The silhouette of his spaceyacht loomed just a hundred meters distant. So close.... How had the thing stumbled out this *far*?

He couldn't take a chance.

The limo was rocketing along, but the hybrid would catch them. Evanston leaned over and jerked the steering wheel, sending the limo careering off at a different angle entirely.

"Evanston! What are you *doing*!"

The limo hit the hybrid so hard it buckled its legs. Its body crashed through the windshield. It shrieked, its hands and claws scrabbling.

Evanston didn't wait to see what would happen next. With the car slowing to a stop, he pushed open the passenger door and jumped out, a peripheral glimpse of jaws closing around the right shoulder of Abner Brookings, Esquire.

Brookings screamed.

Evanston ran.

He ran for all he was worth, and he pulled his wrist up as he did so, hitting a radio stub, already attuned to the proper frequency. When he ran up the ramp, the door would be open on its other end, and the instruments ready and activated. There would be a minimum of preparation for takeoff.

His breath burned in his lungs. He could hear Brookings' cries suddenly cut off. The hybrid wouldn't be able to follow him, though. He'd snapped the creature's legs.

At long last the ship reared before him, beautiful and shiny in the moonlight. He raced up the ramp and sailed gleefully through the door, open as expected.

He cycled it closed.

Safe! Truly safe at last! All he had to do now was run up to the bridge and tap the codes for automatic takeoff! A force field had automatically erected outside the ship, and no one, not Bug nor Predator, not Machiko Noguchi nor the genetic hybrids, could *touch* him. He would take off, return to the center of his true power. Regroup. Recoup. Talk to the Company. Bring in the Marines and wipe these traitors from the face of *his* world. The determination and anger gave him the additional power to climb the steps to the bridge. He stumped through with a happy sigh.

A sigh that changed into a shriek as a form rose from the pilot's chair.

A form without a head.

It finished tapping out its final work on the computer bank and then stood up. "I suggest you not move," said the headless android body. "There will be parties here soon that will bring you back." The voice of Attila.

"No," cried Evanston, frustration replacing his fear. "No, you can't *do* this!"

He pulled out his gun and fired at the android torso. The bullet smashed the chest, pushed back the body. But it did not bring the robot down.

"I suggest you put that weapon down." Machiko's voice. "We've gotten the door open below. There will be a party there very soon to pick you up and take you back."

"Can't we talk about this, Noguchi?" said the man, his voice quavering.

"We certainly can, Evanston. Once you get back here. Once we get things back on-line. Now, I suggest you tell us what we need to know, or you're going to be in deep trouble."

Evanston considered. But not for long.

He told them.

"Thanks," said Noguchi. "See you soon."

Evanston took a deep breath. He sighed. There was nothing more to do. But if he could just stay alive, there would be hope.

He heard the pound of feet in the hold.

Looked up.

One of the Predators strode in. Evanston could smell musk and blood and hate. The thing took off its mask, and bright red eyes burned.

Gore dripped freely from its wounds and from the long knives attached to its wrists.

"Machiko," called Evanston. "Machiko!"

The android's headless body had, however, slumped back into the pilot's chair.

EPILOGUE

O n my mark!" said Machiko Noguchi.

Technician hands hovered over controls.

"Now!"

Fingers flicked switches.

Machiko watched the monitors. On the screen closest to her, one of the Buggers was tearing through a doorway to get at men who had taken shelter.

Its cyborg portion simply blew up, rendering its bizarre body into tatters.

On ten other screens similar bloody and explosive fates met other Buggers.

When the last of the blood and bone drifted down, Machiko got on the all-comm.

"'That was to save your miserable carcasses as well as ours," she said. "The rule of the particular tyrant here has ended. Lay down your arms. The yautja will not harm you if you are not armed! An immediate truce has been called. Headquarters has been captured and Livermore Evanston is being incarcerated. This is Machiko Noguchi. All will be explained in the fullness of time. Call in and report."

"Pretty authoritative," said a voice from behind her.

She turned and saw that Ned Sanchez was standing. He hobbled over and slouched into a chair.

"Ned." She went to him.

"Go back to work. I'll be fine."

"You need something for those burns."

"Yes, I do, but I'm sure that one of these technicians can fetch me something appropriate."

She snapped her fingers, and one of the techies went to a cabinet, pulled out a first-aid kit. As the guy attended to Sanchez's wound, the reports began to come in.

It took a few minutes, but everyone seemed to be willing to throw in the towel.

MacCraken and Marino called in, still hale and hearty, and were given assignments to help take care of the wounded.

"Hey, you sons of bitches. You left me out here to rot!" called the friendly voice of Dick Daniels.

"Hey," said Machiko. "You're alive. You should be grateful for that."

"I seem to have missed most of the fun."

"You okay?"

"Yeah, sure, nothing that a couple of beers won't take care of. Hope you're buying."

"You got a case coming, soldier. Now, get yourself to HQ and we'll put you to work."

"The only ones not to report in are the Hunters."

"I see 'em forming ranks on the vids," said Machiko. "Attila, have you still got that contact with Bakuub?"

The eyes in Attila's head dimmed a moment, then

brightened. "Yes. They're on their way in to talk about what happens next."

"Well, that about wraps it up," said Machiko.

"So to speak," said Sanchez, holding up his newly dressed arm. "What happens next, kiddo?"

"We let the Hunters hunt. We stay out of their way—and put down the guns here. Like I said, these guys will only kill those who kill. It's a part of their honor system, as that system is stronger, believe me, than the high-tech armor they wear."

"What about the settlement?"

She turned to Attila. "I guess we're going to have to ask Mr. Subversive about that."

"I know the correct parties to contact. We shall receive the necessary supplies and armament. This can be a free planet, independent of the Company—free to trade with whom we please. Free to accept the colonies we please."

"You think the Hunters will want to help us?"

Machiko shrugged. "I think the Hunters will do what they want. What I *hope* is that they don't stick around too long."

"After a good look at you, I don't blame you."

"We humans are lucky. We can change." She shook her head. "I don't think they can. I think they like themselves exactly the way they are. And that's why they are the way they are, and have been for a long, long time."

"No interest in psychoanalysts from the Predators?"

"Sure. Give some shrinks guns and send 'em running, and you'll get a lot of interest."

"Monitors are showing the arrival of a Predator party," said a technician. "Can't see them too well."

"Let them in, if you please," requested Machiko.

Appropriate controls were touched, and within moments they heard heavy footsteps outside.

"I believe the next thing to do is let them in," said Machiko.

The appropriate technician looked reluctant, but one proper glare from Machiko solved the problem.

Within moments the big aliens shouldered their way into the room. Attila made the proper greeting noises.

Bakuub stepped forward.

Machiko stepped toward him.

They made a gesture of mutual respect.

"Where's old Evanston?" asked Sanchez.

Machiko could handle that question, and so she asked.

Bakuub gestured to a member of his pack.

A warrior stepped forward.

Held out his hand.

From the hand dangled a net sack, holding a skull with only the spinal column, some flecks of brain, and a dangling eyeball to testify for its freshness.

"Trophy," said Bakuub.

One of the technicians gagged and then was sick beside his station.

"Alas, poor Yorick," said Attila.

"Straight from the horse's mouth," said Machiko.

"We rest now. We talk tomorrow."

Machiko nodded, and the Predators turned and left.

There was a moment of silence as Machiko looked at the blood of Livermore Evanston that had pooled on the floor.

Ned Sanchez looked at her with a different cast to his eye. "Well, Machiko. Looks like you've got yourself a world. What are you going to do with it?"

"Uh-uh, guy. *We've* got *ourselves* a world. And what are we going to do with it." She smiled. "Well, we're going to make it the best world in the universe." She raised her blaster. "Any objections to that?"

"Sounds great to me!" said one of the technicians.

"Me, too," said another.

She grunted. "Good." She poked a free finger at Attila. "In that case I'd like you to meet your new Head of State." She stepped forward, picked up the severed head, and placed it in a chair. "And what, O Head, is our first order of business?"

The eyes traveled around the room.

"I think our first project is exactly what Bakuub is going to be talking to us about tomorrow."

"Which is?" said Machiko.

"Have you forgotten the reason you're here? There are bugs on this planet. And unless I miss my guess, while we've been warring with ourselves, they've been increasing exponentially, as is their wont."

"Right. That's what we'll do. First, though, I think we could use a bit of a rest."

"Oh, and one more personal request," said Attila.

Machiko bowed. "Yes, Your Majesty."

"I really would like to reunite with a certain large part of my physical anatomy."

Machiko nodded. "We'll give it a try. I can't guarantee you anything, my dear friend." She scratched his scalp affectionately. "We'll try."

About the Author

David Bischoff is the author of 10 novels spanning almost every genre: science fiction, fantasy, horror, historical, YA and mystery. He is the author of the *New York Times* bestselling novel **Star Trek: The Next Generation—Grounded.** The scripts he's written for television include two episodes of **Star Trek: The Next Generation.** He lives in Eugene, Oregon.